He's been pa
Patience

MW00529214

GRIT

Melissa Oxford is a widow with a ranch, an orange grove, a goat-obsessed ten-year-old, and not enough time. She doesn't have time to make friends. She doesn't have time to stop and chat. And she definitely does not have time for a boyfriend.

Which is fine, because Cary Nakamura is far from being a boy. Cary's the man who helped Melissa plant her trees. The friend who keeps offering advice even when she's too stubborn to take it.

He's also the man who kissed Melissa in broad daylight on a sidewalk in Metlin, California, smack in the face of God and everyone.

But while Melissa may spend a little too long dreaming about Cary from a distance, she knows the kind of passion he promises is more than she can handle.

She just doesn't have the time.

But sometimes, no matter how busy you are, life makes you stop. It pulls you up short and makes you see things a little more clearly. Things like…

The people you can count on.

The dreams you keep pushing away.

And the passion that can't be denied.

GRIT is a stand-alone, friends-to-lovers romance in the Love Stories on 7th and Main series by Elizabeth Hunter, author of *INK*.

GRIT

A LOVE STORY ON 7TH AND MAIN

ELIZABETH HUNTER

To Annessa —

Best always,

E. Hunter

PRAISE FOR ELIZABETH HUNTER

If you're a fan of contemporary romance and haven't tried the 7th and Main series by Elizabeth Hunter yet, then you have an awesome, satisfying reading experience ahead of you. Emotion, great characters, and a small town vibe that's sure to make you happy.

KYLIE SCOTT, NEW YORK TIMES AND USA TODAY
BESTSELLING AUTHOR

This is no easy love story. It's not a meet cute. It's real, and raw, honest and gritty. To experience the story of hope shown here was perfection.

THIS LITERARY LIFE

This is everything that made me fall in love with romance. This love story wasn't hearts and flowers, this story didn't come with ease. It was beautifully raw, dark and even a bit twisted. It was emotional and it was unpredictable... It honestly took my breath away.

THE SASSY NERD BLOG

I love how this story all unfolded. I had tears running down my face at the end along with laughter because Abby is so funny. I loved the underling theme of this book too about hard-work, responsibly, loyalty: what it really means to love. This is by far my favorite 7th and Main book.

BOOKS AT TIFFANY'S

Grit had a little of everything: second chance romance, friends to lovers. Plus we get a peek at some of our favorite characters like Ox and Emmie. If you haven't picked up a *Love Story on 7th & Main* do so quickly because you don't want to miss a moment.

CATTY JANE BOOK BLOG

I feel like I have so much to say about this book and at the same time I can't think of a single word to properly describe how it made me feel. Cary and Melissa's story just has so many feels packed into it. Loss and grief, beautiful love, frustration, adorable sweetness, the list goes on and on.

RED HATTER BOOK BLOG

Grit
Copyright © 2019
Elizabeth Hunter
ISBN: 978-1-941674-43-7

All rights reserved. Except as permitted under the US Copyright Act of 1976, no part of this publication may be reproduced, distributed, or transmitted in any form or by any means, or stored in a database or retrieval system, without the prior written permission of the author.

Cover: Damonza
Content Editor: Amy Cissell, Cissell Ink
Line Editor: Anne Victory, Victory Editing
Proofreader: Linda, Victory Editing

If you're reading this book and did not purchase it or it was not purchased for your use only, please delete it and purchase your own copy from an authorized retailer. Thank you for respecting the hard work of this author.

Recurve Press LLC
PO Box 4034
Visalia, California
USA
ElizabethHunterWrites.com

To all the single parents
doing all the things.
I see you. I've been you.
Keep going.

PROLOGUE

CARY DIDN'T KNOW how she was standing, but she was. Melissa Rhodes stood across from him, all five feet and a few inches of tough. In the past three years, she'd lost her grandfather, buried her husband, and taken over the family ranch. All the while, she'd continued to raise her five-year-old daughter and take care of her mother.

And now she was standing in front of Cary, doing the one thing he knew she hated more than anything—asking for help.

She stood with her shoulders back, hands in her pockets, staring intently at the ground. "I don't want to ask."

"You wouldn't ask if it wasn't important." Cary cleared the roughness from his throat. "What do you need?"

She blew out a hard breath and looked away. "Just advice, I guess. I have a degree. I know all this stuff on paper, but I have no margin for error. Calvin and I had been talking about this for a while. We have all the money together for the planting."

"You know you're not going to see a decent harvest for a few years, right? You need enough money to float the trees for around five seasons. Can the ranch carry that?"

1

She looked up, and he saw a flicker of the fire he'd thought she'd lost.

Her chin rose. "I can handle it."

"Okay." He leaned against his truck. "I'm not gonna sugarcoat it for you; it's a hard business and the drought has been brutal. The only reason our place has held up as well as it has is that we haven't had to carry debt."

Her blue eyes were steely. "What citrus variety will give me the best return the fastest?"

"You're planting your lower acreage? The Jordan Valley side?"

"Yeah."

Cary mulled it over. "If my dad were still living, he'd argue with me"—he stuck his hands in his pockets—"but I think you should plant mandarins."

"Not navel oranges?"

He shook his head. "I can point you to some hardy varieties of small mandarins, and I think the market is turning hot for them. Plus you'll get a full harvest a year sooner. How many acres?"

"Fifty for now."

He nodded. It was a decent start for a new grower, especially one who already had a ranch. "I can give you advice, but are you sure you have time for this? The ranch—"

"I can handle the herd," she said. "Don't worry about that. I have seasonal workers, and Ox said he can help out more too."

Depending on family was tricky, but Cary knew Ox, Melissa's brother, was solid. "Okay."

The Oxford and Nakamura families had been neighbors for Cary's and Melissa's entire lives. The Nakamuras grew citrus. The Oxfords raised cattle.

Melissa Oxford was twelve years younger than Cary, and as kids, they'd never been friends. They knew each other in passing at best. Nothing had prepared Cary for the gut-punch of full-grown attraction he'd experienced the first time Melissa had come back from college in Texas.

2

She'd left California a leggy teenager obsessed with horses and returned a strong, stunning woman with sandy-brown hair, legs for days, and a defiant smile.

She was also engaged.

It was just as well. Falling for the neighbor girl promised a few too many complications. But Cary was happy to become friends with Melissa and Calvin when they moved back to the ranch in Oakville. Cary and Calvin got close, and the latent attraction he felt for Melissa was solidly locked away.

When Calvin's truck had been hit by an eighteen-wheeler ten months ago, Cary and his mom had been devastated. Calvin, Melissa, and their little girl, Abby, were family. Cary's mother, Rumiko, and Melissa's mother, Joan, mourned together. Cary had dealt with his grief by offering to help, but there was only so much he could do. Melissa was the cattlewoman; Cary grew trees.

And now she was taking fifty acres of their prime grazing land and planting citrus.

"You're sure about this?" he asked.

She nodded. "Yeah. Mandarins sound good. It's always been the plan to diversify."

"Okay. I'm here if you need advice. I don't know shit about cows, but I can help with the trees." He debated asking the question, mostly because it was a sore subject for both of them. "How you doing?"

Her daughter Abby's birthday was coming up.

She shrugged. "I'm fine. Busy. Ready for Abby to start school, that's for sure."

Abby was going into kindergarten, the first of many milestones Calvin wouldn't see. It hurt. And it made him angry. "Seriously, Missy—"

"Don't." She blinked hard. "I'm fine, Cary. I don't want to talk about it."

"Do you talk to anyone?" She didn't have many friends. He

didn't know if she preferred it that way or if she was too consumed with the ranch.

She opened her truck door and hopped in. "I'm talking to you, aren't I?"

He frowned. "I'm not sure that counts."

She slammed the truck door shut. "Sure it does."

"Melissa, don't—"

"I gotta go."

She started the truck, and the engine drowned out his words.

Stop hiding, he wanted to say.

Let yourself grieve.

Let yourself miss him.

I do.

————

HE LOOKED AT HER, her body worn out by hours of labor, rocking back and forth on her mother's porch with a bottle of beer propped between her knees. Her skin was pink from the sun. She'd stripped off her long-sleeved shirt and was finally relaxing in a tank top and jeans, her feet kicked up and resting on the porch rail.

She was sweaty and dirty. It did nothing to detract from her beauty. Her skin glowed and her eyes were dancing. She was exhausted, but she was smiling. He hadn't seen her look so alive in months.

He wanted to kiss her.

He didn't. Of course he didn't. It was just a spontaneous reaction to seeing her so happy for the first time in what seemed like forever. That was all.

Keep telling yourself that, idiot.

"We got a lot done," Melissa said.

"We did."

"Tomorrow, you think?"

"Yeah." He rolled his sleeves up and pushed the rocking chair back and forth with his toe. "I think by tomorrow they'll be done. You'll have some that won't take. You know that, right?"

She nodded. "Second season."

"Maybe a few in the third. By the fourth, you should have a solid grove of pretty little mandarins." He reached his beer bottle across and clinked the neck with hers. "Congratulations, Melissa Rhodes. You're officially a citrus grower."

Her smile lit up the night. "Thanks, Cary. For everything."

———

Two years later...

THE RAIN WAS POURING DOWN, and she could barely see him through the sheets of water. Cary had never been very graceful on a horse, but he was a competent enough rider that he could make it over the hills.

"How'd you find me?" she yelled.

"Ox said you'd be out here." He slid off her mother's gelding, PJ. "I followed the fence."

"Do you have a—" She saw the posthole digger strapped to the side of the horse. "Oh, thank God. I thought I was going to have to ride back."

He waded through the mud to get to her. "You can't use the old hole?"

"The water washed too much of it away. I'll never be able to secure a new post in this storm, and the herd has already tried to break through and go down the hill."

He squinted through the rain. "And we're not letting them because...?"

"More flooding in the lower pastures, and I don't want them

5

crossing the creek. Too many calves. Believe it or not, this is the driest place on the ranch; they've got tree cover here."

The cattle were huddled under the low oaks that spread across the hills of the upper pasture in Christy Meadow. Unfortunately, the storm had already damaged one of the posts securing the fence that kept them away from a muddy road that crossed a rushing creek.

Melissa had thought she was going to have to repair it herself when Ox told her he was stuck in town with a client. She had no idea he'd called Cary.

"Tell me what to do," he said. "I've never done this, but I'm good at following directions."

If there was one thing she loved about Cary, it was his lack of ego. The man was incredibly competent in many, many things, but he had no problem admitting when he didn't know something and he didn't get his ego bent out of shape.

As she shouted directions at him, they managed to repair the fence well enough to last through the storm.

"That's good." She rolled a rock over to prop the new post up. "Can you...?" She pointed to another large rock on the other side.

"Got it." He bent over, his shirt plastered to his torso, and rolled the basketball-sized granite stone over to brace the new post.

As his shoulders flexed, Melissa felt a stirring in her belly.
What?
She hadn't felt that in... a while. Years.
"Just this one?" Cary grunted as he rolled the rock.
"Yeah, one should be enough."

His hair was coming loose from the low ponytail where he'd secured it. Wet strands stuck to the defined line of his jaw and brushed the strong cord of muscle in his neck.

Melissa swallowed the lump in her throat and forced her eyes from his arms as he rose. He must have caught her stare, because he frowned.

"What?"

Oh God, how embarrassing. "Nothing. Thanks—I'm surprised we got that done so quickly."

Cary smiled. "We're a good team."

His smile was a little crooked. Had it always been that way? He turned and reached for the posthole digger, then tied it to PJ's saddle. Her eyes fell to his ass, which was framed by a pair of wet Wranglers.

Melissa forced her eyes away. What was wrong with her? She wasn't a fifteen-year-old girl anymore. This was Cary. Her neighbor. Her friend.

Stop checking out his ass, Melissa!

Once she'd noticed it, she couldn't stop looking. Had he always had that sexy line from his shoulders to his hips? She'd always thought of him as stocky, but he wasn't. His shoulders were just really broad.

"...after we get the horses put up."

She blinked. "What?"

"You feeling okay?" He frowned. "We should get you back to the ranch."

"I'm fine!" She took the roll of barbed wire and walked across the road to the run-down wagon that served as a storage spot. She carefully placed the wire under the old green tarp covering the wagon and walked back to the horses.

Cary was waiting for her, his eyes narrowed.

"What?" she asked. "Do you want to leave the posthole digger here?"

"Do you need it back at the ranch?"

She shrugged, trying to be casual and not look at his jaw. Or his hair, the thick black-and-silver falling across his cheek. Why the fuck was she suddenly noticing all the attractive things about Cary? "We might need it. I can carry it."

"No big deal. It's already on my saddle."

"Okay."

"Okay."

Was it her imagination, or did he look her up and down? Was that a *look* look? Or was he wondering if there was something wrong with her?

Oh God, this is not okay.

Melissa mounted her mare, Moxie, and nudged her down the muddy road.

She wasn't in high school anymore. She wasn't even in college anymore. She was a thirty-one-year-old widow and mother of a seven-year-old who still believed in dragons and had a goat obsession. The kid did. Not Melissa. She had a ranch she could barely handle and a new grove of mandarin trees that was eating up all her savings.

She did not have time to notice that Cary Nakamura was sexy as hell.

Not now. Not ever.

———

Three years later...

"MISSY?"

She was at the hospital. She hated the hospital. Disinfectant stung her nose, reminding her of death. Calvin's death. Her grandfather's death. Her own traumatic miscarriage. Melissa's eyes scanned the room and she saw him.

He was standing. He wasn't on a gurney.

Thank you, God.

Her knees nearly gave out with relief. Wait, there was blood all over his shirt. Why was there blood?

"Cary?" Her pulse was pounding; adrenaline coursed through her. "Why are you covered in blood? What happened? Why didn't you call me?"

"Jeremy is the one who got hurt. He has a compound fracture in his right arm—that's why there's blood."

The rest of his words washed over her.

Jeremy. His rock climbing partner had been hurt, not him. "You're fine? The blood...?"

"Not mine."

Not his.

He was fine. He was whole and healthy. She saw his golden-brown arms held out to her, swirling ink covering his skin. Drying blood stained his shirt, but his arms were the same.

Strong arms.

Steady shoulders.

Strong hands.

She couldn't stop the tears. She covered her face. "Oh my God."

Not his blood. It wasn't his blood.

"Missy?"

No, don't call me that. Don't make me soft. If I give you an inch, I'll fall apart.

She couldn't face him. She turned and shot out the door.

Once she was in the fresh air, she lifted her chin, took a deep breath, and tried to stop the tears.

Get it together, Melissa.

What was Cary going to think of her? He probably thought she was an emotional wreck. Or insane. Maybe insane. And maybe hung up on him.

She didn't have time to be hung up on anyone.

Melissa's legs ate up the sidewalk, heading to the parking garage across from the hospital in Metlin.

"Melissa!"

Shit!

He was taller than her by at least six inches. His legs were longer. And he was strong. So damn strong. He'd be able to catch up unless she ran, and she was not going to run.

9

She stopped and turned, wiping the back of her hand across her eyes. "What?"

He nearly ran into her. "You thought I was hurt?"

"Ox didn't give me details on the phone. He just called and said that you and Jeremy were in a climbing accident. I jumped in the truck and..."

"I'm sorry."

"Not your fault." She cleared her throat. "Is Jeremy going to be okay?"

"Yeah, he'll be okay. Just banged up, and he has to have surgery to sort his arm out." Cary edged closer and his eyes narrowed. "You thought I was hurt."

"Don't..." Her heart started to race again, this time for other reasons. "Climbing accidents can be bad and—"

"You thought I was hurt"—his dark eyes burned into her—"and you drove straight into town."

"Yes." *Turn and walk away. Just turn and walk—*

"You drove thirty miles into town and straight to the hospital because you thought I was hurt."

"Don't do this." She clenched her jaw. "Cary—"

"No, I'm going to do this because that is not the reaction of a woman who told me... What was it? 'We're friends, Cary. Don't let yourself get confused.' Is that what this is?" He reached for her arm. "You feeling a little confused, Missy?"

She could smell him now, past the scent of hospital disinfectant. The warm, sweet scent of orange blossoms he carried on his skin, mixed with pine from the mountains. His strong fingers encircled her wrist. He stepped closer and hooked a finger through her belt loop.

His chest was broad, his shoulders solid muscle. She had to fight the urge to lay her head over his heart. She wanted to hear it beat. Wanted the simple reassurance of his body pressed to hers.

His breath tickled the hair at her temple. "Talk to me."

She shook her head.

"Then tell me to leave you alone."

I can't. Her mind was a jumble of relief and gratitude and need. But she didn't want him to let go.

"Missy, look at me."

"Don't—" She looked up, but his lips stopped any retort she might have mustered.

Oh, fuck it. Reaching up, she grabbed the thick hair that fell to his shoulders and gave in to years of temptation. She reached behind his neck and gripped. She slid her knee between his and pressed her body into his.

He tasted so good. His hand moved from her wrist to grab the small of her back. His fingers curled and dug in. His grip was so tight it would probably leave marks.

So good.

Damn, Cary was an excellent kisser. Way better than she'd ever imagined. It had been six years since she'd kissed anyone, and she didn't even think about fumbling. His mouth was too demanding. His lips were too sure.

For a few sweet seconds, all Melissa thought about was the taste of Cary Nakamura's mouth, the warmth of his hands, and how his chest was just as solid as she'd dreamed.

Oh shit, I'm standing on a sidewalk in Metlin.

Melissa broke the kiss and stepped back. "We can't do this."

"Fuck that," he growled. "We already are."

She shook her head.

"Stop lying to yourself," he said. "What are you so damn afraid of?"

"Afraid?" A bitter laugh burst from her. "Oh... you have no idea." She turned and started walking back to her car.

"Fine!" He yelled. "Walk away, but don't pretend like this is finished, because it's not."

You idiot. This never even had a chance to start.

"I know what you're thinking, Melissa Rhodes. And you're wrong."

11

She didn't have time to argue with him.
Melissa kept walking.
She didn't have time to kiss a man on the sidewalk.
She didn't have time to dream about a sweeter life.
She didn't have time for Cary.

CHAPTER ONE

MELISSA'S EYES were trained on her daughter as Abby waited patiently through the song. She was ten now. She wanted to pretend she was too cool for birthday songs and candles, but the glow of excitement didn't lie.

"Happy birthday, dear Abby..."

There were five ten-year-old girls singing in Melissa's kitchen along with her mom, Joan; Calvin's parents, Greg and Beverly; her brother, Ox, and his girlfriend, Emmie; and Cary Nakamura and his mom, Rumi.

For the small dining room at the ranch in Oakville, it was a full house.

"Happy birthday to youuuuu."

Abigail Caroline Rhodes, ten-year-old cowgirl, goat rancher, avid reader, and light of Melissa's life, leaned over and blew out the candles on her birthday cake.

The party of family and friends erupted in applause, and Joan reached over to lift the birthday cake out of the way.

Abby shot her mom a brilliant smile and shouted, "I'm officially double digits! Can we go out now?" That was her girl. Inside was for sleeping; outside was for living.

Melissa grinned. "After the cake. Did you girls bring helmets?"

"Yes, Ms. Rhodes."

"Uh-huh."

"I brought mine!"

Horse riding would happen, but only with helmets.

"Okay," Melissa said. "Cake first, then horses."

The girls squealed in that particularly earsplitting way that ten-year-old girls squealed. Melissa tried not to grimace. After all, her ears would survive, and she loved watching Abby with her friends.

One more birthday you missed, babe. Melissa sent a thought up to Calvin. *You watching?*

It had been nearly six years since Calvin died. Six birthdays. Six Christmases. Six empty Father's Days. Abby was ten now. Calvin had missed more of her birthdays than he'd witnessed.

The first few years, Melissa had felt Calvin more clearly at those milestones. She felt like he was close. That he was there somehow. But the past few birthdays, his presence had faded. She felt more distant from him on those days, not closer.

"Okay, birthday girl first!" Melissa's mom, a permanent ray of sunshine, handed Abby a generous slice of the carrot cake she'd baked that morning. It was Abby's favorite.

"Just like Calvin." Beverly sidled close to Melissa, who was standing at the back wall of the dining room. "He loved carrot cake."

Melissa smiled. "He did."

"She looks more like him every day."

Melissa kept her eyes trained on her daughter. The chubby cheeks and ponytails of childhood were fading away. Abby was stretching up, her eyes hinting at secrets and inside jokes with her friends. She whispered on the phone about girlhood dramas, horses, and boys in bands.

"She looks like herself," Melissa murmured. "But yeah, there's a lot of her daddy there."

Cary caught her eye from across the room. He was standing next to Ox, but he was keeping his eyes on Melissa and Beverly. Melissa gave him an almost imperceptible shake of the head. Cary and Calvin had been friends. He knew better than most how much tension lived between Melissa and her in-laws.

And how much tension was between Cary and Melissa.

She was pointedly ignoring any and all memory of their kiss outside the hospital months before. It had been a moment of madness. A reaction to stress. It was... a relief kiss. A "super glad you're not dead!" kiss. She and Cary were friends. Good friends. That was all.

Melissa Rhodes, you are a big fat liar.

Beverly broke into her mental accusations. "Have you thought any more about our offer?"

Melissa forced a polite smile. "Bev, it's so generous, but you know this is my family home. Calvin wanted to settle here, and so do I. Abby and I are very happy."

"She'll be going to middle school soon," Beverly said. "The schools on the coast are better than the schools here. We'd pay the full tuition for her to attend Saint Anne's."

The offer sounded kind on the surface, but this wasn't about generosity. It never was with Calvin's parents. It was about control.

"This is our home." Melissa maintained the polite smile. "But thank you so much."

"We built the house for you and Abby. I wish you'd reconsider."

You built the house for me and Calvin, as soon as he told you we'd be living here. He didn't want it, and you know exactly why.

Melissa put her arm around Beverly's shoulders and gave her a one-armed hug even as her mother-in-law stiffened up. "If we ever need it, we know it's there. But Abby is happy here. She goes to a good school and has wonderful friends. And she has the run of the entire ranch. I know that's what Calvin wanted for her."

Melissa knew she had to frame things exactly right, or her mother-in-law would leave in a huff. "You know, that was probably the thing Calvin talked about most often, riding his horse around the ranch growing up. Watching the men work, watching Greg work. Exploring with the dogs." She felt Beverly soften at the memory of Calvin's childhood. "Abby has that here, Bev. And I promise we'll try to visit more. You know you're always welcome here. Anytime."

Beverly was silent, but Melissa knew she'd held off the argument for another day. It was the best she could manage. They'd paid attention when Calvin told them he wanted to live in Oakville, but they acted like Melissa didn't know her own mind, even after six years on her own.

She shifted gears. "Did I tell you I'm planning to convert the old bunkhouse into a holiday cottage? Once it's done, you and Greg could stay on the ranch when you visit, instead of at the hotel in Metlin."

Beverly's eyes went wide. "A guest house?"

"Yeah. For guests and for some tourists. My friends who have converted old outbuildings into rooms can always rent them out to people visiting the national park. It's a nice side income."

Bev's face was frozen, and it wasn't just from the Botox. Her blue eyes blinked over and over. "You're going to have strangers in your home?"

"Not in my home. In the old bunkhouse. After we convert it." Melissa tried not to get frustrated. "I think it'll be cool. We'll meet people from all over."

"Strangers from all over. What kind of people would rent a bunkhouse from strangers?" Her pale face turned even paler. "What about security, Melissa?"

You think I don't know how to take care of my family? Melissa withdrew her arm. "Don't worry, Bev. I have a shotgun and really good aim."

"I would hope so."

Melissa bit her tongue and caught Cary watching her again. His eyes were narrowed. She shook her head again.

Don't get started.

She could read his eyes even though he didn't say a word.

Fine. For now. Cary crossed his arms and watched them.

It wouldn't be the first time Cary and the Rhodes family had fought. The first time had been at Calvin's funeral when Greg and Beverly tried to hustle a grief-stricken and confused Melissa and Abby into a car to take them to their opulent house in Paso Robles. Melissa had been so exhausted she barely understood what was happening, but Cary, Ox, and Greg had almost come to blows.

"Mom! Uncle Ox said he can take us outside." Abby was hastily braiding her wavy brown hair. "Is that cool? Can he take us out to ride? We'll just be in the pasture. I can saddle Moxie and PJ." Her big brown eyes pleaded with Melissa. "Do we need to clean up the dishes or—?"

"Don't be ridiculous," Calvin's father, Greg, broke in. "You shouldn't be washing dishes."

Abby looked between Melissa and her grandfather, unsure of whether she'd been given permission or not.

"Thanks for asking, baby." Melissa smiled. "But it's your birthday. Grandma and I will take care of the dishes. You go out with Uncle Ox."

Cary stood up. "I can help too."

"Thanks."

"Before you skip out on us"—Greg raised his voice to attract everyone's attention—"I think Abby has a present from her grandmother and me to open."

Melissa could feel Beverly vibrating next to her.

Oh boy. A present from the Rhodes grandparents was bound to put anything Melissa gave Abby to shame. She'd learned not to let it bother her. Greg and Beverly gave Abby extravagant presents. Melissa gave her everything else.

"What is it?" Abby was nearly jumping.

"There's an envelope there with your name on it." Greg nodded to a vase of flowers they'd brought. "Why don't you open it up?"

Dear Lord, it wasn't even in a box. What was it this time? A trip to Europe? An iPhone? A car she couldn't drive for another six years?

Abby opened the envelope and pulled out a picture. Her mouth dropped open and her eyes grew to the size of saucers. "Is it...?"

"He's yours," Beverly said. "That's Sunday Picnic. He's sixteen hands, seven years old, and he's on his way from Kentucky right now."

Abby ran over and hugged Greg. "Are you serious?"

"Of course."

"Seriously serious?"

Greg chuckled and patted her back. "Seriously serious, princess. We figured you were ready for a step up from ranch horses. You're an excellent rider, Abby. I know you'll do us proud."

Melissa ignored the slight about ranch horses and focused on her daughter's excitement.

"Mom!" Abby's face was glowing. "Did you see?" She held up the picture.

"I did! He's beautiful, baby." Melissa plastered a smile on her face.

If you keep making that face, it's going to get stuck like that.

Kind of like Bev with the Botox.

Abby ran to Cary's mom, a tiny, elderly Japanese woman who was like another grandmother. "Nana Rumi, look at my new horse!"

"He is beautiful." Rumi's eyes were wide. "But so tall! Are you big enough to ride him, Abby?"

"Yeah, I'm ten now!"

Melissa looked at the picture of the large gelding with a

smartly coated rider on his back, jumping over a rail. It looked like a photograph out of a horse country magazine.

Greg and Beverly had bought her ten-year-old a Thoroughbred. A fancy one. Probably spent twenty grand on it, or more. Never mind that the girl would be better served on a foothill ranch by a hardy quarter horse or an Appaloosa.

Melissa had a bad feeling about this. Greg was looking too smug for this to be a simple present.

"Let me see." Cary put a hand on Abby's shoulder. "That is one handsome horse, kid."

Abby was beaming. "Look at him, Cary. His name is Sunday Picnic, but I'm gonna call him Sunny."

"That's a *great* name for a horse. Think he'll get along with Moxie and PJ?"

"Look at his face." Abby was already in love. "I think he's the sweetest. He's going to love Moxie and PJ."

Beverly's smile was sharp. "I'm sure he would get along with any horse, but he'll live at our stables, Abby. You'll see him there."

Aaaand there it was. Melissa tried not to curse. *You shits.*

Her mother looked furious but was trying to hide it. "Seems a little silly to keep a girl's horse two hours away when she lives on a ranch."

Abby's smile fell. "He's not going to live here?"

"Oh sweetie, he's not a *ranch* horse," Beverly said, trying and failing not to condescend. "Not like your mother's and grandmother's horses. He's a Thoroughbred. Sunday Picnic has been trained as a jumper. You can learn how to jump with him. We'll keep him in our stables on the coast with our trainer."

Greg said, "Desmond has all the connections to get you the very best jumping instructor. He's very excited to start. And once you're ready to compete, there are tournaments and competitions all over the Central Coast."

If they couldn't convince Melissa to move to the coast with their granddaughter, they'd simply try to bribe Abby directly.

Abby was confused. Her friends were confused. Everyone was passing the picture of Sunny the new horse around, and Ox and Cary were glaring at Greg Rhodes like he'd just murdered a unicorn.

Melissa clapped her hands together. "Riding time! Who's ready for riding?"

The squeals started again, and the girls headed toward the door.

Abby ran over to her mother. "Mom, I don't understand—"

"We'll talk about it later." She leaned down, kissed Abby's cheek, and whispered, "Go say thank you. Say thank you to Grandma and Grandpa Rhodes, and we'll figure it out, okay?"

"Okay." A quick hug. "Thanks for the party, Mom."

"You bet, baby." Melissa patted her on the back and watched with pride as Abby walked over and thanked her grandparents for being selfish.

Kidding. Her baby had impeccable manners. Unlike her in-laws.

Cary shot Melissa one more look before he headed out the door with Ox and all the girls. Confusion had been forgotten. They were ten years old, hopped up on cake, and horse crazy. Let them go run off the energy outside.

Cary's mom disappeared into the kitchen with Emmie. Joan and Melissa remained in the dining room with Beverly and Greg.

"I think you should have talked to me before you gave her a horse and then told her she wasn't allowed to have it." Melissa was trying to control her temper, but it was difficult. "Do you honestly not see the problem with this?"

Greg was patronizing. As usual. "She'll see the horse whenever she wants to. You just have to drive her to our house."

"You live two hours away from here. She has school during the week. She has soccer every Saturday through the fall. If the horse lived here, she could ride every day. Instead, you're holding her own horse hostage until she comes to visit you."

"We wanted her to have a quality animal," Beverly said. "And quality instruction."

"I see." The rage was a low roar in the back of her mind. "So her mother and grandmother aren't quality teachers? Four years of junior barrel racing, four years in college, and you think I'm an amateur? My mother and I were riding as soon as we could walk."

"That's not the kind of instruction we're talking about," Greg said. "We'd like her to learn English riding. Receive jumping instruction. She's been talking about it for months, Melissa. I don't know why you're choosing to be offended by our generosity. We all know Abby is a gifted rider. She could have a tremendous future, but she needs the right trainers."

It stung. Just like they intended. Jumping lessons were expensive. Buying the horse was only the beginning.

"I know she wants to jump," Melissa said. "There are stables in Metlin—"

"There are better stables in Paso Robles."

Joan tried to smooth the situation with logic. "If Abby doesn't see the horse every day, who's going to clean up after the animal? Who's going to exercise it?"

Beverly said, "We have staff for that."

Joan looked slightly confused and a little embarrassed. "You'd rather have someone else take care of Abby's horse? Instead of her learning to do it on her own?"

It wasn't the way Joan had raised her kids. Melissa had grown up around horses, but she was only allowed to have her own once she could prove she could take care of it. She woke up every morning for a year to clean stalls and feed her grandfather's horses. When she was twelve, she got her own, a gorgeous little paint mare named Sky.

"You shouldn't have told her you were buying her a horse if she couldn't keep it here." Melissa was finished with the excuses Calvin's parents were trying to give her. "It's not her horse. It's yours. She'll just get to ride it a couple of times a month."

Greg's chin went up. "If you're going to take that ungrateful attitude, then I think we're done here. Also, we'll be getting Abby a mobile phone so we can talk to her directly. She's mature enough to handle her own communication at this point."

"No, she's not," Melissa said. "And you're not. That's not your decision."

"Why are you trying to keep us from our granddaughter?" Beverly's eyes filled with tears. "It's like losing Calvin all over again."

The accusation hit Melissa like a sucker punch, and she was stunned silent.

Joan wasn't. She marched over to Greg and Beverly with fire in her eyes. "Out. Both of you. Shame on you for trying to manipulate your own granddaughter this way. This is still my house, I want you out."

Melissa turned and started cleaning the table. She couldn't look at Greg or Beverly. No way was she going to let them see her cry.

Why were they so cruel? She'd never kept Abby from them, but she wasn't their puppet either. She had her own life, her own ranch, and her own way of doing things. She was trying her best. Every single day, she woke up and did everything she could to hold everything together.

She was it. Her life—and her family—they all depended on Melissa making it work.

But Calvin's parents still saw the woman she'd been six years ago.

She'd been in a fog after her husband died. In the space of two years, she'd lost the grandfather who raised her, her and Calvin's second baby—who died when Melissa was four months pregnant —and then Calvin in an auto accident. She'd been battered by grief, and there were days she could barely function. One day she heard her mother-in-law describe her as "incapable" and talk about how much better off Abby would be living with them until Melissa "pulled herself together."

Melissa wiped her eyes and continued clearing the table, not even looking as Joan ushered Greg and Beverly out the front door.

She glanced out the window at the girl on horseback who was the center of her life. Abby was trotting Moxie around the corral across from the house, waving at Ox and Cary every time she rode past them and shouting greetings as her friends took turns riding PJ.

Her daughter was ten and she was brilliant. She was confident and secure and bright and funny. Abby knew who she was and who loved her. One day her daughter was going to soar.

Who's the "incapable mother" now, Bev?

The beef cattle were turning a profit while Melissa had transitioned from traditional to the grass-fed market, and the citrus groves would pay for themselves in the next two years, giving her a comfortable margin on the ranch.

She needed to find more help on the ranch, but that was always a challenge.

As for a personal life…

She watched Cary jump down from the split rail fence and walk over to help one of Abby's friends mount PJ. His jeans fit snug around slim hips and his button-down shirt was rolled up to the elbows, exposing the new tattoo work on his forearms. His silver-black hair was pulled back in a low ponytail at his neck.

So tempting. So *damn* tempting.

But Melissa didn't have time for Cary. Maybe in eight years, when Abby was out of the house, she could ask him out.

Ha! Like that would happen.

Life wasn't fair, but then her grandfather had always warned her about that. Life was never going to be fair. Luck rolled around, but it rolled around more often for those working the hardest.

ELIZABETH HUNTER

Greg and Beverly's shiny black Range Rover kicked up dust as it pulled away from the ranch house and onto the small road leading back into town. Yet another tense visit from Calvin's family had been survived.

Only this time there was a giant unresolved Thoroughbred-horse issue just waiting to cause more problems.

Melissa had rebuilt her life through hard work and stubbornness. She didn't want to get mean, but if the Rhodes family thought they could guilt her into bending to their wishes, they were in for a rude awakening.

CHAPTER TWO

CARY WATCHED Ox kick the corner of the bunkhouse.

"I mean… it's adobe brick, so it's solid," Ox said. "Her plan's not bad. It's just that it's another thing for her to do, you know?"

"I know." Cary kept glancing between the house and the old outbuilding. The sun was going down, and he could see people moving around inside. Abby's friends had all gone home after the party, the horses had been stabled, and Ox was telling him about Melissa's plan to rebuild the bunkhouse where the cowboys had slept when the ranch ran more cattle.

"She really needs to hire someone full time," Cary said. "She keeps taking on seasonal workers when she needs to hire a manager. Someone who can take some work off her plate."

"You try telling her that," Ox said.

"I did. She nearly bit my head off."

"Did you suggest it or make some irritated snipe about her not knowing what was good for her own ranch?"

Cary crossed his arms over his chest. "Mind your own business."

Ox chuckled. "One of these days, the two of you…"

He lifted his chin. "The two of us what?"

"Hmmm." Ox cleared his throat. "You know what? I'm gonna let you sort it out."

Would Melissa have told her brother about kissing Cary at the hospital? He doubted it. She was fiercely private. She also considered it a moment of insanity that would never be repeated. Which she'd told him in no uncertain terms.

Cary took a deep breath and let it out slowly. "Your sister is going to make up her own mind about all this, just like she does about everything. No one can tell her anything to change her mind once it's made up. Luckily, she isn't wrong very often."

Melissa Oxford Rhodes was one of the most competent women he knew. She was whip-smart and highly intuitive, a combination that made her a very fast learner. She'd come to Cary for advice about her citrus groves a few years ago. Now Cary was frequently tempted to ask her opinion on his own farm.

"Yeah, I guess you're right. She'll figure it out. She always does." Ox continued talking about the bunkhouse project while Cary watched the house.

Lights were burning bright. He could see Melissa and Emmie in the front window, Abby bouncing around in the background. Even the earlier disappointment about her horse couldn't keep that little girl down.

Abby was a complete nut and he loved her.

"Hey, Ox?"

"Yeah?" Ox wandered around the side of the bunkhouse.

"Have Calvin's folks been trying to pull shit again?"

"You mean the thing with the horse?" Ox poked his head around the corner. "Or do you mean the house?"

Cary blinked. "What house?"

"You didn't know about that? They did it years ago. Soon as Calvin told his folks they'd be living over here after they got married. Greg went out and built them a three-thousand-square-foot house on the family ranch, told them it and the land was theirs if they moved back to Paso."

"Why?"

Ox shrugged. "Calvin was pretty forgiving of his parents, but my impression has always been that they're control freaks and want to dictate everything about their kids' lives, even as adults. Melissa drives them crazy."

"I bet." She did have that effect on people. "Wait, is that where they were trying to take her after Cal's funeral?"

"Yeah. If you hadn't pissed her off so much, she might have agreed. She was really out of it. So was I." Ox's face was grim. "Definitely not one of my finest brother moments. But yeah, they pull sneaky shit like this pretty regularly."

"Kinda goes beyond sneaky at this point. Holding a horse hostage is a dick move." It had taken everything in Cary to not give Greg and Beverly Rhodes a piece of his mind. Abby's look of utter elation turning to confusion and disappointment was enough to make him see red.

"Agreed." Ox put both hands up and tested the trim around the door. "And Abby will see through it all eventually. She's smart like Melissa."

"It's still a dick move."

"I know." Ox walked the perimeter of the bunkhouse with his hands slung in his pockets. "This is gonna be good. Might make Mom slow down a little too if she has something to keep busy with close to the house like this. Taking care of paying guests is something she'd enjoy, especially since I've moved into town."

Ox had moved in permanently with his girlfriend Emmie. They lived over their book and tattoo shop in downtown Metlin. It was nice enough, but Cary couldn't imagine living in town. Too many people. Too many cars. He liked the outdoors, and he liked his privacy.

Then again, he also lived with his seventy-two-year-old mother and had since his father passed away. Some forty-six-year-old men might have considered that a burden, but for Cary it had seemed like a no-brainer.

His dad was gone, and Rumi hated being alone. Plus his mom was hilarious and a great cook. She was also more than opinionated about his love life, or current lack thereof.

Cary looked at the dilapidated old building. "Maybe I should build my mom a guesthouse to keep her out of my hair."

Ox's smile was crooked. "Good luck with that."

"No joke." Cary's mom Rumiko was a well-known spitfire. She was an artist who'd moved from Naoshima, Japan, in the 1960s and promptly made Cary's dad, Gordon Nakamura, fall head over heels for her. They'd moved from Gordon's childhood home on the Central Coast and planted orange groves in Oakville. There was enough open space and affordable land for Gordon and enough eccentric company for Rumi.

Oakville was a tiny town in the foothills east of Metlin, full of ranchers and farmers, sprinkled with a healthy population of old hippies, artists, musicians, and odd ducks. There was a bluegrass festival in the spring, a car show in the fall, and a guy who spent all his time making wrought iron dinosaur sculptures to decorate the hills around his house.

Because why not?

Their Fourth of July parade consisted of mostly 4-H kids on horses, and a livestock auction for those same kids was held at the end of every summer vacation.

There were conservation groups and organic farmers, transplanted city people, and lots of folks passing through on their way to the national park.

Oakville residents were passionate about keeping the town rural and original. They didn't want new restaurants or microbreweries like the people in Metlin. They didn't build fancy houses or drive expensive cars. Residents took more pride in their gardens or studios—or dinosaur sculptures—than they did in their bank balance.

Cary couldn't imagine living anywhere else. It was one of the reasons he was still single.

He'd been married in his late twenties, to a chef from the East Bay. She'd tried to start a restaurant in Oakville since Cary refused to live anywhere else. They'd poured time, money, and passion into the place, but it never took off the way his ex wanted it to.

The restaurant had failed. The chef became resentful. She'd moved back to Oakland and the divorce had been amicable—perfunctory, even—leaving Cary to wonder whether they'd been marriage partners or just business associates. They'd never had kids, which Cary was grateful for, and his older sister got to say "I told you so" at all family events in perpetuity.

Ox came to stand next to Cary again. "You know a contractor she could use?"

"Brian Montoya. I'll call him next week and see if he has time. Or he might be able to put one of his younger guys on something like this. The basic structure is solid, just needs shoring up."

"*You'll* call Brian?" Ox looked at him. "You probably shouldn't."

Cary sighed. "Yeah, but I will. I mean I'll give Missy his phone number and call him too. Make sure he's not too busy. He wouldn't mean to blow her off, but he's got a lot on his plate."

"If she finds out, she'll be pissed."

"What's new?"

Cary had dated on and off over the years, as much as a busy independent grower could, but most of the women he knew were already married.

And then there was Melissa.

Cary's attraction didn't give a shit that Melissa was way too young for him or she'd been married to his friend, not that he'd ever shown Melissa a hint of its existence when Calvin was alive.

He tried to keep steady through everything. Through Calvin's death. Through planting her groves. Watching Melissa raise Abby on her own and not being able to help. She didn't need a boyfriend, she needed a friend, so Cary did his best to ignore his feelings.

And when he realized he was flat-out, hopelessly, forever in love with the woman, he drove out to his favorite camping spot and drank himself stupid.

Loving Melissa, like trying to argue with her, was an exercise in futility. She was too stubborn. Too independent. Too convinced she was right. Always.

A failed marriage had taught him a hard lesson: every relationship needed two people willing to bend. He'd been the inflexible one in his marriage, and he'd paid the price. He could recognize that with age.

But Melissa? She'd never bend.

Cary even understood why. She had the weight of the world on her shoulders and a limited number of people she could rely on to help. She probably felt like if she bent, she'd break.

And where did that leave Cary?

Fucked. That left him fucked.

Melissa had stormed out of his photography exhibition when he'd exposed a fraction of his admiration with a portrait he'd taken of her the previous spring. She'd been working in the corral during calf branding. The photograph he'd taken was sexy as fuck, gritty, sensual, and captured her perfectly.

She hadn't yelled at him, but she'd clearly been upset. *We're friends, Cary. Don't let yourself get confused.*

He'd tried falling out of love with Melissa, but he didn't think it worked that way.

But then she'd rushed into town when she thought he was hurt, kissed him in broad daylight, and never spoken of it again.

At this point, Cary didn't know which way was up.

"Hey." Ox nudged his shoulder. "I think you're being summoned."

Cary glanced at the kitchen porch and saw Joan waving at him. His mom had her sweater on and was walking to Cary's truck. "Yeah. Looks like it's time for me to go."

"I'll walk back with you."

"You and Emmie staying here tonight?"

"Nah, we gotta drive back. Tomorrow is farmers' market and we open early." Ox frowned. "Aren't you going?"

"Shit. I forgot about it." He was tempted to be a no-show and just forfeit his table fee for the week, but that pissed customers off, and he'd promised Abby she could help him pour the lemonade they sold at a ridiculous markup. "Yeah, I'll be there."

"You and Melissa still neighbors?" Ox grinned.

"I have a working cooperative agreement with your niece. Your sister tries to pretend I don't exist."

"Uh-huh." His long legs ate up the ground between the house and the bunkhouse. "How's that working for you two?"

"Why do you care, Ox?"

"Dude. She's my sister."

"And I'm your customer. Which reminds me, can we start on my left shoulder next week?"

"You have the drawing ready?"

"My mom already sketched it out, but I'm sure you'll need to modify it."

"No problem. She did an amazing job on that chrysanthemum. I didn't have to do much."

Some mothers, especially Japanese ones, didn't like tattooing. Cary's mom was enough of a rebel to be delighted that her husband and son both liked the practice, even if it was taboo in her family.

Actually, she might have liked it more because of that.

"Let me know." He'd finished both his shoulders and wanted to move on to the water motif he'd planned for the middle of his back. It would be a months-long process between his schedule and Ox's, but the end result was something he'd been dreaming about for years.

He'd told his mother what he wanted, and she'd drawn it out for him on a large piece of sketch paper, using the traditional style he loved.

Cary slowed down as he passed by the living room window, raising a hand to wave at Melissa where she looked out into the darkness.

She waved back, her hand lingering in the air a little longer than he'd expected.

Then she snatched it away like her fingers had been burned and spun around to walk back to the kitchen.

Fire and water. Whoever said that tattoos were a picture of your life wasn't wrong.

CHAPTER THREE

THE NEXT MORNING at the intersection of 7th Avenue and Main in downtown Metlin, Abby shot out of the truck as soon as Melissa parked it.

"Don't leave the market!" Melissa yelled at the disappearing ten-year-old.

"Okay!"

She tried her best not to be overprotective. Abby was friends with at least three other kids whose parents had booths on Saturday morning. She had an uncle and almost-aunt with a shop on Main, along with other known adults up and down the street.

Melissa still worried.

It was hard not to feel like her little girl was slipping away. Abby had a social calendar that had nothing to do with playdates anymore. She had school friends and riding friends. She had book club friends and 4-H friends. Everyone knew Abby and everyone watched out for her.

Which made it feel silly for Melissa to worry, even though she did.

"She'll be fine."

Cary's deep voice made her turn. "I know."

He stood by his grey truck, looking off into the distance, his dark brown eyes piercing. "Doesn't make you worry any less."

"No."

He lowered the tailgate on his truck and pulled out the pop-up shade cover he'd set up for his booth. "You know, when I think about what all I did at that age—"

"Everything." Melissa tore her eyes away from following Abby and reached for her own shade cover, a bright yellow to catch the attention of the crowds. "Our parents let us do everything."

"As long as we were home by dinner."

"Same rule at my house."

"And we survived," Cary said.

Most of us did. Melissa didn't say it. Saying it would only be a reminder of Calvin, and lately it made Melissa more uncomfortable than usual to bring Calvin up with Cary, even though they'd been friends.

The weight of silence hung between them as Melissa and Cary set up their neighboring booths and tables. Market organizers walked around the perimeter, answering questions and handing out monthly forms to report sales. The morning had a chill, but Melissa could smell the threat of heat in the air.

"Gonna be hot," she said.

"Yeah." Cary put out a worn harvest lug of peaches and a box of figs. While Cary's main crop was citrus of all kinds, he planted a few rows of almost everything so he'd have a year-round presence at the market. "You going to the town council meeting tonight?"

"I will if I can, but most of those meetings are just old men bitching about the government, so it's not the highest priority, you know?"

"I can't blame you for that. I'm going though, so if you have time—"

"I'll let you know."

"You thought any more what you're going to do about the horse?"

Melissa didn't hide the derision in her voice. "Nothing much I can do. The horse belongs to them. They can put whatever conditions they want on a gift, including only being able to ride when she comes out to visit them."

Melissa hadn't been growing long enough to have year-round fruit, but she had lemons, grapefruit, and a whatever excess fruit they could spare from the kitchen garden her mother kept. Added to that, Joan's lemon curd and orange marmalade were popular all year round.

Cary kept his eyes on his table. "That was a shit move, giving her a horse like that."

Melissa glanced around to make sure Abby hadn't snuck back within earshot. "Yeah, it was. But it's standard for them, so she's going to have to get used to it. They pulled this stuff with Calvin all the time."

"Ox told me about the house."

She shook her head. "I couldn't believe it. They built us a house so Calvin wouldn't leave. It's still there. No one lives in it. There's just a cleaner who comes once a month unless we've been there to visit."

"So you've stayed in it?"

Melissa shrugged. "Better than staying in their mansion."

Cary frowned as he took a box cutter and sliced off a piece of cardboard from his truck bed. "Mansion, huh?"

"It's weird. Huge place for two people and a live-in cook." Melissa shook her head. "Though I guess Calvin's sister also lives on the property with her husband and kids, so it's not a complete loss."

"There is... so much going on there," Cary said. "But mostly, I'm pissed off on Abby's behalf."

Melissa felt the rush of energy that signaled the return of the Abby.

"Why are you pissed off, Cary?"

"Hey"—Melissa caught her daughter's eye—"don't say *pissed*."

Abby made a put-upon face. "You say it all the time."

Melissa mirrored the face. "And I also drink beer. You can't do that either. Too bad for you."

"So I have to be twenty-one before I can say the word *pissed?*"

Was it a ridiculous thing to be fighting about? Yes. Did that matter? Absolutely not.

"Yeah." Melissa pulled another lug of lemons from the back of her truck. "You have to be twenty-one to say pissed off. And lots of other bad words too. It's the law."

Abby rolled her eyes hard. "It is not." She turned to Cary. "Hey, adult."

"Hey, kid."

"Can I help with the lemonade today?"

Cary glanced at Melissa. "You can help if your mom says you can."

Cary sold fresh-squeezed lemonade from his booth. It was delicious, but Melissa would need that lemonade spiked with a lot more than mint to get her to pay three bucks for a cup.

Abby's eyes turned from rolling to pleading. "Please."

"That's fine, but if I need help, you're over here."

She didn't have anyone to help her in the booth, and every girl needed a bathroom break sometimes.

"I'll cover you," Cary said. "Anytime you need."

It shouldn't have sounded dirty. It really shouldn't have. But then, Melissa hadn't had sex in a long, *long* time. And she had to admit the images that jumped into her head were hardly the first time she'd imagined Cary naked.

"You too." She cleared her throat. "I can cover you—your booth. Cover your booth. If you need something. A break." Fuck, could she sound more awkward? "I can cover your booth for you if you need a break."

Was it her imagination, or did he look amused? Melissa

refused to meet his eyes, ruthlessly organizing the heirloom tomatoes that were Joan's pride and joy.

"Cary, where are the lids?" Abby was digging around in the back seat of Cary's truck.

Melissa glanced over her shoulder. "Abby, you better not be making a mess."

"She's fine." Cary had moved closer. "Look for a big bag under the seat." His booth was set up, and there was still fifteen minutes before the market opened. "Let me help."

He rolled up his sleeves, and Melissa's mouth watered when she saw his forearms.

Not fair!

Did he know what a pair of defined forearms did to a woman? Probably. Asshole.

"Your mom's tomatoes look great."

"You can take some home if they don't sell."

"Your heirlooms sell out every week."

"And at four bucks a pound, I have no idea how."

Cary turned a wooden crate on its side and started piling zucchini in it. "Is this right?"

She glanced up. "Yeah."

"You should teach lessons on how to display this stuff."

"It's not a secret." Melissa felt flustered. "I just do what I see at the grocery store."

"Yeah, but it looks good." He finished setting up the right side of the table and turned, then reached over and lifted the crate of summer squash. "You're observant."

I'm observing the hell out of your ass, that's for sure.

Dammit, she needed to get her mind off Cary's ass. In her defense, he was wearing Wranglers. "Thanks."

"Abby, you find the lids?" he called.

"Yeah!"

"Okay, get everything ready. Market's about the open and people are gonna be thirsty."

Abby jogged from the truck to the booth, carrying a long bag of plastic lids. "Got 'em."

"Okay, put some gloves on and start scooping ice from that bag there, okay?"

Something in Melissa's heart twisted a little as she watched Cary walk Abby through making the lemonades, garnishing with fresh mint, and setting them out in an ice-water-filled plastic tub.

Her daughter was focused and attentive. Abby lived for praise from Cary. She thought he was the epitome of cool.

And Cary was always there for her daughter. Always. After Calvin had died, he'd made a point to be a regular part of her life. Abby invited him to soccer games and school programs, and Cary went to every one he could.

Melissa was both grateful and sad. She appreciated Cary, but she missed Calvin. She missed the grandfather who'd raised her. She missed the life her daughter didn't have with the father who had adored her and wanted to teach her everything.

Abby should have had all those things. The fact that she didn't sometimes gave Melissa random spikes of anger even though she knew her daughter was lucky in so many ways.

Melissa's first customer came to the booth and distracted her. Then a second arrived. Then a third. And in the space of twenty minutes, she'd gone from contemplating the big questions in life to barely treading water selling fruits, vegetables, and preserves to city people with deep pocketbooks.

An hour later, she was able to catch her breath. She popped open the folding chair she'd brought and sat in the shade.

Cary dragged his chair over to hers and sat next to her. "Good traffic this morning."

"Getting those food trucks to park over here helped."

"So did all the businesses opening early on Saturday."

Abby was still perched by the lemonade. "Mom, you want a lemonade?"

"Thanks, baby, but it's too early." Melissa squinted. "I really want a coffee. Is Kathy's coffee cart here?"

Abby ran around Cary's truck. "Yeah, I see her."

Melissa rose and grabbed a small bag, stuffing four heirloom tomatoes inside. "See if she'll trade tomatoes for coffee." She looked at Cary. "You want one?"

"Please."

Melissa stuffed two more tomatoes in and held them out for Abby, who sprinted away on gangly legs, dodging between customers and browsers.

Cary laughed behind her.

"What?" Melissa sat back down.

"That girl is all legs. It's like they stretched out and the rest of her hasn't caught up yet."

Melissa smiled. "I was the same way."

He cocked his head and glanced at her legs. "Yeah?"

"Yep. I was a fast runner for a couple of years at the end of elementary. Then the rest of the kids caught up and I stopped growing."

"You've still got great legs."

She felt the heat in her cheeks. "You can't say stuff like that, Cary."

"Says who?" He got up to sell some peaches to a woman with three kids who were grabbing all the samples on toothpicks.

By the time he sat back down, Melissa had customers. Cary sidled next to her and took orders to the couple waiting in line. He sold two cans of preserves and a couple of tomatoes before they were alone again.

Melissa was hoping he'd drop the legs comment and move on, but it was Cary, who didn't know when to let anything lie.

"So I'm not supposed to say you have great legs?" he asked quietly. "Because you do. And only a blind man wouldn't notice."

"You're not supposed to say that stuff because we're not...

together, okay?" Melissa kept a smile plastered on her face as customers walked by. "We're friends."

"We're friends who kiss each other," he said. "So I'm pretty sure I'm allowed to notice your legs."

"*Kissed*. One time. Why do you keep bringing that up?"

"Because it was a really good kiss and you ran away." He stepped close enough that she could feel his body heat. Smell the scent of his skin and his aftershave. "I think it counts as more than one when I still remember what your mouth tastes like."

Her face had to be on fire. "Please stop bringing it up."

"I will when you tell me you don't want me." Cary's voice dropped. "Tell me you don't want me—that you have no interest in me beyond friendship—and you won't hear another word about it. And remember, I know you well enough that I'll know if you're lying."

Why couldn't she say the words? Why couldn't she just lie?

Abby returned with two coffees in hand. "Sorry it took so long! Kathy had a big line."

"No problem!" Melissa was absurdly glad her daughter was back. "Did she make us lattes?"

"Yeah. That's the other reason it took so long. She said thanks for the tomatoes."

Melissa sipped her coffee even though it was scalding. "Yum. Thanks, baby."

"You're welcome."

Cary eyed her over the rim of his coffee cup with a look that told Melissa she'd only delayed the conversation, not stopped it. Not for a minute did she think he'd forget about cornering her.

But at least she'd stalled him. Maybe by the time he brought it up again she'd have a convincing lie.

Because it would be a lie. There was no way she could say with honesty that she wasn't interested in Cary. She was insanely attracted to him. No other man in six years had even tempted her.

But acting on that attraction? Way too complicated. Maybe Cary didn't see it, but Melissa wasn't blinded by her hormones.

She and Cary had too much history. Too many obstacles. He would always be Calvin's friend, and she'd always be Calvin's widow. Seeing anything beyond that opened her heart to too much pain.

CHAPTER FOUR

MELISSA DIDN'T CALL him before the council meeting that night —which didn't surprise him—but she did show up. She even sat next to him with the safe barrier of her purse resting between them.

"Hey." She grabbed a notebook and pen from her bag. "Did I miss anything?"

"Nope. Bud's still reading the minutes of the last meeting." He glanced at the purse. It was a formidable barrier filled with notebooks, planners, pens—probably some baling twine, possibly a horseshoe—along with various and sundry other mysteries. He poked at the strap. "Do you have any snacks in there?"

"You didn't eat dinner?"

"I was at the packing house until I drove over here."

She raised an eyebrow. "The packing house with all the... fruit? The boxes and boxes of fruit?"

"Do you know how much fruit I eat on a daily basis?" Cary peeked in her purse again. "I bet you have a Snickers or something."

Melissa opened her purse and pulled out a small bag of almonds and a granola bar. "Take your pick."

42

He grabbed both and smiled when she rolled her eyes. "It is forever the purse of mysteries."

"It's the purse of the working mother."

"You were an A student, weren't you?"

She clicked her pen and the corner of her mouth turned up. "Every single year."

He dropped his voice to a whisper. "I only got As in shop class. Drove my parents crazy."

"You and my brother," she whispered. "What's JPR Holdings?"

"What?" He hadn't been paying attention. He'd been looking at her legs, which were nicely encased in a pair of worn jeans.

Cary really loved Melissa's legs. He had plans for those legs.

She nodded toward the front of Veterans' Hall, and Cary turned to his attention back to Bud Rogers, the current council president.

"...followed up their presentation last month with a representative coming to visit tonight, and we thank them for that. Some of my fellow council had a few questions—"

"You could say that." The interruption came from Les Arthur, one of the oldest and most successful orange growers Cary knew. "I appreciate you all showing up tonight. I don't appreciate your pressing for a vote this early."

Cary sat up straight and turned his attention toward the table in front. Les was notoriously quiet, so for him to interrupt meant something needed attention. He was on the council as a favor to the town. At nearly eighty, he was a well-respected member of the community and a local philanthropist. When he spoke, people listened.

"What did I miss last month?" Melissa asked. "What presentation?"

"I don't remember. I was talking with George after the meeting. I remember something about a handout, but I lost track of time and..." *Shit.* More muttering at the head table.

"The very brief introduction we were given to this project last month doesn't even begin to touch on the realities." Tammy Barber, the only woman on the council, raised her voice to speak. "No one mentioned how many houses this developer wants to build. I read every page of this proposal, and I'm concerned—"

"How many houses?"—a shout from the back of the room —"What kind of development are we talking about here?"

Normally Cary hated when people interrupted, but he had the same question.

"Development?" Melissa hissed. "What kind of development?"

"I don't know. It sounded like they were just going to subdivide the old Allen ranch and turn it into a few play ranches, that type of thing. No one even mentioned the word *development*." Cary was really wishing he'd grabbed that handout.

Melissa wasn't shy. She raised her hand a second before she spoke. "I missed the meeting last month, Tammy. Do we still have copies of this handout?"

"How many houses?" The question was asked again. "Just answer that."

Tammy Barber leaned forward. "Two *thousand* houses."

"What the *fuck*?" Cary cleared his throat. "Pardon me, but what?"

"Two thousand?" Melissa was as shocked as he was. "That's ridiculous."

"Well, everyone hold their horses here." Bud raised his hands. "That's why we're talking about it. And that's why JPR Holdings sent one of their top people here to answer your questions. But let's not forget about our budget shortfall last year. This kind of development would be a huge boost for the local economy."

"Bud," Cary said. "Be reasonable. Two thousand houses would nearly double the size of this town. You want to approve something like that?"

Bud raised his chin. "I have to think of the good of the town," he said. "We need to increase our tax base, and I think we all know what the other options would be. No one wants that."

"Are you talking about the marijuana dispensary again?" Melissa asked. "Because not everyone has your hang-ups about weed, Bud."

A few laughs sprinkled the room, but Cary sent Melissa a warning look. Bud could be a blowhard, and his ego was paper thin. The last thing Oakville needed was a bureaucrat on a power trip trying to prove what a big man he was.

"Beyond what anyone thinks about a marijuana dispensary"—Tammy Barber was speaking again—"the fact of the matter is, Cary is right. Two thousand new houses in Oakville would fundamentally change the town."

Myra Dean, the owner of the Main Street Mercantile, raised her hand. "Well yes... but wouldn't that be a lot more people in the shops?"

A more positive murmur made its way through the crowd.

"Yes," Bud said. "That would be a much bigger customer base for all our businesses. Your shop. The hardware store." Bud pointed to the Trujillo brothers, who ran the only remaining hardware and lumber yard in Oakville. "That's thousands more people visiting our stores and shopping. Thousands more going to our restaurants. Staying at the inn." He pointed to Marilou and Walter Fagundes, who ran the Oakville Inn. "Let's face it. We got more young people leaving than moving in. We need to build more housing."

"There's empty houses in town already," Melissa said. "What are you doing to sell those?"

"It's not the same kind of thing at all." Bud was getting testy again. "These would be people with money. The houses wouldn't be built unless they were sold already."

"That may be," Tammy said, "but we need a lot more discussion than just a fancy flyer and a company man coming to sell us on this idea."

"Hear, hear." Les Arthur spoke again. "Let's hear from this fellow. Where is he?"

"There." Melissa nudged him. "That guy. I bet you anything."

"Won't take that bet." Cary knew she was right.

The man leaning against the back wall was too polished to be a farmer, even though he wore jeans and a blue plaid shirt. He pushed away from the wall and walked toward the front of Veterans' Hall.

Bud stood. "I'd like to thank Kevin Fontaine from JPR Holdings for coming tonight to talk to us about the exciting prospects his company has planned for the Allen Ranch area."

"Boots," Melissa muttered.

"I see 'em."

The man's boots were squeaky clean. Cary probably could have seen his reflection in the finish. The boots Cary wore were made for all-day walking. They had orthopedic insoles and were covered in mud. Melissa's boots were made for riding and she wore ankle braces because she'd been riding so long. This guy...

"Greg and Beverly know some Fontaines over on the coast," Melissa said softly. "I've heard that name."

"That's interesting," Cary said.

"Isn't it?" Melissa opened her notebook and began to take furious notes.

Kevin Fontaine walked up to the head table and took his time shaking everyone's hand before he leaned against the old wooden podium.

"Hey, folks." The man's smile didn't falter even though Cary didn't spot a friendly face in the crowd. "I just want to say thanks for having me tonight. I grew up in a small community like this, and I gotta say it feels real good to be back."

"Where?" Cary asked, feeling contrary.

The persistent smile dimmed a bit. He looked over the crowd, trying to discern where the question had come from.

"Where are you from?" Cary raised his voice and waved to the man. "Just curious."

"Uh... Hey there." The smile was back. "I'm from Solvang originally."

"Solvang?" Cary exchanged a look with Melissa. Solvang had some horse ranches and wineries, but it was primarily a tourist pass-through. Was that what this company had in mind for Oakville? Trade its proximity to the national parks for more and more tourist dollars? "Interesting."

Kevin Fontaine's gleaming smile hid whatever his true thoughts were. "The development of the Allen ranch will be a turning point in the future of Oakville, transforming a quaint community known for its orange groves and ranches..."

"Quaint," Cary whispered to Melissa. "Did you know we were quaint?"

"I didn't." Melissa was still taking notes. "Do I need to put doilies on my steers?"

"...into a destination for those looking for a better way of life." Kevin Fontaine's smile seemed to be frozen even as his mouth moved. "Your new residents will be those looking for a slower pace while still pursuing an active lifestyle. They're eager to join a traditional community with strong connections to natural resources like parks. They're people who are already well-established and bring resources with them. Residents who—"

"Oh shit." The realization hit Cary in an instant. "You want to make Allen Ranch a retirement community for rich people."

Melissa's eyes went wide. "What?"

Cary could tell from the frozen look on Kevin Fontaine's face that he'd hit the nail on the head. "That's it, isn't it? You're building fancy houses for rich retirees."

"Active lifestyle, huh? Bet there's gonna be a golf course," Melissa said. "Did I get that right, Bud? You want them to turn some of the best grazing and growing land in Jordan Valley into an overly manicured monstrosity?"

"This town isn't owned by farmers and ranchers," Bud said as

47

ELIZABETH HUNTER

the buzz of conversation grew louder and louder. "Other people live here too!"

"Yeah, but most of them work in farming or ranching." Walter Fagundes spoke, his voice low but booming. "Mari and I may have a hotel for tourists, but this is a farming town, Bud. We like it that way. That's one of the reasons we moved here. You want a bunch of rich city people moving in and—"

"Spending money?" Bud said. "Yeah, Walter. Yeah, I do. New property taxes. New sales taxes and customers for our businesses —including yours, I might add. The bluegrass festival gets bigger every year, but it barely pays for itself. Do you have any ideas for funding the new fire trucks we need? You think the citrus co-op is gonna pay for them out of its own pocket? What about the new plumbing we need at the high school? You think it'd be better if our kids get bussed thirty miles to Metlin 'cause we can only afford to operate the elementary and junior high?"

Cary didn't have the extra cash to donate a whole damn fire truck. They were only a couple of years out of the worst drought in a century. And no one in town knew what to do about the school. He hated to admit it, but Bud had a point.

"You could fund those by loosening up a single restriction," Melissa said. "People up in Foster Valley—"

"I will not have weed sold in this town!" Bud's face was red. "No one wants that."

"No one" was an exaggeration, but Cary knew the idea of a cannabis dispensary in Oakville wasn't popular, even though evidence showed that it would bring in a massive amount of tax money with little to no investment from the town.

The big question was, would adding three thousand new residents prove any more popular?

Cary stood up and folded his arms over his chest. "You know, no offense to Mr. Fontaine, but I want to see details of all this in writing. Isn't that in the town charter? If a new zoning proposal

48

has been made to the council, then it's part of the public record. I want a copy. I want to read through the details of what this holding company is actually proposing, down to the fine print. And I bet I'm not the only one."

Melissa rose. "Agreed. I don't need someone coming in and telling me what the plan is. I want to read it for myself."

Tammy Barber leaned forward. "I make a motion to table any vote about JPR Holdings and the Allen Ranch development until the proposal has been submitted to the public for review."

Les Arthur said, "I second that motion."

Bud Rogers's face was sour. But not even Bud could buck protocol. "All those in favor of Tammy's motion to delay the vote?"

Four hands at the front table went up.

"All those opposed?"

Three hands—including Bud's—went up.

"The motion passes." Bud scowled. "Tammy, you're the recorder. I'll let you sort this out. Meeting adjourned."

The meeting broke up with the two dozen attendees forming small groups, many of them walking to the front to talk to Tammy.

Cary looked at Melissa. "I have a feeling Tammy's gonna be making a few photocopies this week."

"Ya think?" Melissa narrowed her eyes at Bud, who was talking to Kevin Fontaine. "I have a feeling that next month's meeting might be a little more crowded."

Cary scanned the angry faces milling around the room and the brittle smile on Fontaine's face. He was keeping the polite veneer, but it was as fake as his teeth. "Agreed."

"I'm gonna go." Melissa picked up the purse of mysteries. "I want to call a couple of people on the coast."

"I'll walk you out." He followed her out to her truck and waited while she got in. "You gonna tell your mom about this?"

"Yeah. Aren't you?"

"Oh, my mom is gonna be pissed." Cary stepped back as she shut her door. He motioned for her to roll down the window, then said, "You think the Allen family knows about all this?"

Gus Allen had sold the land fifteen or twenty years ago to move into town and be closer to his family, none of whom were interested in running the old ranch. His son, Jeremy, was Cary's regular climbing partner.

"I doubt it," Melissa said. "Gus'd be pissed."

"Think I should tell Jeremy about this?"

Melissa leaned on the steering wheel. "I don't know if Gus could do anything about it. He'll hear about it eventually, but he sold the land. It's not up to him anymore."

"This isn't going to happen." Cary patted the side of her truck. "You know that, right? There's no way people are going to vote to let this pass."

"Maybe not this," Melissa said. "But what if they come back and say they only want to do a thousand houses? Or five hundred? Bud's right. The town needs money."

Cary sighed. "I don't want to believe you, but when I bet against you, I usually lose."

She smiled. "See? You should never bet against me."

"I don't. Not anymore." He leaned closer, intruding on her space. "We gonna talk about us?"

Her smile fell. "There isn't an us, Cary. We're friends."

"Really? 'Cause you're the only one of my friends I want to kiss." Tension hummed in the air between them. Cary felt it, like a shock wire running from her mouth to his. "We're more than friends, Missy. I don't know what we are yet, and neither do you. But we're more than friends."

She put her truck in gear. "I need to go."

"Running away again?" He stepped back. "Eventually I'm gonna keep you in one place long enough that you'll be forced to have a conversation."

Melissa opened her mouth to retort, but nothing came out. She shook her head slightly and rolled up her window. Then she lifted her hand in a slight wave before she drove away.

CHAPTER FIVE

MELISSA WOKE to the sound of chickens clucking underneath her window. It wasn't an unpleasant sound. It was soothing. The chickens clucking meant that someone had already gone out to feed them, which meant Melissa didn't have to do it.

She glanced at the clock and her eyes went wide. Seven forty-five? She bolted up to sitting and ran a hand over her eyes. She'd stayed up way too late the night before. She had to stop reading before bed; it was a recipe for disaster.

She threw a vest over her pajamas and stumbled toward the door. "Abby?"

"Yeah?"

Melissa walked down the hall and saw Abby sitting at the kitchen table eating cereal and reading a book.

"Whoa." Her daughter's eyes went wide. "Uh, are you driving me to school?"

"Yes." She walked to the coffeepot, which was still half-full. "I am." She grabbed a travel mug and poured herself a full cup. "Give me five minutes."

"Okay." She stood up. "Should I warm up the truck?"

"Sure." It was one of the things Abby had started asking when she turned nine, and Melissa let her every now and then. "Five minutes."

"Okay!"

Melissa left the coffee to start cooling on the counter and hustled back to her room at the end of the hall. She threw on a pair of jeans, a tank top, and put her vest back on. Then she tied her hair back in a quick braid, slid her socks on, and walked to the kitchen door.

"Mom?"

"Are you up?" Joan was in the sitting room. "I thought I was going to have to drive her."

"I've got her." She searched desperately for her keys. They weren't on the hook by the door. "Why did you let me sleep so late?"

"I stopped being your alarm clock when you hit thirteen, Melissa Oxford. I'm not going to start that up again."

Abby had the keys! Melissa slammed her feet into her boots and grabbed her purse. She took two steps out the door. "Coffee!"

She ran back inside and grabbed the travel mug before she ran back to the door. "Bye, Mom!"

"Don't drive like a maniac."

She didn't drive like a maniac, but she did speed a little. They made it to school with minutes to spare, prompting exasperated sighs from her daughter, who hated being late.

"Don't roll your eyes. Wake me up next time."

"You know I will!" Abby slammed the door shut, and Melissa watched her run up to the gate of the small country school surrounded by tall oak trees.

All legs. She was like a colt.

I made that.

The thought made her smile. Abby might be a handful most days, but she was a good kid, and Melissa absolutely adored her. She drove her truck through the wilderness of the school drop-off before she got back onto Jordan Valley highway. Taking a long drink of coffee, she turned in to the sun and drove back to the ranch.

She took the few minutes of solitude to enjoy the silence and the coffee before she passed the Nakamura farm. Melissa spotted Rumi taking her morning walk along the road with a broad sun hat and a pair of bright yellow sneakers.

Just the sight of the tiny woman made Melissa smile. She pulled over and rolled down her window. "Good morning, Rumi."

"Melissa!" The older woman walked over to Melissa's truck, her head barely peeking over the window. "You slept in."

"How do you know?"

"I saw you roaring down the road and you didn't even wave at me."

"Sorry. I didn't see you."

"I know. Because you slept in." Rumi winked at her. "Were you reading?"

Melissa couldn't stop the smile. "How did you know?"

"You've been doing the same thing since you were little. Your mother used to complain about it."

"Did she?"

Rumi wrinkled her nose. "Only the way mothers complain about things they think are cute. Like you and Abby and her goats."

"I don't think Abby's goats are cute, I just can't get rid of them without her hating me."

The corner of Rumi's mouth turned up. "You'd never get rid of her goats."

Melissa slumped on the steering wheel. "Why am I so weak?"

Rumi laughed and stepped away from the truck. "You have a good day. I have to keep walking." She held up tiny leopard-print barbells. "I started carrying these now. The doctor said it's good for my bones."

"Yeah? You should tell Mom to walk with you."

Rumi pointed a barbell at her. "That's a good idea! I'm going to do that. She's younger than me. She'll make me walk faster." She waved at Melissa and kept walking, turning right and onto the lane that ran between orange groves and led back to the Naka-mura farmhouse.

Melissa had ridden her horse through the Nakamura groves her entire childhood, marveling at the cool, deep green of the trees and the heavenly aroma of citrus blossoms. She'd watched Cary from afar, harboring a girlhood crush on the handsome young man who kept his hair long and listened to rock music in his Mustang.

He didn't notice her then, of course. She was a child and he was a grown man. But she thought he was the most handsome man ever, and she loved how he teased Rumi, who was one of Melissa's favorite people.

Her girlhood independence had coincided with Rumi's children leaving home, which had led to a sweet friendship that Melissa cherished.

Rumi had taught her how to make rice balls and fried tofu, dishes Melissa had never seen before. Rumi had a light-filled artist's studio behind her house, which Melissa thought was incredibly glamorous and cool. She'd exhibited in art shows and shown Melissa how to paint with watercolors. Melissa still had several of the origami cranes Rumi taught her how to fold.

Melissa had tried to teach Rumi how to ride horses, but the small woman had never grown comfortable around them. They were too big. Too powerful. Rumi liked her bicycle and her walking shoes, though she occasionally joked about buying a donkey.

Melissa slowed down when she reached her own orchard. The four-year-old trees would give their first solid harvest this year. They still had a couple of months to ripen, and Melissa was hoping for a long, warm fall to sweeten the grove. She'd been considering a Pick-Your-Own season before the harvesting crews came in.

Other places picked apples in the fall. Maybe Metlin parents would like to pick mandarins. The short trees were perfect for kids to grab, and the sweet fruit was easy to peel.

Cary was right.

Melissa was happy to admit the man knew his business. He'd turned twenty acres of his own land to mandarins three years ago, right after he'd helped her plant hers. The market for them was hot, and they'd been a solid investment for her.

In another year, she'd be able to pay off the balance of the loan she'd had to take from Calvin's parents, and then she'd be completely in the black. It was a good feeling. Even though Greg and Bev had never let the note hang between them, she still felt the pressure of owing money to Calvin's family.

She parked her truck on the edge of the road and walked through the groves for a bit, looking at the insect-monitoring stations. She breathed in the scent of the trees and felt the ground under her boots.

It was good. What she was doing was good. It would be more stable than the cattle, though she never wanted to give the ranch up completely. But diversity was good. If the U-Pick operation went well, then maybe they'd do the pumpkin patch her mom had been talking about. Heck, maybe she'd let Abby get more goats and open a petting zoo in the fall.

Okay, maybe not more goats.

She walked back to the truck and headed home. The horses had to be fed and exercised. She was late checking the herd too.

She needed to hire another hand to keep track of the cattle, but she'd been running on the tightest budget possible while she still owed her in-laws. Once the loan was paid off, then she'd be able to hire someone full time. She had feelers out already, touching base with some of her grandfather's friends in Northern California, Idaho, and Texas. Most cowboys were looking to leave the state with its high cost of living, but Melissa was hoping a few might be looking for warm weather and minimal snow.

She'd barely opened the gate when she saw an unfamiliar truck parked by the house.

Melissa immediately went on alert. She pulled up next to the truck, which was an old Ford F-250, clearly meant for hauling a trailer, and hopped out.

"Hey, Mom?" She walked around the unfamiliar truck once. Idaho plates. Current tags. Big hitch. "Joan?"

She walked up to the porch and heard laughter coming from inside.

Melissa opened the door and heard her mom's voice coming from the kitchen. "Hello?"

"Hey, sweetie! Come on back!"

She knew her mother was a trusting person, but Melissa was not. She hoped these were old friends and not random people stopping by. She hung up her purse and walked into the kitchen.

She immediately saw an older man in his midfifties and a woman around the same age sitting at the kitchen table, cups of coffee in their hands. The man had a long handlebar mustache that was reddish-grey. His face and posture said cowboy, and Melissa spotted a hat sitting on the chair next to him.

"Hey there." She tossed her truck keys on the counter.

The man rose and nodded. "Ma'am."

The unfamiliar woman turned and smiled. "Good morning."

Joan rose and walked to Melissa. "Honey, this is Stu and Leigh Hagman, and they've just come from the Brady Ranch outside Twin Falls. I've known Leigh for ages. We worked in Monterey together when we were younger."

"Oh cool. Welcome to the ranch. Garret Brady?" Melissa smiled. "How's he doing?" Old Mr. Brady had been a good friend of her grandfather's. "I haven't seen any of the Bradys in ages."

"Well, Old Man Brady passed last year," Stu said, his voice a deep baritone that indicated a lifelong smoking habit. "But he'd been ill for a while, so it wasn't a surprise or anything. His daughter's running the ranch now."

Joan sat back down. "That'd be Carla?"

Leigh said, "Yep. And she'd doing great. She and her husband have three kids. Real nice people." Leigh turned to Stu and nodded. "In fact, Carla's the reason we're here." She smiled at Joan. "Other than wanting to catch up with Joan."

"It's so nice to see you." Her mother patted Leigh's hand. "I can't believe it's been twenty years."

Stu rose and reached in his back pocket. "Used to work for Carla. She didn't have any work for us at the ranch." He pulled out a folded envelope. "But she mentioned she'd heard from the Tanner Ranch that y'all might be looking for some help. Leigh and I are both experienced, and we're looking for a fresh start if you need help."

Melissa let out a long breath. "Oh man. I wish—"

"We're definitely looking," Joan said.

Melissa sighed. "Mom, we can't afford it."

Stu jumped in. "We work cheap. I'm even happy to give you a few weeks free to see if we suit the place. All we need is a place to park our motor home and pasture for our horses."

Leigh smiled. "We don't need much. We just like working."

"I can't *not* pay you." Melissa took the letter Stu handed her. "It's not right, and I don't think it's even legal." She scanned the letter from Carla Brady, which offered a glowing recommendation for both Stu and Leigh.

One of the hardest-working couples I know.

...package deal.

...great cook.

...way with horses.

...twenty years' experience, at least.

I'm tempted to lay off a couple of my younger guys to hire them back, but that's not really fair. If you're looking for good people you can trust with your herd, I can't recommend them enough.

Melissa was crushed. Why couldn't Leigh and Stu have shown

up six months from now? She looked up from the letter. "Oh you guys, I wish I could, but until the mandarin harvest—"

"Melissa, can I talk to you?" Joan stood, her mouth in a flat line, walked over to Melissa, and pulled her out the kitchen door and into the hallway.

"Mom," she whispered, "we can't."

"We can afford it," Joan said. "And you need the help. I read that letter from Carla Brady. The two of them could run that entire herd. It is not that big. They're looking for work. You need help. God sent them to us."

"I can't make money magically appear!"

"I'll pay them," she said. "I can help. I've got Social Security and Medicare now, and what else do I have to spend money on? Nothing."

"Even if I pay them minimum wage—which is just insulting for an experienced guy—that's nearly two thousand a month for one of them to work. There's no way we can pay for both."

Joan sighed. "You know, once upon a time if a man wanted to work with his wife and wasn't asking for much, you just let him."

"Well, when you were growing up, Grandpa didn't have be afraid of the labor board."

"Oh, for heaven's sake. These people are looking for work and a place to get away from the snow now that they're older. They're not gonna take you to the labor board."

Melissa bit her lip. It was tempting. So, so tempting. With two trusted employees, she could take a vacation. She hadn't done that in eight years. She could take Abby to the beach. Or call the friends who'd probably forgotten she existed. She could have a *life* outside the ranch and the orchard.

She suspected her mom was right. This couple probably didn't need four grand in monthly income, especially if she could give them rent free parking and use of the pastures and barn. "What if we hired one and let the other one... contract as needed?"

Joan nodded slowly. "That could work."

"Honestly, I'm still going to be working. If I hired Stu to take on some of the ranch day to day, then Leigh could work with you around the garden and help with the house and just bill us for her time."

"That's fair! And if you could pay Stu, then I'll pay Leigh. It'll be between her and me."

"But if she's an independent contractor, then that means she can take other jobs too. You can't give her a schedule she's got to keep to. Nothing like that. She's in charge of her own schedule."

"Rumi might have things she needs help with," Joan said. "That's likely to work out fine." Joan nodded. "Let's see what they say."

Melissa had a knot in the pit of her stomach. "I still don't know about this. It's a lot of money for us and not that much for them."

"We're doing fine. You're just manic about getting that loan paid off, and you shouldn't be. You've got three more years. If we keep things tight, then by next year's harvest, you'll be done with them."

"They're Abby's grandparents," she muttered. "I'll never be done with them. But the sooner I get out from under that loan, the better."

Melissa came to a decision and pushed open the swinging door to the kitchen. "Okay, Stu and Leigh, here's the deal. I can hire one of you full time—minimum wages is all I can afford right now, but that's twelve bucks an hour here in California—and we can probably take on the other on a contract basis for filling in."

Stu and Leigh exchanged smiles. "And our motor home?"

"Job comes with free rent. You're welcome to park here. There's room in the pasture behind the barn—there's even hookups my grandpa put in—and you'll have space to stable your horses. We've got four empty stalls right now, so that's not an issue. You have your own trailer?"

"Sure do," Leigh said.

The couple looked like they'd won the lottery.

"You won't be sorry," Stu said. "This suits us perfect. It's exactly what we've been hoping for, a family place where we can feel at home. Honest work." He swallowed hard. "You won't be sorry, Ms. Rhodes."

"Just Melissa, please." She felt bad she couldn't pay them more, but if you had few expenses, then you didn't need much. "So you've got free rent and stable here, and we've got a big kitchen garden. You're welcome to help yourself to anything you need from that."

"I love gardening," Leigh said. "I can get my hands dirty with Joan."

Joan beamed. "That would be great."

"There's always beef in the freezer," Melissa said. "And eggs. Lots of eggs."

Stu reached his hand across the table. "All sounds good to me. When can I start?"

"Today," Joan said. "Why don't you borrow my horse and Melissa can show you around the place. I'll help Leigh get you guys settled."

Stu's face was red and he looked close to tears. Melissa looked away and led the man out to the porch. She cleared her throat and pointed to the stables. "The horses are probably about ready to murder me. I was late waking up this morning."

"You'll be able to take a few more mornings off from now on." Stu cleared his throat. "Take a vacation with your girl even. You can depend on me and Leigh."

Melissa nodded and walked out to the barn with Stu, hoping the man was right. If the two of them worked out, they could change her whole life.

CHAPTER SIX

CARY TURNED from the row of potted citrus trees he'd been experimenting with. "You did what?"

"I hired someone," Melissa said, staring at the tree. "I think you need to prune that lemon back more. It's a Eureka and they'll take over the world if you let them."

"Forget the lemon. You hired someone? Who?"

"Couple out of Idaho. They used to work on the Brady Ranch. Oh! And you'll never guess who had time to squeeze in a project." She did a little dance. "Brian Montoya came through. I gave him a deposit for materials and he's starting on the bunkhouse this week."

"Is this someone you know?"

She frowned. "Brian?"

"No, this person you hired."

"I don't know them, but my mom knows the wife. And Old Man Brady and my grandpa were friends."

"Did you check references?"

"They had a letter from the Bradys." Melissa sidled next to the tree and held her hand out. "Give me those clippers. I want to try something."

"Where are they living?" Cary handed over the clippers.

"On the ranch." She began snipping branches. "You've got to be tougher or—"

"*On* the ranch? With you and your mom and your daughter?"

Melissa looked up. "No, over on the Allen ranch with all the rich retirees, Cary. Yes, my ranch. They've got a motor home, and you know Grandpa put in those hookups behind the barn. I can't pay them much, so it's a fair trade." She left the tree he'd been working on and moved to the next. "What are you doing with these?"

Cary frowned, wondering how her brain moved from topic to topic so quickly. "Um, if I can perfect the grafting, then I'm going to sell them to backyard gardeners who don't want three different trees. You'll get a lemon, an orange, and a grapefruit all on one tree. You just have to be brutal about pruning so one type doesn't dominate."

"That's a great idea."

"But getting back to the mystery cowboy, can we talk about how you don't know these people from Adam? I would agree what you worked out is a fair deal if you'd checked these people out." He took the clippers from her. "Right now you don't know them."

"My mom knows Leigh. What's the problem?"

"That you're too trusting? Why did they leave Idaho?"

"Looking for warmer winters."

"Is that what they said?"

"Not... exactly." Melissa cleared her throat. "My mom mentioned avoiding snow, which was probably from something Leigh had told her. I didn't hear it from them, but this is someone my mom knows, okay?"

And most murder victims know their killers. "Not okay. I think you should know why they left Idaho."

"The letter from the Bradys just said that they were looking for a fresh start. It's not any of my business why. And it's really not any of yours! Carla Brady also said she'd hire them in a heart-beat if she had any jobs available."

"That's a real easy thing to say from thousands of miles away." He started pruning again. "Why didn't you check them out? Do a background check? Did you even make them fill out employment applications?"

"Stu helped me move the herd from Badger Hollow over to Christy Meadow," she said. "Does that count as a job application? Because it took me a quarter of the time it takes me on my own. We also managed to fix three fence posts in the same afternoon. I got to eat dinner with my mom and Abby in the middle of the week. And they have a dog, Cary. A trained cattle dog. Do you know how much help that's gonna be?"

Cary bit back a sarcastic retort. It wasn't that he didn't trust her judgment, but Melissa could be overly trusting of anyone who could ride and rope well, as if cattle skills gave you inherent virtue. "I'm just saying that you have these people living on your ranch now. You're not the least bit concerned that there's something you should know that they might not have told you?"

"No, I'm really not."

He cut two branches in quick succession. "You drive me absolutely crazy."

Melissa examined the graft on the navel orange branch. "Why?"

"Because when it comes to me and you, you're the picture of suspicion. You overthink everything."

"Oh, so this isn't about safety at all." Her chin jutted out. "This is about the nonexistent relationship you insist—"

"This *is* about safety! Your safety and Abby's." He cut her off before she said something that would start a completely different fight. "You're suspicious of me, whom you've known basically your entire life. But when it comes to hiring complete strangers who happen to know about horses, you're fine. 'No problem,

64

Cary. They're saints and angels, randomly showing up on my doorstep to make life easier. They even have a dog.'"

She glared at him. "They do have a dog. And you and me? We're not a thing. I've been telling you that for months now. Just because we—"

Cary dropped the clippers, walked over to her, and kissed her just to shut her up. Her mouth was sweet. She'd been eating a nectarine in his office.

It only took a moment for her to respond. She went from stock-still to melting in seconds. A small sigh escaped her throat, and her fingers curled against his chest. She slid one hand around his waist, and her fingers spread against his back.

Her lips were urgent and soft. Her tongue tasted like sugar and coffee. He could feel the tension that lived in her vibrating under her skin. She was a volcano. Melissa had so much pent-up energy, touching her skin might light them both on fire.

Cary was willing to risk it.

Her body was pressed to his, her hips snug against his and her breasts tight against his chest. Before things went too far, Cary released her mouth and nibbled her lower lip, then drew back. "You were saying?"

Melissa blinked. "What?"

Was his smile smug? Maybe just a little. "You and me aren't *what?*"

She looked away, her face guilty. "You have to stop doing this."

"Why?" He played with a piece of hair that had escaped her ponytail. "I like kissing you. And I've been waiting a while to do it."

She frowned. "What does that mean?"

Shit. He shouldn't have said anything. "Just... that we have chemistry. We've had it for a long time. That's all I'm saying."

"Did you think...?" Her face turned red. "Not when Calvin was alive, we didn't. I would have *never*—"

"I'm not saying that." He rubbed his temple and took a step

back. "I'm not saying there was anything when Calvin... I didn't think of you that way then. Not actively. Or intentionally, I mean. Even if I had been attracted to you in some way, you were his wife, and I would have never—"

"You know what?" She motioned between them. "You keep asking what I'm afraid of. Why I don't just... I don't know, let go and have a wild, crazy fling with you or something."

His jaw clenched. "You think I'm interested in a fling?"

"It's because of this, Cary. Because I'm always going to be Calvin's widow. And you're always going to be his friend. And he's always going to be there, okay?" She swallowed hard. "He's gone, but he's never gone. Do you get that?"

"I can't get that, because I've never been where you are. But that's no reason—"

"You can't have a relationship when there's another person in the middle of it! Calvin is Abby's father. He'll always be there. That's not fair to you. Or me. Or... anyone. It's not fair, but it's the reality, okay?"

She turned and started to walk away.

Cary yelled, "I don't..."

She paused, but she didn't turn around.

You don't what, genius? You don't have an answer for her because she's right?

"You're not right, Melissa."

She turned around. "Why not?"

"I don't know right in this exact moment; you're just not." He motioned between them. "This is not over."

"Cary, it shouldn't even *start*."

"Do you want me?"

The look in her eyes tore him to pieces. "It doesn't matter."

"It doesn't matter what you want?" He cleared his throat. "I disagree. Very much."

She smiled a little, but she looked like she wanted to cry. "What's new?"

Melissa looked at him for a few more minutes, then she shook her head, turned, and walked away.

Cary watched her until she disappeared into the trees.

Well, at least she wasn't running. That was an improvement.

Kind of.

———

HE FINISHED PRUNING the grafted citrus and worked a little in the greenhouse he was using for propagation. If there was one thing he liked about being a farmer, it was the endless experimentation. Every plant behaved a little differently. Every orchard was a slightly different microclimate. Nothing was predictable. Nothing was boring.

Kind of like Melissa.

How could they go from talking about citrus grafts to arguing about her new employees to arguing about their relationship to kissing to more arguing?

The woman didn't just drive him crazy, she gave him whiplash.

And while there might have been an arguing theme in most of their interactions, it didn't discourage Cary. He was pretty sure that would just make things more interesting in bed.

Because that was where they were headed. One way or another, their self-control wasn't going to hold out forever. Something was going to snap. He just hoped they were in a relatively secluded place when it happened.

God, she was so damn stubborn. What did she think? That their attraction betrayed Calvin?

He thought about his friend as he examined grafts. Pictured Calvin's ornery face in front of him. Cary had loved that kid—missed the hell out of him—but Calvin could be more than a bit of an ass. He was a rich kid from the coast who knew far less about cattle ranching than his wife did.

To Calvin's credit, he didn't let that bother him. Much. Cary could see the tension between them at times because Calvin dismissed Melissa too often. Most of it was youth, but some of it was upbringing. Despite his faults, Calvin had loved Melissa and adored Abby. Just like Cary did.

He walked through the greenhouse and into the office at the far end where he kept a desk and his computer. He sat down and leaned back in the creaking chair. *Sorry, Calvin*—he stared at the stained ceiling tiles in the old building—*but you're gone and I'm in love with your wife. I'm not going to back off in honor of your memory or some shit like that.*

And what would Calvin say?

I just want you both to be happy.

No, Calvin would not have said that.

I hope you know what you're in for.

That was more likely.

Then again, Melissa had never been a live wire to Calvin the way she was with Cary. Being on her own had changed her. Holding everything together with sheer will and endless work had shaped the woman she'd become. She was more stubborn. More single-minded. More determined.

Do right by my family, asshole. Or I will haunt you.

Cary had to smile. That sounded like Calvin.

Do right by my family.

Cary could do that. In fact, he *would* do that.

He picked up the phone and called Joan's mobile phone. "Hey, Joan! It's Cary. Yeah, Melissa told me. That's fantastic. Uh-huh. ... Sounds like the right kind of people. What are their names again? Stu and..." He jotted down notes as Joan raved about their new employees.

And neighbors.

Cary wasn't worried about the ranch. Melissa was more than competent when it came to that. If someone fucked up, she'd fire them. But these people were living in a trailer next to the house where Abby slept. You better believe he was going to be suspicious.

"So they were up in Idaho before they came down here?" He wrote more notes, grateful that Joan was the chatty type. "Oh, Oklahoma too? I didn't know there was much ranching there." He couldn't stop the smile. "I know. It's very obvious I don't own cows. Cattle. Whatever."

He got all the information he needed to start a background check. Full names. Last address he could figure out. A few past employers. It was enough to start with.

"Melissa?" He frowned. "Yeah, she was over here. She's not home yet?"

Fuck. Where had she gone?

It wasn't his business. She was a grown woman. She didn't need watching.

"Hey, Joan? Yeah, I need to go. Let me know if she doesn't get back before dinner, okay?"

He hung up the phone and immediately dialed another number. Paused while it rang.

"Kern County Sheriff's office."

"Can I speak to Mark Guzman, please?"

"Just one moment." The receptionist put him on hold while Cary tapped his pen back and forth on his desk.

He was going to find out just who these people were. If they were good people, then no problem. If they were dangerous? If the wrong kind were sleeping in a trailer and working around Abby?

Problem. Massive problem.

"Hey, Mark." Cary tapped his pen on the pad of paper where Stu and Leigh Hagman's names were written. "Good to talk to you too."

CHAPTER SEVEN

MELISSA WOKE early on Saturday morning, hoping to get in a longer ride during the coolest part of the day. She walked out the door in the blue light of the late-summer morning and saddled Moxie, nodding to Stu in the distance when she saw him heading up the road to the north pasture with his border collie, Dex, trailing behind.

Stu nodded back, raised a hand, and kept riding. He'd been introducing the herd to Dex gradually, and so far Melissa was pleased with what she saw. The cattle seemed less stressed, and she hadn't seen any of the anxiety she'd been worried about. Stu's calm commands were enough to move Dex, who herded with confidence but wasn't aggressive.

It had only been two weeks since Melissa had hired him, and Stu hadn't given her reason to doubt him once. So far he'd been as knowledgeable as promised. He had a good instinct for cattle, worked well with others, and was an excellent horseman.

She'd even been able to take Abby over to the coast to see her grandparents the weekend before to meet the famous horse that sort of belonged to her. They'd stayed two full days, and Abby had gotten to know Sunny, the gelding who really did seem sweet as apple pie.

It broke Melissa's heart driving her daughter away from her new love, and she was sure that was exactly what Greg and Beverly were after. They wanted Abby to be on the coast permanently, which wasn't going to happen.

Melissa left the developed part of the ranch behind and followed an old trail that led along the rocky hills beside the creek that flowed through Allen Ranch. Come the rainy season, it would be a rushing stream, but this late in the summer it was bone dry, with nothing but stones and oak trees revealing its course.

She took a deep breath and inhaled the scent of sweet grass and wild roses. Birdsong filled the air as she rode. Two hawks circled the meadow to her right, hunting in the long grass.

Though it had been ranchland for fifty years, the edges of Allen Ranch had always been undeveloped. Gus Allen had liked it that way, liked his children and grandchildren to experience the unaltered wild of special places. Since he'd moved and no one had run cattle on the land, it had quickly returned to its natural state.

Melissa rode along the edges of the ranch, noting the frayed barbed wire fences and toppled fence posts. Whoever had bought the ranch wanted to sell it, but they didn't seem keen on maintaining anything. It was a good thing no one but Melissa and a few other neighbors used this trail. It was becoming a hazard.

She rode for an hour, across the foothills that bordered Jordan Valley and along the dry creek. She hadn't gone looking for Cary, but when she came across his quad bike, she wasn't surprised. There was a stretch of tumbled granite at the end of Jordan Valley where he liked to climb.

She hadn't really talked to him since their argument about Stu and Leigh, though she'd seen him in passing and he'd been up to the house to have lunch with her mom and Abby last Saturday when her brother was at the ranch.

He'd been avoiding her calls too. And though he couldn't ignore her texts, his replies had been mostly monosyllabic.

She missed him, not that she'd ever tell him that. But she did.

Melissa rode a little farther and spotted him in the distance, clinging to the side of a giant black granite boulder called Halsey Rock. His hair was tied back in a low ponytail, and his shirt was stripped off. He wore nothing but olive-green pants and a bandana tied around his neck.

Melissa dismounted Moxie and tied the horse's lead to a fallen sycamore near the creek. Then she walked over to a shaded patch near the boulders and sat near Cary's pack, leaning her back against the cool granite that was still shaded by the hills. The sun was rising behind the mountains, casting long shadows on the foothills and the valley.

Melissa rested her head on the rock, her eyes trained on Cary as he moved.

With clothes on, Cary reminded her of a solid block. His shoulders were square and his chest was deep. He didn't move with any particular grace when he walked through his orchards. He moved like a farmer. His arms seemed a little long for his body, and his legs were sturdy.

Stripped to the skin, clinging to the rocks and moving across the face of nearly black granite, he was art in motion. The definition of his back and shoulders was a thing of utter and complete beauty. His rolling muscles were decorated by brilliant ink. His broad shoulders narrowed to a trim waist.

Cary's fingers flexed and reached with grace and precision. His arms stretched wide as he found footholds in the tiniest crevices and seams.

She watched him in silence. Even the birds were observing. His legs hung only a few feet off the ground, but every movement was imbued with tension.

When he reached the far side of the granite face, he hopped off the rock and flexed his hands before he stretched his arms up and out.

Wooooow.

Cary turned, wiped his forehead with a handkerchief, and froze when he spotted her.

Melissa raised her hand in a slight wave, but she couldn't find it in herself to make a snarky remark or biting quip. The silence was too precious.

Cary walked toward her, wiping his hands on the bandana he'd taken from around his neck as he searched her face. His hair fell around his shoulders, which shone with sweat. A fine sheen of it covered him from forehead to waist, making his skin glow in the swiftly growing light.

Without saying a word, he knelt in front of her and nudged her knees apart. He braced his hands on the rock she leaned against and lowered his mouth to hers.

It was the third time they'd kissed, and surprise had turned to anticipation. His mouth was slow and luxurious, moving as smoothly as he'd traversed the boulders. His full lips covered hers, caressing each in turn. His tongue moved at the seam of her mouth, parting her lips as he explored her.

Cary tasted like tea and honey. Melissa put her hand on his cheek and enjoyed the rough texture of his stubble against her palm. The edge of his jaw rested in her hand as he angled his mouth to kiss her deeper.

She spread her jeans-clad legs and allowed him to press his body into hers. The rock was at her back, and his warm skin was against her breasts. Her hand relaxed, and she ran it from his shoulder all the way along his arm. He smelled like clean sweat and Cary, an indefinable blend of orange blossoms and earth.

She felt a sigh leave her throat; his mouth moved to her neck and he kissed her again. She closed her eyes when the sun hit her face, only to open them again so she could watch her fingers—

silhouetted against the morning sun—trail over the burnished bronze skin of his tattooed shoulder.

Beautiful, beautiful man.

Her head fell back as Cary kissed slowly along her collarbone.

He still hadn't said a word, and she was grateful.

Maybe this is the solution, Melissa. Neither of you talk. Just kissing and sex. No talking means no fighting.

She was near bursting when he drew back and placed one more soft kiss on her lips.

"Good morning."

Melissa let out a long breath. "Hey."

Cary moved his backpack and sat next to her. He unzipped it and brought an olive-green canister out. "Tea?"

"Sure."

She watched him fill the lid of the thermos and hand it to her. She took it and he brought out a water bottle, drinking half a liter before she could take a sip of tea.

Melissa watched him, watched the easy slope of his shoulders and the fine creases around his eyes. His silver and black hair was loose around his shoulders. There was no tension between his eyes. "I think this is the most relaxed I've ever seen you."

Cary opened his mouth, then closed it as he smiled. "Bouldering is a nice way to start the morning."

"You were going to say something else."

"Yes." He glanced at her. "But we've gone ten whole minutes without fighting, and I don't want to break the streak."

"What was it?" She leaned her head against the rock to watch him, enjoying the cool granite against her cheek. "I've never seen you so relaxed..." She smiled a little. "Because I've never seen you after sex?"

He smiled, and a rarely seen dimple appeared at the corner of his cheek. "Was that a suggestion?"

"A guess. That's what you were going to say, isn't it?" The dimple told Melissa she was right.

"How do you know so much about men's brains?"

"I've spent my entire life on a cattle ranch. How do you know how to kiss so well?"

Cary set his water bottle down. "Look at us. We're actually having a conversation."

"Kind of." She shifted toward him. "You're ignoring my question."

"That's not a question you ask." He lifted his arm and moved to put it around her but paused. "I'm sweaty."

"And I smell like horses."

Cary shrugged and moved his arm to encircle her, shifting her so she was sitting between his legs and leaning against his chest. It wasn't the first time they'd sat close. It wasn't the first time his arm had been around her. But everything in this moment felt new. Untested. Fresh like the morning they'd intruded on.

Cary reached into his backpack and brought out a nectarine, then he unfolded his pocketknife and sliced off a piece before he put it to her lips.

Melissa ate it and enjoyed the burst of flavor against her tongue. It combined nicely with the green tea and honey he'd poured for her.

"So, Melissa Oxford Rhodes"—he sliced off another chunk of fruit and ate it—"are we ever going to talk about the two of us without you running away?"

"I keep coming back." She took a deep breath and relaxed against his chest.

"Yeah." He reached for the tea. "You do."

"So." She handed him the cup.

"So what does that mean?"

She rolled her eyes. Why were men so dense sometimes? "It means I keep coming back."

He nudged her lips with another piece of nectarine. "I was thinking about what you said. About Calvin."

Why did you have to bring that up?

"You're not allowed to feel guilty for kissing me," Cary said. "Not now. Not ever. Calvin's been gone six years and there was never *anything* other than friendship between us when he was alive. His death never made you stop living before. You're choosing to make it different this time."

"I told you, you can't have a relationship with another person—"

"Missy, do you know how old I am?"

She frowned. "Uh... I don't think I do, actually."

"I'm forty-six."

"Really?"

"Really."

Okay, that was older than she thought, but Cary must have good genes because he was sexy as hell and he climbed mountains, for heaven's sake.

He cut off another piece of nectarine and fed it to her. "I've never had a partner die. Not a wife or a girlfriend. But I was married before. I've had serious relationships that ended. Some of them pretty badly."

"I remember when you married Aneesha." Teenage Melissa had been crushed. And then she decided that Kyle Robinson was going to take her to her first high school dance. She wore a purple dress.

Cary said, "And I remember when you married Calvin. I was there, in fact."

"I was at school when you and Aneesha broke up," she said. "I remember Mom telling me about it though."

Melissa had been sad, but not overly interested. She'd already met Calvin and had decided it was fate that they'd met in Texas, two ranching kids from California. Melissa had planned her wedding years before it happened, utterly confident that her life would go exactly as planned.

"Life is weird," she said. "And unexpected. And weird."

"Life is long," Cary said. "And you know what I've learned since my marriage to Aneesha fell apart?"

Melissa shifted so she could see his face.

"I've learned that every person we meet changes us. Sometimes in good ways. Sometimes in bad. Sometimes both. But we're changing all the time."

"What does this have to do with Calvin?"

"You're not the woman you were when you married Calvin, Missy. I'm not the man I was when I married Aneesha. Which is good, because I was kind of an arrogant bastard back then."

"Really?"

"Yeah. I was. And getting divorced knocked a lot of that out of me. Aneesha changed me. Changed who I am."

Melissa frowned. "But she didn't *die*, Cary."

"No, but in a lot of ways—important ways—I am who I am because of her. And in that sense, she's still with me all the time. So is my dad, who taught me how to be a man. So is Jenny Christiansen, who taught me how to kiss—you did ask—and every other person I've been with. Every other person I've loved."

"So you're saying Calvin is always going to be with me."

"Of course he is." Cary moved her hair to the side and kissed her neck, making Melissa shiver. "Not only with you, but with Abby. With your mom. On the ranch. He put his mark all over that place."

"I forget his voice sometimes," she blurted out. "Forget the sound of my name when he said it. Is that terrible?"

"No. It's normal. It's been six years."

She rubbed her knuckles over her eyes. "But then I feel close to him when I'm riding in the north pasture. He loved going up there in the spring to see the wildflowers. We took Abby there for a picnic when she was only a baby. Sometimes when I'm there, it's like... if I turned around, he'd be sitting on the fence. Waiting for me."

"I think that's beautiful," Cary said softly. "And I'm glad. Do you think that bothers me? Why would it bother me? He was my friend." Cary blinked hard. "And I miss him, but that doesn't keep me from wanting you. Or recognizing what's been growing here for years."

Melissa cleared her throat. "I don't know if I'm ready for what you want, Cary. Even if I can accept what you're saying—"

"What do you think I want?" he asked. "No, don't tell me yet, because I can almost guarantee you're going to get it wrong." He put a finger over her lips when she opened her mouth. "No. Stop. Just... don't assume."

She batted his hand away. "Don't assume what? You pretty much told me we're not friends, so—"

"Bullshit." He glared at her. "When did I say that?"

Melissa opened her mouth. Closed it. Okay, he hadn't said they weren't friends, he'd said they weren't *just* friends. Which... Okay, judging from how much they were kissing that morning, it was a fair statement.

Cary continued before she could respond. "As far as I'm concerned, we'll always be friends. Nothing about that has changed."

She rolled her eyes. "Seriously?"

"Seriously." He propped his arm on his knee. "Missy, I know you like arranging shit and putting everything in the right drawer. Your office organization is ruthless." He leaned over and kissed her mouth, savored it. "But don't try to organize us. For now, let's just keep being friends."

She raised both eyebrows. "Friends?"

He shrugged. "Friends who kiss."

"Is that a thing now?" It was entirely possible. Melissa hadn't been on a first date since 2004. She didn't know how anything worked these days. There were apps for everything. Friends Who Kiss was probably a relationship status on Facebook.

"It's a thing." He wrapped his arms around her and rested his chin on her shoulder. "It's a thing for us."

CHAPTER EIGHT

CARY GOT off the phone with the agency his friend Mark had recommended. Background checks on Stuart Hagman hadn't taken as long as Cary anticipated. None of the information had been buried. Most of it was public record, in fact.

The real mystery was how to approach Melissa. He'd just broken through the hard shell of her resistance to a relationship; he didn't want to sabotage his progress.

"Friends who kiss."

Sure, Melissa. Friends who kiss. That's all.

It wasn't ideal, but he could work with it. The woman was cautious by nature, and life hadn't been kind to her. He respected her caution; he just wished it was directed at those who might be actual threats.

Like Stu Hagman. Potentially.

There was no getting around it. The man hadn't been up-front with Melissa, and she needed to know. Cary wasn't willing to jeopardize Melissa's, Abby's, and Joan's safety because the woman he loved might get pissed off at him for interfering.

Check that. She would definitely get pissed off at him, but there was nothing else to do.

Then again, maybe he didn't need to talk to Melissa. The more he thought about it, the surer he was.

He didn't need to speak to Melissa. He needed to talk to Stu.

He ran a quick hand through his hair, thinking about the best way to approach the man. "Phil?" he called to his foreman.

Phil stuck his head in the office. "Yeah, boss?"

"Going over to the Oxford ranch. I've got my phone."

"No problem." Phil disappeared again.

It was a quiet time on the farm. They'd finished picking the Valencias and had a few months for pruning and cleaning the groves before they'd be ready to harvest the navel oranges and mandarins. Phil was trying to contact pickers and line up everything for harvest in advance, but many contractors didn't want to be booked that far out or commit to a price before they knew how high labor demands were going to be.

"Phil!"

Phil appeared again. "Yeah, boss?"

"You touch base with Teresa yet?"

"I left her a message, but she hasn't called me back."

Cary grunted. "Okay. I'm going over to Oxfords."

Phil grinned. "Yeah, you said that."

"What are you smiling at?"

"Nothing." The old man wouldn't stop grinning. He'd been hired by Cary's dad, so in Cary's mind, he was a fixture. No one could fire Phil. Not that they'd want to. He was a nice person and his wife made excellent brownies.

Cary glared at Phil as he walked out the door. "Just shut up."

"Wasn't saying anything!"

"Yeah, well... stop smiling."

"Say hi to Melissa!"

Cary turned and flipped the man off before he opened his truck door. He drove the three miles from his farm office over to the ranch, taking his time to survey his groves along the way. His father's original five-hundred-acre orange farm had been expanded over the years. Cary had bought pieces of property here and there. This one was good for Valencias. That one for lemons. Another had both his current office, a greenhouse, and was certi-fied organic, which gave him a bridge to that market while he transitioned his other groves to more sustainable practices.

His property was scattered, but the original farm still surrounded his mother's house, which sat in a grove of oaks and sycamores that ran along Halsey Creek.

Cary drove past his family home and turned left on Jordan Valley Road to get to the Oxfords' ranch. He glanced at his watch. If he was correct, she'd be gone this time of day and he might be able to talk to Stu on his own.

He was driving past the house when he saw Abby waving from the porch. The smile was automatic. He might be a cranky bastard at times, but that child was pure sunshine and he'd do anything for her. He stopped and got out of the truck.

"Hey, kid."

"Hey, adult."

He put his hands on his hips. "Don't you have school today?"

"Nope." She climbed up on the porch railing and swung her legs. "Teacher work day. Mom's not here. Grandma's in the house."

He leaned against the post near the front step. "I came to talk to Stu."

"Oh." She hopped down. "Stu's nice. I like him and Leigh. Want to see my new goat?"

"You got a new goat?" He followed Abby as she skipped to the goat shed behind the house. "Yeah, I want to see it. I thought your mom said no more goats."

"We didn't buy it." Her cheeks turned red. "Aslan got Princess kind of pregnant and so Princess had a kid."

"That does happen sometimes when you put goats together."

Abby's cheeks were still a little red. "You have no idea."

Cary muffled a laugh and stuffed his hands in his pockets.

"I'm just glad this one made it," Abby continued. "Rosie had a kid last year, but it didn't live for very long."

"I'm sorry." He hadn't heard about that. "That's sad."

She shrugged. "It happens. Generally speaking, goats are very hardy animals."

"I don't know much about them. I never had any when I was a kid."

Her eyes went wide. "Really?"

"I told you before. No animals."

She looked at him with eyes of sincere pity. "Well, goats are very fascinating creatures. Did you know they were some of the first animals humans ever tamed? People have probably had goats longer than they've had dogs."

Cary nodded. "That makes sense. Dogs are nice, but they don't give milk or wool."

"Exactly!" Abby shook her head. "But there's like... millions of dogs in America but hardly anyone has goats."

"That's crazy. I don't know what people are thinking."

"I know, right?" She opened the metal door and let Cary in the shed. A wide corral filled with large rocks, a picnic table, old children's toys, and various and sundry crates had been built off the side of the shed, which shielded the goat corral from the afternoon sun. It was not the neatest setup. He and Melissa had patched it together over the years as Abby's goat obsession grew.

As they approached, happy bleats of excitement greeted them as six goats jumped and skipped over to see their favorite human.

"Hey, guys!" Abby rubbed the heads of all six goats before she walked deeper into the barn. "Princess," she sang. "Hey, mama goat! How are you?"

Cary followed Abby into the small kidding pen, which was separate from the main corral. A floppy-eared doe lay in straw with a tiny kid next to her. Cary bent down and watched as Abby filled a plastic tub with oats and brought it to Princess.

He squatted down to examine the new addition to the herd as Abby fed the mother goat. "Pretty cute, kid."

Abby looked up with a brilliant smile. "Which kid are you talking to?"

"Ha ha. I'm talking to you, human kid. And I'm talking *about* goat kid. Boy or girl?"

"Girl. I think I'm gonna name her Lala. I was hoping it would be a girl because I want to learn how to make goat cheese, and if we get more boy goats, that doesn't do much for me. I already have two boys, and Mr. Tumnus is starting to fight with Aslan. They nearly broke the fence last week."

"You want to make goat cheese?"

Abby stood. "Yeah. I like goat cheese, and Paula at the farmers' market said she'd teach me how to make it if I want. And even though I can't sell goat cheese at the market, I can sell goat-milk *soap*, and I looked online how to make that and I don't think it's very hard. I bet people in Metlin would buy goat-milk soap. Especially if I made it smell really nice."

She was standing with her hands on her hips in a posture Cary had seen a million times. Though Abby was a combination of both Calvin and Melissa, her expressions came entirely from her mother.

Abby caught his smile. "What?"

"Nothing." Cary stood. "I think it's cool that you like goats so much. And you already have plans to do something smart with them. Some kids want a regular job, but your ideas are way better."

"Thanks." She sighed. "Mom doesn't like goats."

"I think she has more issues with little girls who let their goats out into the garden and aren't responsible about putting them back."

"None of them have gotten into Grandma's garden since last year!"

"So." He rested a hand on her shoulder. "Give her time to forget. They did destroy all the roses."

"The roses grew back."

"Just give it time." He walked back out to the main goat pen. "Tell me more about the wonder of goats."

"Did you know they have four stomachs?"

"I did not."

"They do. And no upper teeth."

Okay, that was interesting. "Really?"

"None at all," she said. "See? Goats are fascinating animals."

"They really are."

———

JOAN CALLED Abby into the house for lunch, and Cary got back in his truck and drove to the barn, parking beside the worn structure before he walked to the trailer in back. He knocked on the door and stood back so whoever was inside could see him through the windows.

He'd waited a couple of minutes before he saw the door handle turn. A woman around Joan's age peered out.

"Can I help you?"

"Yes, ma'am. I'm looking for Stu Hagman."

Someone else was in the trailer. Leigh glanced over her shoulder, and a lanky, weathered man came to the door. He wiped a handlebar mustache and stuffed the napkin in his jeans pocket.

"I'm Stu Hagman. C'n I help you?"

"I'm sorry if I interrupted your lunch. I'm Cary Nakamura. Friend of Melissa's from down the road."

Stu nodded. "I've heard your name. You got the orange groves next door. There a problem with the fencing I need to know about?"

"Fences are fine. Can we...?" Cary nodded toward the shade structure behind the barn with a picnic table underneath it.

Stu and Leigh exchanged looks. Leigh looked nervous. Stu looked solemn.

"Sure." He nodded toward the picnic table. "You want something to drink?"

"I'm okay. Thanks."

They walked to the shaded area and sat.

Cary braced his elbows on the table. "I've been friends with Melissa a long time. Our families are close."

"Miz Rhodes is a good woman."

"Yes, she is. So is her mother."

Stu cleared his throat. "Can I ask what you're doing here, Mr. Nakamura? Did Miz Rhodes—?"

"Melissa has done nothing but sing your praises," Cary said. "She thinks you're a good worker. Likes how you ride and likes the work you're doing with your dog. Says you're a good cattleman."

"I've been doing it for a long time." He crossed his arms over his chest.

"Yeah, you have." Cary drummed his fingers on the table. "But not for the past ten years or so."

Stu's face was frozen.

"Did you tell her?"

The older man's face gave nothing away.

Cary persisted. "Did you tell her you've spent time in prison?"

"I've been on probation five years," Stu said quietly.

"Yeah, and before that you were in prison in Oklahoma." Cary drilled his eyes into Stu's. "And you were an addict."

Stu was silent a long time. Then he sighed deeply and leaned his elbows on the table, looking away from Cary. "*Am* an addict, Mr. Nakamura. Once an addict—"

"Always an addict. Trust me, I know. I got some guys working for me who've had their own issues." Cary waited for the man to look back at him. "I'm not judging you, Mr. Hagman. I admit, I was worried. And when I first started reading the report, I was pretty damn mad to think you'd kept that from Melissa. But I kept reading, and from what I can tell, you're not a violent guy except when you're using."

The man's face was fixed in a stern expression. "They charged me with assault, but it was a bar fight. I was drunk. I never intended for it to go that far."

"You know what?" Cary leaned on the table. "I understand that. And from what I can find, you've walked the straight and narrow since you got out. Your wife stuck by you. Your friends didn't abandon you. That says a lot."

"I'm training dogs again."

"Dogs are good judges of character, though Abby might tell you goats are better."

The corner of Stu's mouth turned up. "That girl does like her goats."

Cary's gut told him Stu Hagman was a good man who'd made his mistakes, but he'd paid his debt and was working on redemption. He wouldn't be a threat to Melissa, Abby, or Joan. He was probably too grateful to even consider putting them at risk.

He was also pretty sure that Melissa didn't know a damn thing about the man's record.

"Mr. Hagman," he said, "I don't have anything against you. None of this is personal. I'd run a background check on anyone I didn't know who moved onto Melissa's property and lived within spitting distance of that little girl, because I'm a suspicious asshole who doesn't trust many people."

Stu nodded. "I understand that."

"Did you tell her anything? Does she know even a little bit about the drugs and the assault and the prison time?"

Stu hesitated before he shook his head. "I told the Bradys. They sent Leigh a little money when we were trying to get back on our feet, so they knew."

Cary didn't believe in secrets. Secrets were a killer, even when intentions were good. "Did the Bradys tell you *not* to tell Melissa?"

"They didn't. But they didn't include it in the letter either."

Cary nodded. "I didn't go to her with this. I came to you because you need to be the one to tell her. She may decide she's fine with you staying on. She may decide different. But she needs the information. You living here without telling her where you've spent the past ten years is as good as lying if you ask me."

"I see." Stu cleared his throat. "She doesn't know you ran that background check, does she?"

"No, she does not." Cary tried not to visibly cringe. "And you probably know her well enough by now to know how she's going to react to my butting in." Cary shrugged. "But it wasn't really a matter of choice for me."

Stu nodded.

"I'd like you to tell her. Doesn't have to be today, but it better be soon. If you don't, I will, but it'd be better coming from you."

Stu took a deep breath. "Felt wrong not to tell her, but..."

"I expect it's not an easy thing to talk about, but think of it this way. Life'll be a lot less stressful if you don't feel like you're hiding your past, don't you think?"

He opened his mouth, closed it, then nodded. "Yeah."

Cary stood and held out his hand. "Mr. Hagman, you seem like an honest person and you've paid your debt. But Melissa has a right to know."

Stu stood and took his hand. "And I understand why you'd do the background check. We protect the people we love."

Cary shook his hand and released it. "Well, I'm glad you understand, because she's going to be mad as hell."

CHAPTER NINE

MELISSA WAS SO bored her eyes were starting to cross. She'd agreed to be on the Committee to Save Jordan Valley, but so far the co-chairs were disorganized and didn't know quite what they wanted to accomplish.

Did they want to stop the Allen Ranch development from putting two thousand houses on one of the prettiest stretches of the Jordan Valley?

Definitely yes.

Did they want to stop all development of the property? Even a smaller number of houses or small ranches? Keep it ranchland? Push for a conservancy?

No one quite knew that part, and plenty of old-timers were very wary of telling anyone what to do with private property other than making it clear that two thousand houses on one piece of land was not acceptable.

Joan and Melissa were sitting in the back, listening to the debate while Abby sat next to them, drawing her favorite subject —the new baby goat—in her drawing pad. She'd finished her homework and was probably bored. Unfortunately, the meeting showed no signs of ending.

"I think we should approach it from a conservation perspective." Sherry Granger, one of the co-chairs, was speaking. "We don't have the water for that many people. It'll push down air quality. A lot of people in Oakville are here because the air is better than in the valley."

Melvin Raphney, one of the oldest members of the committee, grumbled. "I want to know what it's gonna do to the roads. We already have park traffic. That's bad enough."

"Do we know that'll change with more houses?" someone asked. "Wouldn't they have to build roads if they build houses?"

"There's only one road in and out of Jordan Valley," Melissa said. "You go far enough and there's a dead end. It doesn't connect to anything. Never had to. It's ranchland."

"Can they build something more? Put a road over to Granite Creek? Something like that?"

"I don't know," Sherry said. "But it seems like roads would be a problem."

"The problem is we don't *know* anything." Joan was sitting next to Melissa and stood to speak. "Because they haven't done a report on anything. We don't know how much water this place will suck up. How much stress it's gonna put on our roads. What would a golf course do? Is that going to affect local wildlife? I think that's the first thing we need to push for, some kind of environmental study."

Murmurs of agreement around the room.

"Uh…" Sherry smiled nervously. "Joan, do you know how to go about doing that? Who would do an environmental study in Oakville?"

Joan looked at Melissa. "Honey?"

Her eyes went wide. "You're asking me?"

"Is that something you can look up online?"

"Uh…?" Her mother's search engine skills definitely needed an upgrade. "Maybe talk to Adrian Saroyan in Metlin? He's an honest guy and he's sold a lot of the property in downtown Metlin that's been developed."

Someone asked, "That Jan Saroyan's grandson?"

"I think so."

Joan said, "Yes, he's Jan and Ana's grandson."

More murmurs of agreement.

Melissa said, "A lot of stuff he's sold is property that changed uses, like from industrial to residential. That kind of thing. He might know where to start. I think what we need is an environmental *impact* study. See what kind of effect this would have on the air and the water—"

"And the roads!"

Melissa rolled her eyes. "Yes, Melvin. They would check the roads."

The old man crossed his arms over his chest. "Didn't up and move to this place so I could sit in traffic like it was a goddam city. Pardon my language."

"I don't think we're in any danger of turning into Los Angeles."

"Mom." Abby tugged on Melissa's sleeve. "Are you almost done?"

"Soon, baby." She pulled Abby's ponytail. "Give me... fifteen minutes. If it's not over then, we'll leave."

Sherry Granger stood, her hands clutched in front of her. "Okay, I think that's a good first step. Either Maria or I will contact Adrian Saroyan and ask him for advice on what the best steps might be for this committee."

Joan said, "And I'm going to call the paper in Metlin. Have any of you read anything about this in the paper?"

"Nope."

"Not me."

"I haven't."

Joan nodded. "Seems like it might be a local story they'd be interested in. Lots of people in Metlin come up for the bluegrass festival and for shopping and the Christmas markets."

Melissa made a mental note to call Adrian and fill him in. He likely had no idea what was going on in Oakville, but she knew he was pretty outspoken about responsible development in Metlin, and he might be willing to get involved in this, especially if it landed his name and picture in the paper.

The meeting switched from dispersed muttering to outright chatter, and Melissa picked up her purse and held her hand out for Abby.

"Mom." Her ten-year-old rolled her eyes. "I'm not a baby."

"Sorry." Would she ever get used to having a preteen? Just the word made her shudder. "Get your stuff together and we'll go." She looked for her mom. "As soon as Grandma is finished talking to Melvin."

"Melissa?" Sherry walked over to her. "I wanted to ask you, because someone said you knew Kevin Fontaine? The rep from the holding company who spoke at the council meeting?"

"I don't know him." Melissa took the file Sherry handed her and started paging through it. There were news clippings of Kevin Fontaine breaking ground on a golf course in Santa Maria. A printout of the man in a suit at what looked like a board meeting. "I know the last name, but I don't really know him."

Abby jumped up on the chair next to Melissa and leaned over her shoulder. "Is it that guy?"

"Yeah." She tugged the edge of Abby's T-shirt. "Abby, don't jump on the chairs."

"I know him." Abby pointed to the picture in the file. "He's one of Uncle Devin's friends."

Melissa turned to Abby, forgetting about the chair. "What?"

"Uncle Devin, Aunt Audrey's husband."

"Yeah, I know who your Uncle Devin is." Calvin's younger sister, Audrey, had married the slimiest of slimy salesmen. Devin would do anything for a buck, but he sucked up to Greg and Beverly, which meant that Audrey and Devin were family favorites.

Abby pointed to the picture of the smiling man in the file. "That guy's one of Uncle Devin's friends. I've seen him at Grandma and Grandpa's house."

"When was this?"

Abby scrunched up her nose. "The last time I was there without you, I think. They had a party. There were so many people."

"That was six weeks ago." Melissa glanced at Sherry. "Long before the council meeting."

Sherry's mouth formed an O. "Well... that's unexpected."

But was it? It wasn't hard to imagine that Greg and Bev would try to interfere with Melissa's life if they couldn't get her to bend to their whims. There was definitely something going on, and she would be calling Greg as soon as she saved up enough aspirin for the headache it would cause.

"Let's go." She patted Abby's back. "Thanks, kiddo. Grandma and I will take care of it." She looked at Sherry. "I'll let you know when I do, okay?"

Sherry nodded. "Sorry. It's always complicated when it's family."

"Nothing I can't handle." She turned and followed Abby out of the church social hall where they were meeting.

Dammit, Calvin. Of all the things to inherit, your parents have got to be the most work.

Melissa walked to the truck and started it, waiting for her mom to join them.

"Mom?" Abby piped up from the rear seat.

"Yeah, honey?"

"Is Uncle Devin being shitty?"

She winced, fairly certain Abby was repeating something she'd overheard from one of her own conversations. "Don't call Uncle Devin shitty. But... possibly yes."

Abby sighed. "He doesn't like goats."

"Uncle Devin?"

"Yeah. He thinks my goat-milk-soap idea is stupid."

Melissa turned. "Did he say that?"

Abby rolled her eyes. "No. But I can tell. Just like I can tell that you really like goats even though you say you don't."

"They're not my favorite animals, Abby. But I think your soap idea is great and sounds like a good weekend project."

"And I can make money."

"Yes, you can, tiny capitalist."

Abby's eyes gleamed. "And with all my money, I can buy more goats."

Melissa couldn't stop her laugh. "Nice try. But no."

"Cary thinks my goat-soap idea is great too." Abby's face pinked with pride. "He says it sounds really smart."

Melissa felt her heart beat a little faster. "That's because Cary is also very smart, and smart people recognize other smart people."

"But Uncle Devin thinks goat soap is stupid."

Melissa said, "Uncle Devin is a shitty person and you shouldn't listen to him."

"Mom!"

"What?" Melissa realized what she'd said. "Oh. Right. Don't use that word."

Abby was shaking her head sadly. "I think I need to report you to Grandma."

"You better not, you snitch." Melissa swung her arm over the seat and managed to land a pair of fingers in Abby's armpit, tickling her daughter until she wiggled away, laughing. "Don't forget, I know where you sleep."

Abby was panting and laughing. "I know where you sleep too."

"Truce then."

Abby let out one last giggle. "Truce."

Melissa hoped her mom wouldn't talk too long. She closed her eyes, took a deep breath, and imagined Cary half-naked, climbing Halsey Rock. Mmmmm. That wasn't a bad way to pass the time.

Was that legal for "friends who kiss?" Would Cary like that she was imagining him half-naked?

All the way naked?

Melissa felt her cheeks go hot. She was too old to be feeling teenage flutters when she nearly had a teenager herself, but Cary Nakamura made her feel like a goofy high school girl.

No, she hadn't felt this kind of flutter even back in high school. In high school and college, she'd been focused on her future. On school. On getting a degree. On remaking the ranch.

Then she met Calvin and she'd been focused on building their life together. Not that they didn't have fun, but her head was full of plans for the future. Graduate. Get married. Have a baby or two. Save for the future.

Everything had gone according to plan until nothing did.

In a split second, Calvin—and everything Melissa thought her life would be—was gone. Now Melissa had her own ranch. Her own farm. Her own family.

And along came Cary, promising... things. Kisses. Romance. Thoughts that left goose bumps all over her skin.

What was she doing?

She rubbed a hand over her face and glanced at the glowing church door. Her mother still hadn't emerged. "So Abby, when did you tell Cary about your soap idea? At your birthday party?"

"No! A couple of days ago when he came by the ranch to talk to Stu."

Melissa's brain froze. "What?"

"Sorry. Mr. Hagman, not Stu."

"No, when did you say Cary came by the ranch?"

"When I had that day off school. You were gone and he came by to talk to Mr. Hagman."

About what? If any of the cows had gotten loose in Cary's groves, Stu would have told her. If there was an issue on their adjoining land, Cary would have talked to her.

The passenger door opened, and Joan hopped inside. "Sorry!

Let's head home, ladies. I don't know about you, but I need a piece of that coffee cake before I hit the hay. What do you think, Abby?"

"I vote yes for cake!"

"Melissa?"

Melissa wasn't thinking about cake. She wasn't thinking about sleep. Or half-naked Cary. Or romance. Or shivers.

Why the fuck had Cary come to talk with her ranch foreman? And why had neither of them mentioned it for two days?

She put the truck in drive and headed back to the ranch.

She didn't know.

But she would.

———

SHE KNOCKED on the door to the Hagman's trailer as soon as Abby was in bed, knowing that Stu might have already turned in. He rose before the sun to start work, so he and Leigh kept an early bedtime.

Too bad. She needed to know what was going on.

He answered the door in an undershirt and immediately caught that Melissa was not there to chat. "Hold on." He closed the door and opened it a few minutes later with a flannel on over his shirt. The nights in Oakville were always cool even if the day was blazing.

"Sorry to bother you so late, Stu."

"That's fine." He ambled out to the picnic table. "Been meaning to talk to you. Just got busy with the pump guy."

The water pump in Christy Meadow had been malfunctioning, and thirsty cattle took priority over almost everything.

"That's fine." She sat down at the table. "So why did Cary come by?"

"Did he call you?"

"No. Neither of you did. My ten-year-old daughter mentioned he'd come by to see you." She folded her hands and tried to remain calm. The idea of two men she respected going behind her back pissed her off, but she needed to know if they had a good reason. "We got an issue on the ranch I need to know about?"

"No, ma'am." Stu cleared his throat. "Mr. Nakamura came by because he found out that I'd been in prison a few years ago in Oklahoma."

Dammit. Melissa schooled her face. "You didn't think you should mention that to me and my mom?"

"I know I should have, and I didn't. I apologize for that." Stu's shoulders sagged. "I guess I'll tell Leigh we should be moving on."

"Don't jump to conclusions, Stu." She took a deep breath and contemplated her options. She'd never thought Stu had a lily-white past. You didn't move states to "start over" if everything in your life had gone right.

But she hadn't expected this.

"Did Carla know all this when she sent me that letter?"

He nodded.

"What were you in prison for?"

"Possession of a controlled substance and assault." Stu's face was stony. "I was using when I got into a bar fight. Hurt someone pretty bad, and he was... kind of important. Locally, I mean. They threw the book at me. I served five; got clean in prison. Been out on probation for a little over five."

"What kind of drugs?"

"Oxy." He cleared his throat. "Other stuff when I couldn't find that. Started with a back injury at work. I'd been roughnecking. Got hurt, but the oil company denied my claim, so no rehab. Doctors put me on a bunch of pills." Stu made a face. "Just... took on a life of its own. I can point to all the reasons why, but it don't excuse it."

"That's powerful stuff, Stu. You're not alone." Oakville and Metlin didn't have opioid problems as bad as other places in the country, but it was still plenty bad. "You clean?"

Stu nodded.

"You sure?"

He looked up. "Leigh'd leave me if I used again, Ms. Rhodes. I lose her; I lose everything. So yeah. I'm sure."

She nodded slowly. The truth was written all over Stu's face. She'd seen the two of them together. Seen how Stu looked at his wife. Melissa suspected Stu would sooner cut off his own arm than lose Leigh.

Melissa took a deep breath. "Well, this sucks."

"If you need to fire me, I understand and I don't have any hard feelings. Please don't blame Leigh though. She's been—"

"You legal to leave Oklahoma?"

He blinked. "I... Yes, ma'am. Free and clear."

"You in a program or something?"

He nodded. "Twelve-step. You can talk to my sponsor if you want. He's back in Oklahoma, but we talk regular. He's trying to connect me to someone out here."

Melissa nodded. "Why California?"

"We headed to Idaho first. Thought we could head back to where we had friends and just work to make a living. Nothing fancy. Just work. I just wanted to be around good people, you know? Oil fields are a different kind of folks. Went to the Bradys first. They sent me to you."

"So the Bradys knew all about your record?"

"Yes, ma'am."

She was annoyed that Carla hadn't trusted her enough to share the information, but then Carla's dad and her grandfather had been close. She and Carla only knew each other by reputation.

Melissa frowned, processing everything Stu had said. "Your back injury... You good to be on a horse?"

"I'm good." He nodded firmly. "I'm better now. I can get a report from a doctor if you want, but believe it or not, I met a physical therapy assistant in prison. He was a good guy. Showed me some exercises, and I was real steady about following his instructions. He knew his stuff, and I don't feel anything around

97

the old injury anymore, except when it gets real cold. One of the reasons Miz Brady thought California'd be a good place for me."

Melissa watched the man—his hands were folded, his shoulders hunched. The lines of his face told the story of a hard life, but the straightforward way he spoke told Melissa he wasn't hiding anything anymore.

"Sometimes life shits on you," Melissa said. "Trust me. I've been there."

"Yes ma'am. I know you have."

"A whole lot of it is pure luck. Who you're born to. Where you're raised. Who loves you." Melissa stared into the distance, watching the stars that filled the sky. "You know how people say they're blessed by this or that? I'm not sure if I even know what that means anymore. My grandfather died, the baby I was expecting died, and my husband got hit by a truck. All in about a year and a half." She turned to Stu. "Does that mean I'm not blessed? You think God's got something against me?"

Stu shook his head. "I don't think so. I don't think God works that way."

"Your back got injured and you didn't get the right treatment. That's bad luck, Stu. Nothing more than that. It could have happened to me or my mom. My brother. Anyone."

Stu nodded.

"I'm not gonna fire you. I wish you'd told me up front and I didn't have to hear all this because Cary found out."

"He was just—"

"You don't need to defend Cary to me. I'll deal with him." She stood. "Anything else you need to tell me?"

"The fight was a one-off. I swear it. I've never beat someone like that in my life. I was high and had just been laid off. One of the executives came in—"

"Wait, you beat up an oil executive?"

Stu shrugged. "Pardon my language, but he was an asshole. Came into that bar the end of every week to try to pretend he was one of the guys. Self-made. All that shit. He wasn't, but most of 'em ate it up. Made 'em feel important that the big boss wanted to drink a beer with 'em. I shouldn't have lost my temper—"

"Oh, I don't know." Melissa hooked a hand in her pocket. "My grandpa used to tell me that some men's faces could only be improved by a fist."

Stu cracked a smile. "Well, Leigh wasn't too pleased with me."

"I imagine not." She took a deep breath of cold evening air. "Stu, I think we're good."

He waited, hands still folded on the table. "You sure, Miz Rhodes?"

"I told you to call me Melissa." She held out a hand. "And yeah. You keep everything up-front with me and we're good. I'm gonna let you get back to sleep because we're gonna have to move the herd across the creek tomorrow and the water's still running. I want to start early."

"Yes, ma'am." Stu shook her hand. "I don't want you to be mad at Mr. Nakamura though. He's right. I should have told you from the beginning."

She grimaced. "That may be, but Cary needs to learn to mind his business. This isn't the first time he's pulled something like this."

"I suppose." Stu stood. "But I reckon he thinks you and your family *are* his business."

That brought her up short. "Did he tell you that?"

The corner of Stu's mouth turned up. "Not in those words."

What did that mean? For a plainspoken guy, Stu could be cagey.

"I'll figure out how to deal with Cary," Melissa said.

How? She had no idea. She'd probably be up half the night thinking about it.

Come to think of it, if she wasn't going to get any sleep, Cary didn't need any either.

CHAPTER TEN

WHEN CARY MOVED BACK into his mother's house after his dad died, he converted the back bedroom into a suite with a separate door, washroom, and small dining area. He might have been fine living with his mom as an adult, but she didn't need to know when he came and went. And he definitely didn't need to share a bathroom at age forty.

Most days he was grateful for the separate entrance. But when Melissa decided to come knocking at ten thirty, he wished she had to use the front door.

Because she was too polite to use the front door, and then he could sleep.

Cary rubbed his eyes and stared at the ceiling. She wasn't banging, but the knock wasn't soft either. He'd heard her truck just as he was drifting off to sleep and knew the knock was coming even though he'd turned out the lights.

He sat up in bed and swung his legs over the side. He walked barefoot to the door and swung it open. "Hey, Missy."

She glared at him. "I need to talk to you."

"Yeah, I bet." He pointed to the rack by the door. "Shoes."

He hadn't been raised by Rumi and Gordon Nakamura to let

any disgusting boots or street shoes into his home. Melissa had been over to the house enough times that she didn't bitch about it. She pulled off her boots as Cary went back to the bedside table and grabbed a glass to get some water.

"I'd offer you something to drink," he said, his voice rough, "but you banged on my door after ten o'clock, so fuck it."

"You know why I'm here."

"Yep." He downed the glass of water in one long gulp and set it back on the table. "And? It couldn't have waited until tomorrow?"

"No." She put her hands on her hips. "If I have to sit up thinking about you interfering in my life and what the hell I'm going to do about it, then you don't get to sleep either."

He scratched his chin. "I don't really get that, but okay."

"Why did you...?" She glanced at his chest. "Can you put a shirt on please?"

The night was warm and he was wearing a pair of basketball shorts and nothing else. Cary glanced down at his bare chest. "No."

"You're not going to put on a shirt?"

"It's hot. Is my chest offending you?"

"It's... distracting."

"Then I'm definitely not going to put on a shirt." He sat on the edge of the bed and leaned back, careful to sit right in Melissa's line of sight. "So, what's up? You here to be pissed at me about doing a background check on Stu?"

"Yes. If you had concerns, you should have come to me."

"I did, and you blew me off."

"When?"

"When we were pruning my grafts."

She frowned. "When?"

"The time I kissed you by the greenhouse and you got mad at me and stormed off."

"Right." Some of the anger deflated. "I forgot about that."

"Was it because I kissed you?" The corner of his mouth turned up. "Don't answer. I'm going to assume it's because I kissed you."

"Ha ha." The anger was back. "This is so easy for you, isn't it?"

That woke him up. "Excuse me?"

"It's so easy for you!" She looked around the room. "You've got your nice independent life. Your successful farm. Your awesome mom who cooks and cleans and does your laundry for you."

Cary stood and put his hands on his hips. "Are you trying to imply that I'm lazy?"

"You have enough spare time to mess with my life, so maybe you need a new project to keep you busy."

I do have a new project. In fact, you're a project and a half, Melissa Oxford.

She continued in her rant. "You have enough time to go behind my back, investigate a man who has done *nothing* to you that would make you suspi—"

"This is not about me!" He stopped just short of yelling. "This is about you. And about Abby. Do you honestly think there is *anything* I would not do to keep you and your family safe? Do you think there is anyone I wouldn't check out? Big Bird could move behind your fucking barn and I'd do a background check on him, Melissa."

"So you think I can't protect them?" She slapped a hand on her chest. "You think I'm... what? Careless? Naive? A bad mother? Trust me, you're not the first person who's said it, but I don't give a shit. I know I'm a good mother. All I do is work for my family. That is my whole life. You sleep soundly over here, and I lie in bed every night worrying—"

"You think I sleep soundly?" He swung his arm toward her ranch. "You want to know what I lie awake at night worrying about? I worry about strangers living behind your barn. I worry about someone doing something to hurt Abby. I worry about you working yourself into complete exhaustion because you're too damn stubborn to ask for help. I worry about your fucking in-laws making your life so difficult you think mourning Calvin has to be a full-time job six years after he died!"

She got in his face. "I never asked you to worry about me, and dealing with Calvin's parents is none of your concern. I will handle this. I'm not some whiny little—"

"Why?"

She stopped short and blinked. "What?"

"Why do you have to handle *everything*?"

The sound she made was halfway between a laugh and a cry. "Because I have to, Cary. Don't you get it? There's no one else. This *is* the backup plan. There isn't a plan C. If I don't make this work, then I have nothing. I don't have any other options. I have one ranch. One chance to make something for myself and my daughter."

He crossed his arms over his chest. "And you have to do all that on your own?"

"Yes."

"Why?"

"Because it's my responsibility."

"Even when other people are offering to help?"

"I have to do it myself."

"Why?"

"Because I have to prove that I can!" Tears sprang into her eyes. "If I don't, then... they'll be right. The plan didn't work. And Calvin died for nothing. It would have been better if he stayed with his family and never married me!"

"What?" Cary grabbed her shoulders. "What are you even saying? You think it's your fault he died in a car accident?"

She said nothing.

"Melissa, what the hell are you thinking?"

She swallowed hard and the tears came fast. "They don't have fog in Paso Robles. Not like here. The truck would have seen him."

"Dammit, Melissa." Cary pulled her into his chest and hugged her so hard if she was anyone else, she might have broken. "You know that's not rational. You *know* it."

"I tell myself that." Her voice was muffled against his chest. "But every time I see Bev, I just hear her, over and over, what she said after the funeral..."

Damn, he'd forgotten all about that. Beverly had railed at Melissa, shouting at her for insisting on living in the country, living on the ranch. She had blamed Melissa for Calvin's death, even when Melissa had been shattered.

"Calvin's mom never should have said that. There's no excuse for it."

"But Cary, she lost her baby. I don't know what I'd do or say if anything happened to Abby. I can't even think about it because it takes me to such a dark place that—"

"Shhhh." He kissed the top of her head. "Stop. Don't even let the thought enter your head." Cary held her for a long time, rubbing her back and wishing that grief took a rational path. He couldn't count the number of times he'd blamed himself for not being at the farm when his own father had passed.

"What happened to Calvin..." Cary ran a hand over Melissa's hair. "Accidents are accidents, Missy. They happen everywhere. Marrying you? Living here? It didn't cause anything. You know that."

She wiped her eyes. "Most of the time I do."

He held her for a long time, until her breathing evened out and her shoulders stopped shaking. "You know," he said softly, "I still feel guilty I wasn't on the farm when my dad died."

Melissa pulled back and looked at him. "What?"

"I was at a growers' conference in Texas. And even though I know it's not logical, I still feel like... if only I'd been here."

"'If only' is the devil's chorus. That's what my grandpa used to say."

"If only I'd been at the farm and with my dad instead of being in Texas, maybe I could have gotten him to the hospital and saved his life."

"If only Calvin and I had decided to live in Metlin and not Oakville after Abby was born." Her smile was sad. "Lot shorter trip to the store when you run out of milk."

"He was going out for milk?"

"Yep."

"Damn." Cary sighed. "If only I'd bugged my dad about going to the doctor to get regular checkups, we would have known he had a heart condition."

She sighed and laid her head on his chest. "If only I hadn't insisted on buying a white truck because they're cooler in the summer."

"If only I had listened when my mom started talking about Dad's dizzy spells." He kissed the top of her head. "Come here."

Cary walked backward to the bed, Melissa still in his arms. "Sit." He sat on the bed and leaned against the headboard, settling Melissa between his legs. "Times like this, I really do wish this room was big enough for a couch."

She sniffed. "It's okay. I already know you're trying to get me into bed."

The laugh grew from his chest and he couldn't stop it. He laughed hard, the feeling of release like a salve. Melissa started laughing too, grabbing a tissue from the box by the side of the bed.

She was laughing and crying at once, shaking her head over and over. "Sorry. That was just wrong."

"No, that was perfect."

"I know what you're saying is right. About the accident. But..."

"Grief isn't rational." He smoothed his hand over her hair, playing with the long braid that lay over her shoulder.

"Yeah." She wiped her eyes again. "And I don't *mourn* him, Cary. It's not like that. It's been six years. I can remember the good stuff and not just the heartache. Lately, I've been feeling more guilt than grief."

"Guilt?" His hand froze. "About what? About us?"

She frowned. "No, not because of… us. Or this. We still need to talk about… this."

"Nothing to talk about. We're just going along. Being friends. Who kiss."

Was that side-eye? Yeah, that was definitely side-eye.

Melissa said, "I feel guilty because I'm kind of pissed at Calvin."

"Why?"

"Because he died, and now *I* have to deal with his parents!" She let out a strangled laugh. "How is that fair?"

"It's not." He stroked her back, enjoying the solid feel of the muscles under her shirt. "You're so damn strong."

"Yeah?" She let out a hard breath. "Sometimes it's exhausting being strong."

He cleared his throat. "Okay, you *are* strong in many ways, but I was being superficial and talking about your muscle tone." He slid his fingers under the back of her shirt and ran his fingers up the small of her back. "I mean… damn. Have you been lifting? It's sexy as hell."

She shivered. "You know what I do for a living."

"Is it the riding? Does that…?" He slid his finger just under her waistband before he pulled his hand back. "Sorry. Not the time."

She turned her eyes up to his. "Why not?"

Oh, don't look at me like that. Not right now. "Because you're upset."

Melissa turned and sat up on her knees, tilting Cary's face to hers. "So distract me… friend."

Cary fisted his hands on his legs, but Melissa took each one, unfurled his clenched fingers, and placed them on her hips.

"Melissa, I don't think—"

Her mouth stopped his words. Her kiss was unexpected and sweet. It was the first time she'd initiated anything since their heated kiss at the hospital, and everything in Cary's body came to attention.

Yes, finally! battled with *Not a good idea!*

She pulled back. "What's wrong?"

He looked her straight in the eye, but he didn't move his hands. If she was going to run, he figured he'd at least be able to slow her down. "You said, 'Distract me.'"

"And?" Melissa bit her lip, and dammit if that wasn't as sexy as the curve of her hips under his palms.

Cary wanted to flip her over, cover her body with his own, and fulfill about a dozen fantasies in one night. He wanted those legs wrapped around his body. He wanted his mouth between her thighs. He wanted to make her absolutely mindless with pleasure. She desperately needed stress relief, and he'd been thinking about how to provide it for years.

He flexed his hands and felt the give of her flesh. It would be so easy to give in and be her distraction, but that wasn't what he wanted. "I want... a lot of things, Missy. But I don't want to be a distraction for you."

She draped her arms over his shoulders and frowned a little. "You *are* distracting. I was waiting in the car the other day and all I could think about was you naked." She glanced down. "Kind of like you are right now."

He'd never been happier that he lifted weights. Granted, it was mostly because he was getting older and he wanted to keep mountain climbing, but impressing Melissa was a definite bonus.

"And when I think about kissing you..." She sank lower and let her lips hover over his. "You *are* distracting, but you're not *a distraction*. Does that make sense?"

Well, when she put it like that...

"Yeah, that makes sense." He put his hand on her nape and pulled her mouth to his. Cary wasted no time sliding his hand from her hip back to cup her ass.

The sound she made in her throat was both shock and pleasure. Cary left his hand there, massaging the round curve as he devoured her mouth. He put his arm around the small of her back and pulled her close.

Her breasts were against him, and she slid her arms around his neck. He slowed down, savoring her mouth, tasting her over and over. He didn't want to go too far—it was the first time she'd initiated anything, and he wanted her to lead.

She rose to her knees and kicked one leg over his, pressing closer. When she brushed against his erection, Cary let out a hard grunt.

"Oh." Her voice was breathless. "Hey."

"Ignore him." Cary squeezed her ass. "He has no sense of timing."

"I didn't plan—"

"I told you." He shifted his hips. "Ignore him. Come here."

He kissed her over and over, running his hands up and down her back until he felt her shiver. The stiffness in her back disappeared and she melted against him.

Thank fuck.

"I know you probably need to get home," he whispered against her lips. "Just stay with me a few more minutes."

"Okay." Her eyes were closed and her lips swollen. She played with the thick hair at his nape. "I love your hair."

"Good." He liked his hair too, and he'd always worn it long. Some women didn't like it, but there was nothing like the feel of a woman running her hands through it—like Melissa was doing—or gripping it when he went down on her.

Another time.

Cary lost track of time. Melissa tasted so good, and she was soft and hard at the same time. He loved the dip of her waist and the curve of her breasts. They were just enough for a handful. She liked it when he teased her nipples and squirmed when he licked her neck. Her legs were muscular. Her arms were lean. He really wanted to see her naked back.

He was in the middle of imagining possible sexual positions when Melissa pulled away.

"What is it?" he asked.

"It's midnight."

He frowned. "We've been making out for two hours?"

"Don't be silly. We were fighting. Then I was crying. Then we were talking. Then we were making out."

"Oh." He kissed her again. "I'm glad we're so efficient when we have time to see each other. We really get a lot done. A note for future meetings? You're very fun to kiss."

"You too, friend."

"Friend?" He remembered. *Friends who kiss.* "Right. You're very fun to kiss... friend."

The corner of her mouth turned up and told him she knew he was full of shit.

"I need to go," she said. "I have to get up early with Stu tomorrow. I should have been in bed two hours ago."

He took a deep breath and felt his eyes drooping. "I'd love for you to just sleep here, but I also know that's not going to happen."

"Yeah... not. Probably ever."

"Right." He rubbed his eyes. "When is Abby's next weekend in Paso?"

"This one. Why?"

He tugged her hair. "Because I want to take you out on a friendly date, friend."

Melissa blinked like the idea didn't compute. "I..."

She was imagining the gossip. Imagining the tongues wagging and the whispers. They were inevitable in a town the size of Oakville. The fact that the entire town probably knew Cary was in love with her was not even on her radar. She was thinking about school-mom gossip.

"Just think about it," he said. "We could go into Metlin."

"Okay." Her eyes were still cautious. "I'll think about it."

"Good."

CHAPTER ELEVEN

MELISSA GRABBED a cup of coffee from the pot on the counter. She'd been out at dawn with Stu, but the herd was moved to the upper pasture and out of the worst of the heat. They'd checked the water pump in the north pasture, and it was still working fine. They'd tagged two sections of fence that needed mending, but Stu said he and Leigh would take care of it later since it wasn't urgent.

And suddenly, at ten in the morning, Melissa had time to sit down across from her mom with a cup of coffee.

"Hi."

Joan smiled. "Fancy seeing you here."

"I know." She sipped the coffee. "Stu'll have lunch with Leigh and then they were going out to fix some fence. Said they didn't need me though."

"How about that?" Joan put down the newspaper. "What will you do with your life?"

Melissa blinked. "I have no idea. You need some help in the garden?"

"Nope. Weeding's done and it's too hot to do more today."

"Have you checked the goat pens?"

"Goats are happy in their jail."

"Are the accounts done?"

"Finished them yesterday. I told you. You don't remember?"

"Huh." Melissa drank more coffee. "What do people do in the middle of the day when they don't have a million things to do?"

"Have lunch with their friends—remember when you had those? Quilt. Read a book. Day drink? I don't know. Maybe you should take a nap." Joan's eyes were smiling. "You've been out late a few nights this week."

"At the committee meetings?"

"I'm pretty sure there was at least one other night you were late." Joan tapped on her chin. "Now where were you?"

"Mom, stop."

"I'm just going to say... it's about time."

"I have no idea what you're talking about."

"Okay." Joan opened her paper again. "Maybe I'll head over to Rumi's for lunch. See what's up over at the Nakamura place."

"Mom..." No. Please no. This was exactly what she didn't want.

"What?" Joan's face was pure innocence.

"You know what? I should go into Metlin." Melissa forced a smile. "Pick out bathroom tile and paint. Want to help?"

"Nope." She smiled. "I'm not going to Rumi's. I'm meeting with Sherry and Maria for the Jordan Valley Committee. I just felt like giving you grief."

"Thanks so much." Melissa grimaced. "That reminds me. I need to find out what's going on with Devin and this company working on Allen Ranch. I have a bad feeling about it."

"Nothing your brother-in-law does ever feels all the way legal."

Melissa shrugged. "He knows how to walk right down that line, but I know what you mean. He's..."

"Slimy."

She grimaced. "Yeah. He is."

Joan sipped her coffee. "You just be careful."

"With Devin? I'm not worried about Devin."

"With everything." Joan rose and walked behind her, bending down to wrap her arms around Melissa's shoulders. "Do you know I want to wrap your heart in Bubble Wrap and hold you like I did when you were Abby's age?"

"I'm thirty-four."

"Doesn't matter." She kissed Melissa's head. "You're still my baby."

"Love you, Mom."

"Love you, Lissa."

She squeezed her mom's arm for a few moments until Joan straightened and walked away. Melissa adored her mother, but for the first time in years, she wished she had someone other than Joan to talk to. She didn't really have friends.

She'd had them once, before life turned upside down. But she was isolated on the ranch, and after Calvin died, the few friends they'd had drifted away. She had a couple of college friends she kept in touch with online, but they mostly lived in Texas. She was friendly with some of the moms at Abby's school, but they weren't *friends*. Not really.

Melissa had Joan and Abby. She had Cary. She had Rumi. She had her brother, Ox. And she had no one she could talk to about possibly starting a romance with her neighbor.

But she could drive into Metlin and keep working. Working was what she did best. She'd call Brian Montoya and see if he had time to pick out materials for the bunkhouse. They were making good progress, and she didn't want to hold him up.

She could go by Tacos Marcianos for lunch. Go into INK and grab a new book for Abby. Maybe spend a few minutes with her brother.

She finished her coffee, grabbed the bunkhouse binder from the row of notebooks on her desk, and headed for her truck. On the drive into Metlin, she blared Pink on the radio and rolled the windows down before the day turned scalding.

It was nearly eleven when she pulled onto Main. After parking her truck by INK, she walked into the store and immediately looked for her brother.

Emmie spotted her. "Hey, Melissa!"

"Hey." She walked over and gave Emmie a one-armed hug. "How's it going?"

"Oh my God, she did *not!*"

The outburst from the office behind Emmie made Melissa and Emmie both turn their heads.

Emmie's best friend, Tayla, was ranting at the computer screen in her converted office, which was open to both the bookshop and the tattoo studio where Emmie and Ox worked.

"Emmie, you'll never believe what idiotic celebrity had a *Handmaid's Tale*–themed birthday. *Who does that?*" Tayla spotted Melissa. "Oh hey, Melissa. What are you doing here?"

"Rethinking my birthday plans now."

Tayla rolled her eyes. "Seriously though."

Melissa grimaced. "Yeah, that's a new level of clueless."

Despite the grimace, everything about Tayla made Melissa smile. The girl was hilarious and whip-smart.

Emmie, on the other hand, was smart, quiet, and low-key sarcastic, which suited Ox perfectly. Despite outward appearances, her brother was a big softie, and Melissa couldn't have custom designed a better girlfriend for him. Emmie was exactly the person Ox needed.

Her brother had a heart of gold, but he could be horribly unorganized and wasn't the best on follow-through. Falling in love with Emmie had given him focus.

"Anything new for Abby?"

Emmie's eyes lit up. "Did she like *Song for a Whale?*"

"Loved it."

"Okay, so it's a graphic novel and I don't have it, but I know Jeremy has it across the street at Top Shelf. It's called *Sea Sirens*, and it's amazing. I almost picked it up for Abby the other day, but I didn't know if she was still liking fantasy and magic stuff."

"Everything. She reads everything. She even reads to the goats. She says it's soothing."

Tayla said, "Your daughter is painfully adorable, Melissa."

"Thanks. I like her." Melissa glanced across the street. "The new book is at Jeremy's?"

Emmie nodded. "I just saw it the other day."

Melissa nodded. She hadn't been inside Jeremy's comic shop since last spring when Cary exhibited some of his photography for the monthly Art Walk hosted by the city.

She'd gone in expecting some cool ranching pics she could pick up for the house and walked out feeling like Cary had stripped her bare and left her hanging naked on the wall. Nothing about the picture was revealing—she'd been wearing work clothes —but something about Cary's perspective had made her feel completely naked.

Melissa turned to Emmie and lowered her voice. "Um... the pictures Cary took at the ranch—"

"You mean that hot-as-fuck portrait your smokin' silver-fox neighbor took of you and hung up for the town to see?" Tayla said. "It's not there anymore."

She could feel her cheeks turn red. "Right. Okay, thanks."

Tayla walked over to the counter and sidled next to Emmie. "Soooo, Melissa."

"Yeah?"

Tayla wiggled her eyebrows. "You and Cary. What's going on there?"

Had she been wishing she had girlfriends to talk to about Cary? She was an idiot. She didn't need anyone to talk to. Talking was overrated. "Uh, Cary and I are friends."

"Friends?"

Friends who kiss.

Emmie put a hand over Tayla's mouth. "Ignore her. She respects no boundaries."

Tayla shoved Emmie's hand away. "There's something going

on. I can tell. Look at her face." Her eyes lit up. "Look, look, look! Things have happened, Emmie!"

"You think?" Emmie's eyebrows went up. "Oh, she's blushing."

Melissa started backing out of the store. "Okay, so I'm gonna go grab that book now."

Emmie held up a hand. "Um, Melissa, maybe you should—"

"I'm good!" She waved as she walked out of the shop. "I'm good. Going to get that book. Bye!"

She walked past Café Maya and waited at the crosswalk, staring at the ground and trying to get her face under control. She hated blushing and only did it when Cary's name was mentioned. Apparently.

Shit.

She crossed the street, heading for Jeremy's comic book shop.

"*Sea Sirens*," she muttered. "Is that the same as mermaids? Is it a mermaid book?" She wasn't sure how much Abby would like mermaids, but she wasn't going to go back to Emmie's. Not for all the books in— "Oof."

She wasn't looking and nearly ran into the door as someone opened it.

"Melissa?" Cary held the door open. "Hey."

Of course Cary was in Jeremy's shop. Of *course* he was.

"Hi." She glanced in the shop, and the memory of last spring's Art Walk came rushing back.

His face lit up. "I didn't expect to see you today." Without another word, he let the door to the comic book shop close, stepped up to her on the sidewalk, put one arm around her and kissed her.

She lost her head for a second, just like she always did when Cary kissed her. All she could think about was how his lips felt and how he smelled. After a stunned moment, she pushed him away.

"Hey." She looked around. "Hi. Um, I didn't know we were doing… that. In public."

He looked amused. "Doing what? Kissing on the sidewalk in Metlin is practically a tradition for us. Of course, we weren't fighting before we kissed, but I feel like we could skip that part."

"One time," she hissed. "One time is not a tradition."

He smiled. "Two times now. That's getting closer."

She glanced over her shoulder toward INK. Were Emmie and Tayla watching? Probably. *Just kill me now.* "What are you doing here?"

"Going over a new climb with Jeremy. Want to come? Tayla, Emmie, and Ox are camping with us. You and Abby could come too."

Melissa was too confused to think. "I… can't think about that right now. Abby's going to her grandparents this weekend."

"It's next weekend, so perfect." He tucked her hair behind her ear, his fingers brushing her cheek. "What are you doing in town?"

"I had some free time, so I set up a meeting with Brian about the bunkhouse." Half of her wanted to push his hand away and the other half wanted to lean into it and purr. She kept flashing between kissing him at Halsey Rock. Kissing him in front of the hospital. Kissing him on his bed.

Okay, that seemed like a lot. Maybe they were kissing more than average, but what was average for friends who kissed? She had no experience with any of this.

She shrugged her shoulder and he dropped his hand. "So… what are you doing here?"

He grinned. "Going over climbing plans with Jeremy. Like I just said."

"Right." She was an idiot. Her brain was gone. Why did Cary do this to her? It was probably all the kissing. "So there's a book Emmie told me Jeremy has, and she thinks Abby would like it. That's why I came over."

"Nice." He looked her up and down. "You look great today."

"I'm wearing dirty jeans and a tank top."

"I know." He leaned closer. "But I'm choosing to imagine you naked."

"Cary!" She looked around. "You can't say things like that."

"Why not? Are you imagining me naked now?"

Of course she was. How could she not be? The man was evil. "You are…" She opened her mouth. Closed it. "You're in a mood today. And I'm going to go buy that book for Abby." *And not imagine anyone naked for a while.*

"Okay." He opened the door for her. "I'll help."

"I don't need help."

"Hearing *that* is definitely a tradition." He walked close behind her and hooked a finger in her belt loop. "We could lose that one though, and you could just let someone—me, mainly—help you out from time to time."

"I don't need help picking out a book for Abby."

"Want to go to lunch? What time is your meeting with Brian?"

"One, and I'm going to Tacos Marcianos for lunch."

"Sounds good to me." He peeked in her purse.

"What are you doing?"

"Nothing." He grabbed a granola bar from the outside pocket and opened it. "I love that you carry snacks with you all the time."

"You know, those are for my *kid*."

He finished it in three bites. "You should keep my energy up." He raised one eyebrow. "You never know when you might need it."

Okay, she was leaving that alone. Melissa scanned the shop for anything that looked like kids' stuff. "If you happen to also go to Tacos Marcianos for lunch, then I will see you there."

"Hey, Melissa!" Jeremy waved from behind the counter. "Let me know if I can help you find anything."

"Thanks. I wanted a book Emmie mentioned about sirens or something?"

"Oh, that's in the—"

"I'll help her," Cary said. "I know where it is."

"Okay."

"What is with you today?" Melissa shot an annoyed glance at Cary. "You can let go of my jeans now."

The corner of his mouth turned up. "But I like getting in your pants."

"Do you say things just to shock me? Because—"

"It's so easy?" He herded her toward a stand of books near the front windows of the shop. "I'm not going to lie; I like it when you make that face. Gives me all sorts of ideas. And I love shocking you because you're just so..."

"What?"

"Unflappable. I think that's the word. You're always together. Always on top of everything."

"Not on top of you." The words slipped out before she could stop them.

Cary barked a laugh. "Just tell me when and where. Where do you want to go this weekend?"

"What?"

"On our date."

"I didn't actually agree to that. I said I'd think about it."

"You've had a few days to think." He let go of her pants and put his arm around her to turn her toward the books. "Is this the one?"

It was. There was a little girl underwater holding a cat. She looked adorable, clever, and sassy, not unlike her daughter. "How did you know?"

"'Cause I saw it earlier and thought about buying it for her." He picked it up and flipped it over. "There's a talking cat. Abby would approve of a talking cat."

Melissa stared at Cary. He was cocky, cranky, and infuriating, overly confident and utterly charming. And he was staring at a middle-grade graphic novel with the sweetest expression on his face.

Without a word, she hooked her arm around his neck, pulled

his mouth down to hers, and kissed him. She stepped into his body, waiting for his arms—those strong, steady arms—to wrap around her.

There.

She was enveloped by him, surrounded by solid strength. She let out a long sigh and kept kissing him. The tension that lived in her back drained away. Her mind quieted.

There you are.

She closed her eyes and let go, knowing that he would hold her up. When their lips finally parted, all the cockiness was stripped from his expression, and he was the one who looked shocked.

"Café Georgette."

He blinked. "What?"

"I want to go to Café Georgette this weekend. I love their french onion soup. Let's go Saturday. I want to dress up, so you better pick me up looking fancy."

The corner of his mouth turned up. "I'll be there."

CHAPTER TWELVE

EARLY ON SATURDAY MORNING, Melissa loaded a sleepy Abby, a crate of vegetables from her mom, and a head full of worries in her truck and pointed it west toward Paso Robles. She coasted down the foothills and across the valley, making the hour-long trek to Kettleman City, where Abby's grandfather or grandmother would meet her.

After Calvin died, Melissa had been keenly aware that Abby was Greg and Beverly's last link to their son. And while she didn't always get along with her in-laws, she knew they adored her daughter. Melissa might have never felt like family in the Rhodes clan, but Abby was. She would grow up understanding a level of privilege that Melissa didn't. When she reached the age of thirty, she'd receive a trust fund worth more than Melissa and Joan's entire ranch was worth.

How did you raise a levelheaded kid when one side of their family told them they were a cut above the rest of the world by no more virtue than the name they were born with?

She glanced over at her daughter, watching as Abby slowly roused herself from slumber and rubbed her eyes. She recognized the exact moment when Abby remembered where they were going by the spark of excitement that lit her eyes.

Abby sat up straighter. "I'm going to see Sunny today."

"You sure are."

"And I have my first jumping lesson tomorrow."

Melissa kept her voice level. "Yes, you do. Now, you realize you're not going to go jumping over rocks and rivers right away. You remember that, right? There's an entirely different set of skills you need to—"

"I remember, Mom."

Melissa *felt* the eye roll even if she didn't see it.

Fine, kid. Pretend your mom knows nothing and Antonio the Great knows all.

From the way Abby spoke about him, Melissa was fairly sure the Spanish riding instructor that Beverly and Greg had hired was not only an expert in jumping and dressage but also walked on water.

She kept her eyes on the road, bypassing the turnoff for Metlin and cruising under the 99 freeway. She turned up the radio, leaving the music on the easy, rolling rhythm of "Tiger Striped Sky." On days she took Abby to the coast, Joan opened the booth at the farmers' market, though Melissa would be able to join her by nine or ten.

She shoved a fruit smoothie toward Abby, followed by a granola bar and a container of yogurt. Once the preteen lump had been fed, she magically transformed into her usual energetic self.

"I've been doing all the exercises Antonio recommended." She sat up, nearly wiggling in her seat.

"That's good." She kept her eyes on the road. "Is anyone taking lessons with you? Or is it just you and Grandpa?"

"Me and Grandpa mostly. Sometimes Grandma."

"Does Aunt Audrey ever join you?"

"Aunt Audrey?" Abby's brow was furrowed. "Aunt Audrey doesn't ride."

"What?" Melissa's eyes went wide. "Sweetie, yeah, she does. She was a competitive jumper in high school. Your dad even thought she might make it to the Olympics; she was that good."

"Really?" Abby sat up straighter. "Why didn't she?"

"She took a fall and injured her knee. Had to have surgery to put it back together. After that, she couldn't really compete anymore. She never told you about that?"

Abby shook her head. "Nope. Not even a little."

"That's too bad." Melissa glanced at Abby. "I might call her. I had no idea she wasn't riding at all. I kind of assumed that you got interested in jumping from talking to her."

"Nope. I just saw it on TV and thought it looked cool."

"Who was watching jumping?" They didn't watch it at the ranch.

Abby smiled a little. "Aunt Audrey."

"Huh." That settled it. Melissa was definitely calling Audrey. "You know, even if she can't ride, she probably would have some great ideas about your lessons. If I can't be there, I can't think of anyone I'd rather have watching the instructor."

"Why can't you be there?"

Such an innocent question. Such a complicated response. "You know, kiddo, sometimes Grandma and Grandpa and I have our disagreements. And when you go to visit them—especially for something as exciting as your first jumping lesson—I want it to be about you and them, not me and them. Does that make sense?"

"I guess so." She propped a bare foot on the door panel. "I don't understand why you guys can't just get along."

"I absolutely hate telling you things like 'you'll understand when you're older,' but I kind of have to in this situation. Sometimes there are people in the world who just don't see things the same way. And that's me and your grandparents."

"Did you and Dad see things the same way?"

Melissa smiled a little. "Mostly."

"Just mostly?"

"Well, if we thought about everything the same way, what would we talk about?"

"I guess that's true." Abby crossed her legs on the bench seat, bending in ways that Melissa vaguely remembered being easy when she was ten. "I still wish you'd come and see me when I'm jumping."

"I definitely will. When you're ready for an audience, I'll be there."

"And Grandma Joan?"

"Absolutely."

"How about Nana Rumi and Cary and Ox and Emmie? If I win a trophy at a jumping competition, I want everyone to see me."

Melissa smiled. "Why don't you focus on learning how to jump and not on your inevitable competitive glory, okay?"

Abby put her fist under her chin and leaned on the center console. "I guess."

"Okay." She passed through Hanford. Halfway there. "And when you're ready for the winner's circle, I'll make sure everyone is there."

"Good." The foot on the side panel began to tap. "You know we have a house at the ranch, right?"

Oh boy. "Yes. I know your grandparents built us a house."

"So we could live there if we wanted."

Melissa kept a smile plastered to her face. "Did your grandpa tell you that?"

"Yeah. And Grandma."

Lovely. Thanks, Bev. That was professional-level undermining. "Abby, I know your grandparents would love if we lived closer to them, but who would take care of the ranch if we lived on the coast? Who would take care of your goats?"

"The goats could come with us."

Melissa kept her eyes straight ahead. "I know Oakville isn't as fancy as Paso Robles, but it's our home. And that's where we're going to live, okay?"

"Okay." The girl stared out the window as flat rolling fields passed by.

It was late summer in the valley, and fields that had been green and growing were drying out, nearing harvest time. Wide-leafed cotton and spiky safflower. Dairies and tomato fields. Everything grew in the valley, and currently everything was dusty.

Ten minutes of silence passed before Abby spoke again. "Uncle Devin and Aunt Audrey are fighting a lot."

Oh man. "I'm very sorry to hear that. Fighting is never fun."

"Do you think they're going to get divorced?"

"Abby, I wish I could tell you, but I can't. Sometimes people fight. It doesn't mean they're going to get divorced." But it could, and with Devin and Audrey, nothing would surprise Melissa.

Another ten minutes of silence as Abby contemplated the almond orchards they were driving past.

"Jessie's mom and dad got divorced," her daughter said, "and now she has to sleep on the couch at her dad's house because she doesn't have a room there."

"That sounds... not great. I'm sorry to hear that." Melissa wasn't sure who Jessie was. It seemed like Abby was friends with the entire Oakville Elementary some days. "Is Jessie in your grade?"

"No, she's younger than me, but she lives next door to Marta."

"Got it." Marta and Abby had been friends since first grade. "You know what I think?"

"What?"

Melissa took the turnoff for Kettleman. She drove two blocks and pulled over into the parking lot where Greg or Bev would meet them. Then she turned to her daughter. "I think you are a wonderful, empathetic person and Jessie is lucky that you're thinking about her. She's probably having a really hard time right now, and older girls who are smart and kind like you and Marta could make a big difference. You could be a good friend for her to have."

Abby's face turned from suspicious to beaming. "Thanks, Mom."

"So can you do that? Be thinking about Jessie and make sure she has good friends around her?"

Her daughter nodded vigorously. "Definitely."

"I want you to remember something important." How to get this across to a ten-year-old? "Sometimes in life things go wrong, and even if we want to, we can't make them better." She brushed Abby's hair back. "Dads die in car accidents. Parents get divorced. Pets die. We can't do anything to prevent those things. Whether we're kids or adults."

Abby's brow was creased in worry.

Melissa continued. "What we *can* do for the people we love is come around them. Kind of like... You know the wire supports Grandma puts around her tomato plants?"

"Uh-huh."

"Kind of like that. You and Marta and Jessie's other friends can be right next to her while she'd growing through this. Keep her branches from drooping. Let her have a safe place to rest and have fun while she's going through something hard. Does that make sense?"

Abby's frown disappeared. "Totally. We can do that."

"Awesome." Melissa saw Greg's Range Rover pull into the parking lot. "Looks like your grandpa's here."

Abby reached across the cab of the pickup and squeezed Melissa around the neck. "Thanks, Mom."

"For what?"

"For driving me out so I can see Sunny, of course." Her face was beaming. "I'm gonna tell Grandpa to send you pictures, okay?"

"Please." She handed Abby the duffel bag from the back seat. "And what do you say if they try to buy you a cell phone?"

Abby's face took on an innocent expression. "Please and thank you?"

Melissa narrowed her eyes. "Kid."

She heaved a great sigh. "'No, thank you, Grandma. My mom says I have to wait until I'm thirteen.'"

"That's right."

"Even though I really, *really* want one."

"You got a horse. You can wait on the phone." Melissa jumped out of the pickup and grabbed the crate of vegetables from the back seat. "You get in the car. I've gotta talk to Grandpa."

"Okay!"

She walked over to a smiling Greg Rhodes, who was wearing a perfectly pressed golf shirt with his hair swept back into a silver wave.

He grinned and bent down to Abby. "Hello, princess."

Melissa hated when Greg called Abby princess, but she bit her tongue.

"Hey, Grandpa!" Abby gave him a quick hug and jumped in the passenger seat of the Range Rover. "Mom wants to talk to you."

"Great." Greg kept his smile in place when he turned to Melissa. "How things going at the ranch?"

"Good." She handed him the crate of veggies. "Mom packed some stuff for Bev. The tomatoes are amazing."

"Fantastic." Greg took the crate and gave Melissa a one-armed hug. "So, what's up?"

She put her hands in her pockets and assumed the "casual rancher talking shop" pose she'd perfected by watching her grandfather. It always put old men at ease. "You hear anything about this Allen Ranch project over in Paso?"

Greg frowned. "An Allen ranch in Paso?"

"No, over by me. I was wondering if you'd heard about it?"

Greg kept frowning, but something about his expression put Melissa's instincts on alert. "Can't say... Ah, you know, I think I've heard the name, but not much else."

"Huh."

"What's up?"

"Developer looking to put a few thousand houses on the old Allen ranch next to mine. Like a… fancy retirement-community kind of thing."

"Huh." Greg nodded. "Well, I can see why the town would be interested in that. Big boost to the local economy, right?"

"It's not real popular so far. Folks don't seem too keen on developing open land like that."

"That so?" Greg stuck his hands in his pockets, mirroring her stance. "What are you and your mom thinking? That ranch is right next to yours. It'd up your property value by a lot."

Melissa shrugged. "More neighbors equals more problems, you know? Isn't that why you and Bev built out in the hills?"

"We do like our privacy." A crack appeared in the facade, and Greg's smile twisted a little.

Melissa kept going. "So you haven't heard of it?"

He shrugged. "Nothing specific."

Liar. She knew it down to her toes. "That's interesting." She started to turn and saw Greg's shoulders relax. "You know—"

His shoulders tensed.

She turned back. "The spokesman for the holding company who bought the ranch is named Kevin Fontaine. Isn't he a friend of Devin's?"

Greg looked like he smelled something bad. "I'm not an expert on Devin's friends, Melissa."

"Oh, I was just thinking you could probably ask him about it." *You know all about it, you lying liar.* "If you wanted to know more, I mean."

"Other than Abby, I'm not too interested in what goes on in Oakville." His eyes turned calculating. "Now, if you're asking for a favor—"

"Nope." She'd rather die. "I'll find out the information I need. Just thought it was interesting. Right now Allen Ranch is the talk of the town."

"Well, that's not too difficult."

"Right." Melissa smiled wide. "You guys have a great weekend. Ask Bev to send me pics, okay?"

Greg nodded. "Melissa."

"Greg."

She walked back to her truck and started the engine, watching as Abby and Greg pulled away.

What did Greg know about Allen Ranch? Because one thing was sure.

He knew exactly what she'd been talking about.

———

MELISSA STOOD in front of the mirror in her room, staring at the dress she'd put on and trying not to panic.

It was too short. Had it always been so short? It wasn't like she'd grown taller in the six years since Calvin had passed. When had she bought this thing? It couldn't be that old. Had it shrunk? It fit everywhere else, it just seemed way too short.

"Melissa?" her mother called from the kitchen. "What do you want to do for dinner?"

"I'm going out, remember?"

"Oh, that's right!" Joan sounded overly cheerful. "Who with?"

Melissa sighed. "A friend, Mom."

That was true. Cary was a friend. A friend she kissed and regularly fought with, but definitely a friend.

"Okay."

The lack of more questions told Melissa that Joan knew exactly what she was doing. It was probable that Cary had told Rumi they were going on a date, and Rumi would have immediately told Joan.

Melissa tugged on the hem of the dress. No good. It was hopelessly short, and there was nothing more to be done. If she stayed in her room any longer, she'd change back into her work clothes and call the whole thing off. And she wasn't going to do that. She wasn't a chicken.

She walked to the door and turned the knob before she paused.

Cluck, cluck, Melissa.

She opened the door and walked to the bathroom. Then she proceeded to do something she rarely did. She put on makeup. Not a lot, but enough to make it obvious.

This is a date.

I am dressing up.

I will be kissing you at the end of the night.

Maybe more?

She paused while applying blush.

More?

She'd... leave the door open for more.

Wait, was she ready for more? The idea of "more" with Cary Nakamura sent a shiver over her entire body, but when she started to think about details, she panicked.

This was so nerve-racking! Dating in college hadn't been this nerve-racking, had it?

You were a different person then.

In college, Melissa had been wildly confident. She knew she was a pretty girl and she used it. She dated who she wanted. She hung out wherever she wanted, whether that was a club, the library, or a frat house. She was the designated driver. The friendly, smart girl. The one who could hang with anyone. Where had that girl gone? She'd been so much braver when she was clueless about life.

She finished a sweep of plum over her eyelids that made her blue eyes vivid. Then she put on a coat of mascara and zipped a lip balm into her purse. She tugged the seam of her dress one more time before she walked down the hall and into the kitchen.

Joan closed the cupboard door and turned when she saw

Melissa. Her mother's smile lit up her entire face. "You look beautiful."

Melissa tugged the hem of her dress. "Are you sure? This dress seems too short. I think it shrank."

"It didn't. You just got self-conscious about your knees."

"My knees?" How did her mother know she hated her knees? "Seriously, it shrank."

"Nope." Joan walked over to her and took her by the shoulders, pointing her toward the door. "Do you dislike the dress for any reason other than it feels too short?"

"No, it's just—"

"Good. You look beautiful. It's a classic dress and you look like a million bucks. Go have dinner with Cary."

She walked to the door only halfway of her own volition. "Did Rumi tell you?"

"No, you did."

Melissa squawked. "What?"

"Every time you look at that man, I can see it. So just go. Have fun. I will be going to bed early tonight with a brand-new book Emmie got me because my granddaughter isn't bouncing around the house and keeping me busy. Enjoy your date." And with that, Joan nudged Melissa out the front door and onto the porch.

Melissa turned to the closed front door. "Mom, keys!"

Joan cracked the door open and tossed Melissa's keys at her. Then she shut it in her face.

"Gee, thanks." She felt her phone buzz in her pocket. It was Cary.

Heading over to pick you up.

She typed back. *I thought we were meeting there.*

We live a mile from each other. Why would we take two cars into Metlin?

She had nothing to say to him. She had no idea why she'd been thinking she'd meet him there. Before she could think of a good excuse, she saw his headlights turning onto her road.

Normally she'd run down and open the gate at the cattle guard, but fuck it. She was in heels tonight. She perched on a rocking chair and waited for him.

Her date.

What had she gotten herself into?

CHAPTER THIRTEEN

CARY HAD A REALLY hard time concentrating on driving. He tried to think of the last time he'd seen Melissa's legs in anything other than jeans.

There'd been the Fourth of July swimming party a couple of years ago that they'd both been invited to. Cary had nearly had to leave because his fortysomething body suddenly decided he was a teenager when he saw Melissa in a bathing suit. He'd ended up sitting at the outdoor bar the entire night, trying to ignore her completely.

And now she was sitting next to him in his truck, dressed like a goddess. Wearing makeup of all things.

"You look fucking amazing." He cleared his throat. "Did I already say that?"

"Yes." She smiled. "But thanks again. You look great too."

He was wearing dress pants and a fitted grey button-down. He'd put on more muscle climbing this summer, and the shirt felt a little tight in the shoulders. "Does this shirt look too tight? I haven't bought dress clothes in a while."

She shook her head. "It's really not. It looks... good."

"Are you sure?"

"Very sure."

"Okay." He swallowed hard when he caught another glimpse of her legs as they passed under a streetlight while going through town. "So, Café Georgette?"

"Did you make a reservation?" She winced. "Shit. I didn't think about that. We might need a reservation on a Saturday night. I've only ever been for lunch, so—"

"Relax. I made a reservation." He reached across the cab and took her hand, playing with the fingers before she could start to worry them. "As soon as you told me, I called. We're good."

Her fingers stilled. "Oh. Thanks."

"I'm taking you out. The least I can do is make a phone call." He grinned. "This isn't nearly as elaborate as Jeremy and Tayla's first date. Did you hear about that?"

"No. What did he do?"

Cary recounted everything he'd heard about the world's most elaborate lakeside picnic his climbing partner had pulled off last spring. It had worked. He'd convinced the city girl to stay in Metlin and give him a shot.

"You know"—he released her hand so he could adjust the air conditioner in the truck, then he picked it up again—"I probably shouldn't be telling you about the over-the-top exploits of my friends when I'm just taking you out to dinner, which is the least imaginative first date ever."

"Counterargument: the lake would be dry and dusty right now. Also, any meal I don't have to cook is the height of luxury. Also also, I don't have to do dishes tonight either." She smiled. "Dinner is great."

"Good."

She shifted her legs and he bit his lip. Fuck. How was he going to make it through an entire meal in public this way?

Acting on impulse, he pulled the truck over on the side of the road near a small grove of mandarins.

"What's up? Did you forget something?"

"Yeah." He flipped up the center console on the truck, slid across the cab, and slid his arm behind her neck. "Forgot to kiss you hello."

"Oh right." The corner of her lips turned up and he took it as an invitation, angling his mouth over hers as he pulled her closer. His hand ran from her waist, over the soft curve of her hip, to the sliver of skin just above her knees. He pulled away from her mouth a fraction. "Have I told you I love your legs?"

"Yeah." Her voice was breathless.

Praise the god of skinny black dresses, she crossed her legs and hitched the right one over his knee, placing one leg within reach. He ran his hand over the soft skin, down the muscled calf, and teased the sensitive skin at her ankle with the lightest touch.

"Fuck." He breathed out. "So good."

Her fingers curled into the muscle at the top of his shoulder. "Oh my God, *so* good."

Cary nudged her chin up so he could put his mouth on her neck. "You smell amazing."

"You smell…" Her voice was high. "…different."

He pulled back. "What?"

Her smile was shy. "Okay so… I really love the way you normally smell, which is kind of like dust and oranges."

"And you like that?"

Her cheeks got a little darker. "Yes?"

Cary couldn't stop the grin. "But tonight I took a shower and put on cologne."

She leaned forward and smelled his shirt. "And it's very nice. It just smells different. Kind of like cedar trees and leather? And I like both things, it's just different. But nice!"

"Would you like to say nice again?"

She smiled. "Very nice."

He started laughing and he couldn't stop. Luckily, Melissa started laughing too. She put her forehead on his shoulder, and he could feel her breath against his neck.

"I feel like a dork now."

"Did you call yourself a dork?" He laughed harder. "At least you're a dork with the sexiest fucking legs I've ever seen." He still had his hand on her ankle. He ran his fingers lightly up the back of her leg, behind her knee and just above it, teasing the skin on her thigh.

Melissa stopped laughing and her whole body shivered.

Cary turned his head and whispered in her ear. "I'm glad you like how I smell."

"I'm glad you like my legs."

"I'm glad we're going on a date." He kept his voice low. "I've been wanting to do that for a while."

"I'm glad too." She lifted her head. "Should we go?"

"It's either that or we cancel our reservation for a dinner we don't have to cook or clean up after and make out for a couple hours in Sandy Strathmore's tangerine orchard." He shrugged. "I'm good with either."

She gently pushed him away. "You better feed a girl, Nakamura."

He ran a hand over her leg one more time. *Goodbye, ladies.* "Fine," he said. "But only because I've seen how mean you get when you're hungry."

"You are not wrong."

———

LIKE MELISSA, Cary had only had brunch or lunch at Café Georgette. During the day, it was a small restaurant with a pretty, flower-filled courtyard covered by umbrellas.

At night the umbrellas were removed and sparkling lights and candles decorated the walls surrounding them, lending the bricks, flowers, and trees a fairy-tale atmosphere. Small candles burned in the center of each table. Most of the parties were couples or tables of four.

Cary took Melissa's hand and walked to the hostess stand. "We have a reservation for two. We're a little late."

"Oh!" The hostess smiled. "The name?"

"Nakamura."

"Let me just check and see if your table is ready."

She walked away, and Melissa curled her fingers around his. Cary felt the rightness of it down to his bones. Her hand was relaxed. Her shoulders were relaxed. The line that lived between her eyes had disappeared.

He knew she was capable. She was capable as hell. He knew she was strong. She was so strong sometimes that he thought she could take on the world with one hand, all while nursing a premature calf and fixing a barbed wire fence with the other. He often suspected she hid a third arm somewhere on her person, because he didn't know it was possible to do everything she did with two.

He just wanted her to breathe.

Cary desperately wanted to just take a couple of things off her plate sometimes so she would just be still and relax. He found his stress relief on the side of mountains. She found hers on the back of a horse.

When she wasn't working. Which was almost never.

He squeezed her hand. "Are you relaxed?"

Her eyes went wide. "Uh... kind of?"

"Only kind of?"

She stepped closer. "I'm a little nervous about being on a date. I counted. It's been over thirteen years since I've been on a first date."

"You're doing great; it's been a few years for me too."

She narrowed her eyes. "Why is that?"

"Do you really have to ask?"

Her eyes relaxed. Her whole face got softer. "Really?"

"Pretty sure you're the only one surprised by any of this. I think I was pretty obvious."

"Is it clueless of me to say that I was too busy to notice?"

"No." He kissed her forehead. "It's not clueless. That's your reality. Now your reality is you can't ignore me anymore."

"I never ignored you."

He smiled. "True. But you only wanted to talk about oranges."

The hostess came back and grabbed two menus. "Your table is ready. Thank you for waiting."

Melissa leaned close to Cary and said, "So you're saying you don't want to talk about the new irrigation system and potential yield improvements that—"

He turned his face and kissed her hard and quick. "Nope. Don't even bring it up."

Melissa's laugh was low and wicked.

There it was. He knew she had an evil side. Now he just had to get it to stay out and play.

———

"THAT WAS GREAT." She stretched her legs out in the truck and leaned her head back. "Their food is so amazing."

"That dessert was amazing."

"Thank you for liking chocolate nearly as much as I do. It makes picking dessert much easier."

He smiled, one hand on the wheel and the other holding hers. "You could have picked your own."

She made a face. "Too much rich food."

"But the best company."

Melissa turned her head and smiled. "It was good company."

They'd spent an hour and a half at the restaurant, taking their time, enjoying the atmosphere, and not talking once about citrus trees.

It was a revelation.

Cary learned things about Melissa he'd never known, like she'd barrel raced competitively in college and really enjoyed drawing, which was a skill both she and her brother had inherited from their father, an old cowboy in Montana who'd never remarried after he left their mom.

She didn't like carrots but ate them around Abby because she thought it was responsible.

She desperately wanted to visit Chile and spoke pretty decent Spanish.

She'd only ever had two serious boyfriends. One in high school. One in college, whom she married as soon as she graduated.

And me. He didn't say that part when it came up in conversation. He'd let her figure it out on her own.

They were nearly at her ranch. "When are we going to do this again?"

"Uh… Abby goes back to her grandparents in a couple of weeks."

Cary frowned for the first time in hours. "So you don't want to go out again until Abby leaves town?"

"I just assumed—"

"I'm not interested in hiding this—in hiding *us*—from your daughter."

"It's not that." She sat up, and he saw the tension return to her shoulders. "But this is all new. And I've never dated before. And I want to talk to her about it because she sees you as a close family friend, but not… whatever it is we are now."

Cary let her ramble until they were at the ranch. He got out, opened the gate, and drove through it. Then he repeated the process in reverse, not saying a word once he was back in the truck.

"I'm not going to budge on this, Cary." Her back was up now. "Abby is my daughter, and she only has one parent now. She has to be the priority and—"

"Did I say I disagreed with you?" He kept driving toward the house; a low anger simmered in his belly.

"You're doing the silent thing."

"I'm a quiet person."

"You haven't been quiet all night, and now you're being silent, so what was it? Me not telling Abby about us right away? Me making her the priority? Me—"

"You're trying to fit us in boxes again." He parked the truck and turned to her. "She sees me as a close family friend. I'm still a close family friend. That's not going to change."

"But if we keep dating, it will change. That's what I'm saying. And then if things don't work out—"

"You already planning on that?"

She shook her head. "I'm not saying that. But I have to think about it as a possibility."

Cary was quiet for a long time, absorbing what she was saying. *She had to think about the possibility.*

Of course she did. She had to think about every possibility. He probably should have thought about it too.

The problem was Cary couldn't even imagine a future where he wasn't in love with Melissa and nuts about her daughter. So the possibility of her trying him on and deciding it wasn't a good fit just pissed him off.

"You should show me the bunkhouse." He opened his truck door and walked around to hers.

"What?" She opened her own door.

He helped her out of the truck. "You should show me the bunkhouse."

Melissa blinked. "Is that code for something I should know?"

He crowded her against the side of the truck and caged her with both arms. "I don't know. You all right with me kissing you right here where your mom could see from the windows?"

Her cheeks turned red. "I should show you the bunkhouse."

CHAPTER FOURTEEN

MELISSA HAD SPENT weeks cleaning and organizing the bunkhouse so that renovations could begin. The cobwebs were gone. The dust had been chased away. The large room was mostly empty, but there was still some old furniture out there. Nothing plush like the retreat she envisioned for ranch guests, but bed frames and a few dressers.

She pushed open the door, Cary's heat at her back, and flipped on the single light, which was nothing more than a bare bulb at the far end of the structure.

"So... this is the bunkhouse."

"Nice." Cary put his hands on her waist and spun her around. He backed her up to a sturdy dresser on the far wall until she bumped into it. "Tell me more."

She hitched her hips up on the edge of the dresser, and Cary stepped between her legs. "Uh... planning to take out half the bunks, shore up the others, and add a queen bed on..."

She couldn't concentrate when he nudged her chin up and started kissing her neck. Her heart was racing. She put her hand on his shoulders to steady herself.

"Where's the bed going to go?" His hands had landed on her

hips, and his fingers flexed as if he was testing the give of her body.

"Far wall. Opposite corner. Thought I'd give parents... ah." Her nipples went hard when one hand skimmed along the edge of her breast. "Um... privacy. Parents need privacy."

"I totally agree," he murmured a second before his lips landed on hers.

The sound she made was halfway between a moan and a sigh. Kissing Cary was like sinking into a pool on a hot day. His lips were full and firm, moving expertly over her mouth. She didn't feel nervous anymore. She hooked an arm around his neck and pulled him closer, reveling in the tight control she felt in his body.

He wanted her, but he couldn't have her. Not yet. He was letting her have the reins.

She'd forgotten what it felt like to hold that draw for a man. She was heady with it, full of the knowledge of how his body felt against hers and how her body was responding and welcoming him.

It was a delicious, decadent hunger to want Cary this way. To crave his kisses and the sound of his voice when his lips were against her skin.

He kissed her neck, the edge of her jaw, the sensitive skin behind her ear, her collarbone. He dipped his tongue in the hollow between her breasts and ran it up her neck until his mouth met hers again.

Melissa hooked her fingers in his belt and tugged him closer, eager to feel the hard press of his erection between her thighs. She didn't want sex—didn't feel ready for that—but she was imagining what it would be like with Cary.

Would she still know what to do? It would be different with him, but the basics were the same. Would her body respond the same way?

Cary's hands had been still, firm but unmoving. One at the small of her back. One on the curve of her hip.

Melissa pulled away from his mouth. "Touch me," she whispered.

"I am touching you."

"Touch me more."

He froze, let out a rough breath, and his lips landed on hers again. He moved impossibly closer, and the hand that had been on the small of her back moved to her side.

He cupped her breast, teasing the nipple hidden beneath her dress and bra. "Like this?"

She nodded and kept kissing him. She was addicted to his mouth. And maybe his hands too, because that thumb was criminally talented.

The hand at her hip began massaging her thigh.

"Your hands are so strong." Her eyes rolled back, just from the feel of his fingers on the bare skin of her thigh.

"My hands are very strong." He bit her lower lip. "But don't worry. They know what they're doing."

The tips of his fingers were callused but smooth. Was it the rock climbing? Nothing was rough about them. She'd been expecting rough.

The thumb on her breast didn't stop, and the hand teasing her inner thigh moved higher.

"Like this?" he whispered against her lips.

All Melissa could do was nod.

"How about this?" His fingers teased higher, but not as high as Melissa wanted.

Just to make sure he got the message, she spread her legs wider, the fabric of her dress straining.

She pulled away from his mouth and looked him dead in the eye. "Like this."

He didn't make a sound, but his lips formed the word *Fuck* and his dark eyes lit with greed.

Cary's mouth landed on hers with new urgency. His hand

moved up her inner thigh and teased the fabric of her panties before he moved them aside and his fingers were on her.

She moaned in his mouth, and she wasn't quiet.

He nudged her legs wider and moved closer, teasing her as his thumb worked on her breast.

Melissa felt light-headed from the rush of pleasure. She couldn't think. Couldn't reason. The churning thoughts in her mind fled. There was only this.

Cary's mouth.

Cary's hands.

Cary's fingers between her thighs.

Two of his fingers dipped inside her, not deep, just a teasing promise of things to come while his thumb worked her clitoris, and she nearly wept from the pleasure.

She couldn't even think to kiss him. She pressed her face to his neck and let the tension build and build until the wave crested and her body took possession of her mind.

"Let me see." Cary let go of her breast and grabbed the hair trailing down her back. He tugged it until she fell back against his arm. "Missy, look at me."

Melissa met his eyes, but she wasn't thinking of anything other than the waves of pleasure coursing through her body.

"Fucking gorgeous," he muttered.

The pleasure went on and on, and Melissa couldn't speak. She could barely breathe.

Cary's fingers slowed and eased from her, working her down from the high of climax. "You are so beautiful."

"So are you." It was the first thing that came to her mind and it tumbled out.

He smiled the purest smile she'd ever seen from him. "I'm beautiful?"

"Handsome, I mean. You're handsome."

"I don't mind being beautiful if that's what you want to call me."

She hugged him, hiding her face against his neck. *You are beautiful.*

Beautiful, beautiful man.

Steady man.

Sexy man.

Good man.

She sighed, and it felt like her whole body was loose. Her thigh was pressed against the erection beneath his slacks, and she started reaching for him, only to have Cary bat her hand away.

"Not tonight."

"What?"

He kissed her long and sweet. As he did, he adjusted himself and moved from between her legs. He smoothed her dress down and ran his fingers up and down her knees.

He pulled away from her mouth. "Tonight was about you."

"How about you?"

The corner of his delicious mouth turned up. "Tonight was about me too."

"Cary—"

"When can I see you again?"

"Uh…" She tried to make her brain work. "We have the Jordan Valley picture thing tomorrow morning, remember?"

He planted his hands on the dresser, caging her in. "When can I *see you* again?"

"Oh, you mean…?"

"Yes."

"Um…" Was she actually making plans to see Cary just so they could fool around? She wouldn't have time for dates in the middle of the week, but the idea of going two weeks without having his hands on her had suddenly become kind of torturous. "Text me on Tuesday?"

"Good." He stepped back and held his hand out, helping her off the dresser. His eyes were fixed on her legs. "Have I mentioned how much I like that dress?"

She suddenly felt self-conscious again. "I feel like it's too short."

"It's not." He took her hand and led her to the door. "Trust me, it's not."

———

DRESSES AND KISSES were the last thing on Melissa's mind the next morning. It was hot as Hades in the middle of Cooper's Field, but dozens of families had gathered under a stand of oak and sycamore trees on the far edge of Melissa's property near Jordan Valley Road. Allen Ranch was in the distance.

Cary had thought of a fund-raiser to both collect money for fighting the development company and to raise awareness in town about what the council was voting on in a few short weeks.

Joan had set up a booth with homemade lemonade and iced tea with a big sign overhead. SAVE JORDAN VALLEY. SAY NO TO ALLEN RANCH! She was passing out drinks and handouts with a summary of the development plan along with the names and phone numbers of all the Oakville council members. On the bottom of the handout, it said in giant letters: MAKE YOUR VOICE HEARD!

To attract people, Cary was taking family portraits for free, spending a few minutes with each family that showed up and taking beautiful pictures against the rolling fields and oak trees of Jordan Valley, while other volunteers led hikes and showed visitors around.

Melissa was wrangling the volunteers who had shown up, handing out information and lemonade and talking with a reporter from the *Metlin Gazette* while they walked around. Emmanuel Ortiz was a guy she'd gone to high school with and he'd grown up in Oakville, which was the only reason he was paying any attention to the situation.

"Didn't the Oakville city council have a budget shortfall last year?" Manny asked, pointing his voice recorder in Melissa's direction. "There's been talk of the high school closing. Possibly the middle school too. Are you saying that these empty fields and hills are more valuable than Oakville students? The development would solve the budget shortfall with new property taxes."

Melissa had been expecting that question. "I'm sure it would, but it would also tax our water supplies and infrastructure. Because the council has rejected our request to hire an independent firm for an environmental impact study, we don't really know what the effect of two thousand new tract homes, a clubhouse, and a golf course would have on our community. That's a lot of people and buildings to put in an area that you can see right now." Melissa pointed toward the distant foothills. "See where that dark granite rock juts out?"

The reporter squinted. "Yes."

"Imagine a line going from there to the road. That is the southern boundary of Allen Ranch. Now imagine two *thousand* houses and four *thousand* people crammed into that area. Look at the road. Do you think it's going to accommodate four thousand more residents? It's a two-lane road."

Manny had to smile. "That's a lot of traffic."

"Exactly. So they're going to want to expand the road. Look at the farms along the road. Are the farmers going to want to sell their land to expand the road for what is essentially a country club they can't visit? Who's going to make them? The federal government?" Melissa knew if there was one thing the residents and Metlin and Oakville shared, it was suspicion of the federal government. "If anyone tries to take good productive farmland for a road we don't need to a place we don't have any say over, people will sue. And who will be defending those lawsuits? Where will the money come from?"

Manny was nodding. "So you're saying that the money the town will make in new property taxes might get eaten up by lawsuits from residents?"

"I don't know if the town will get sued. I'm not saying that. But I find it impossible to think it's not going to cost us money." Melissa put both hands in her pockets. "I'm not antidevelopment, but it's just not a good site. Why here?"

Manny spread his hand out. "Beautiful, empty land? The same reason people are taking pictures out here?"

"It's not empty. It's grazing land. There are creeks and hiking trails. Bird-watching areas. Picnic spots. There are houses on that land that have been there for over a hundred years. Not to mention that there are two Yokuts sites on the Allen ranch that Native people have been visiting for like two *thousand* years."

His eyes glinted. "There's Yokuts land over there?"

Melissa spread her arms wide. "Come on. This is *all* Yokuts land, but the sites on Allen Ranch aren't formally Yokuts property. They shouldn't have to be. The Allens and the people before them just had mutual respect, okay? They didn't need to make it a legal thing, because they respected the people who visited and didn't disturb the sites. Is JPR Holdings going to respect that? Or are they going to build a golf course on it?"

Manny said, "I might have to make an appointment with the Yokuts council to see what they think about this."

"I think that's a great idea."

"Thanks, Melissa." Manny held out his hand and turned his voice recorder off.

"Thank you. We really appreciate the coverage."

"So your last name is Rhodes now, right?"

"Yes. My late husband was a Rhodes."

"I was really sorry to hear about that." Manny put his recorder in his backpack. "I remember that accident, but I didn't realize that was your husband. What do you think he'd think about all this?"

Melissa shook her head. "He'd be appalled. He loved Oakville. Loved the hills and Jordan Valley."

Manny squinted. "I was talking about the Rhodes family and JPR Holdings."

Melissa froze. "What about them?"

Manny's eyes went wide. "Oh my God. Do you not know?"

Self-preservation took over. "Manny, are we off the record here?"

Manny spread his arms out. "Dude. You danced with me at senior prom when everyone else was ignoring me. I'm not gonna be biased, but I'm not looking to ambush you."

"I had a feeling that they knew something because Abby recognized the guy they sent to the council meeting, but honestly, my in-laws and I don't have the best relationship. So no, I don't know what you're talking about."

Manny scratched his chin. "Shit. So... I did some digging to find out who were the actual owners of JPR Holdings because it sounded dodgy to me, and I thought it might be an angle."

"Is it?"

He shook his head. "Not really. It's just a bunch of different people. Nothing even close to illegal. The guy who actually bought the property put it together once he realized ranching wasn't a weekend sport, you know? He decided to develop it, and he went looking for investors."

"Where do the Rhodeses come in?"

"Kind of on the ground floor. They know the guy and were some of the first people involved." Manny grimaced. "I hate to tell you this, but all in all, your in-laws own about a quarter of the company that's trying to turn Jordan Valley into houses."

———

MELISSA WAS livid when she showed up in Kettleman City later that afternoon to pick Abby up. She gritted her teeth, smiled, and waited until her bouncing daughter had bounced herself into the truck.

Then she approached Greg. "You're part of JPR Holdings."

His eyes narrowed. "Yes, we are."

"Why would you do this?" Melissa no longer had any fucks to give. "Why would you do this to Abby? You know how Calvin felt about our ranch. Do you really think money you don't need is worth this? What's the game plan? Make us so miserable we want to leave and move to the coast?"

Greg's smile was patronizing. "Not everything is about you, Melissa."

"Bullshit. This is definitely about me. About me and Calvin refusing to be under your thumb. About us choosing to raise Abby in Oakville instead of near you. Well, I can tell you one thing, it's not going to happen. This Allen Ranch thing? It's dead. My mother and I—"

"Wrong." Greg's smile never left his face. "You and your mother aren't going to do a damn thing to oppose this. In fact, you're going to dissolve the little protest committee you have going. I want you to make it happen."

Melissa was incredulous. "Are you nuts? Why do you think you have any right to—"

"I have every right." His voice rose. "You're going to shut up about Allen Ranch, Melissa. You're going to shut right the hell up or I'm going to call in the note. And I know you don't have an extra seventy-five thousand dollars to pay us back. Not yet."

Her chin rose. "We have a contract. Calvin drew it up. He didn't trust you either."

That stung Greg—she could see it in his eyes—but his smug smile never wavered. "My son was brilliant. Far too brilliant to have married you. You're right. You did have ten years. That ten years is up."

"It's been seven."

"It's been seven since you took the money," Greg said. "But we signed the contract ten years ago in May, Melissa."

Melissa's stomach fell. "What?"

"He signed the papers long before he brought it up with you. You were about to have Abby. He didn't want to put another thing on your plate. He signed the contract ten years ago. Just because he waited three years to take the money doesn't mean the contract isn't valid."

Greg stepped back, and Melissa was still frozen.

"So you're going to shut up about Allen Ranch. You and your mom. You're going to shut up about it, or I'm going to call in that note, take your ranch when you can't pay it, and develop the whole damn Jordan Valley into houses I can sell off bit by bit." He walked to his Range Rover and turned. "But don't worry. I'll let Joan live with you and Abby in Paso."

Melissa couldn't move. Greg drove away, and she was still standing there, baking in the hot sun, ice running though her veins.

Abby opened the truck door and poked her head out. "Mom? What's wrong?"

CHAPTER FIFTEEN

CARY DIDN'T KNOW what to think when Melissa knocked on his door at nine o'clock on a Monday night. He'd texted her earlier in the day, but she hadn't mentioned getting together.

"Hey." He opened the door and let her in. "What's up?"

Something was definitely up. Her expression was frozen and blank. She walked wordlessly to the bed and sat down on the edge, her eyes staring at something he couldn't see.

Cary dragged over a chair from the table by the window. "Melissa, seriously, what's up? You're freaking me out. Is Abby okay?"

She nodded.

"Your mom?"

"Mom's fine."

"What is going on?"

She covered her face with both hands, leaned forward, and breathed out a rough breath. "I fucked up, Cary. I fucked up so bad."

His heart raced. "What the hell is going on?"

"I finally read the contract. He said we had ten years, and it didn't even occur to me to doubt him. Now the money is spent and I have nothing. I have no wiggle room. All the savings I'd socked away went to rebuild the bunkhouse because I thought it would be a good investment, and now—"

"I don't understand what you're saying." He shook her shoulder. "Start at the beginning. I can't help if I don't know what's happening."

She looked up and her eyes were red. "A little over seven years ago, Calvin and I borrowed one hundred thousand dollars from his parents to complete the planting for the orchards. It should have been more than enough. We should have had time. Ten years should have been enough, even though I didn't start right away because of the accident. I thought I had eight years left on the note when I planted the trees."

"Okay." Cary nodded. "Why isn't eight years enough? How much do you still owe?"

"Seventy-five thousand."

That wasn't great, but profit from her acreage could take care of that in a year. "You planted four years ago. You still have three years, and you'll have a full harvest next season. You're making it right now operating the ranch with what you have, so if you put all the harvest profit into paying off the loan, you should be fine."

"That was the plan. But I don't have three more years," she said. "It's already been ten years since it was signed, and the contract says the note is due ten years from *signing*. Not ten years from receiving the money."

Cary felt like his stomach had dropped to the ground. "Missy, why on earth—?"

"Calvin signed it before Abby was born." She shook her head. "He didn't tell me at the time—he waited until she was about a year old. Then he waited to get the money from his dad, and by the time we actually had the funds, it had already been three years, but I had no idea."

Cary leaned back in his chair. "And you didn't think to read the contract after he died because...?"

"Why would I? I trusted what Calvin said. The money was there, and I was desperate to get started. We were already behind schedule. I'd waited over a year, and I knew I needed to start. To move on. Keep going." She shook her head. "Now Greg can call in the note anytime, and if I don't pay it, he and Bev can take the whole ranch."

So many things were wrong with this, but the timing bothered Cary. They hadn't come to Melissa when the note was due. She said it had been agreed to before Abby was born, and Abby had celebrated her tenth birthday well over a month ago.

"What do they want?" he asked. "This isn't about money."

"Good catch." Her smile was bitter. "They're part of JPR Holdings. They're the ones who are trying to build the Allen Ranch development."

He closed his eyes. Yep. That sounded like Greg Rhodes. "So that's why the Fontaine name sounded familiar."

"Kevin Fontaine is a friend of my brother-in-law. I have no doubt Devin's hands are all over this. He's probably the P in JPR Holdings."

"Devin Peres," Cary muttered. "Peres, Rhodes. Wonder who the J is?"

"Don't care." She waved a hand. "Doesn't matter. All I know is that Greg is saying that if I don't shut up about Jordan Valley and dissolve the protest committee, he's going to call in the note on the ranch. Which... I can't even do that. I didn't start the committee. It's not in my power to dissolve it."

"Unbelievable." He closed his eyes. "Actually, it's sadly believable."

He and Calvin had been friends, and none of this came as a surprise to Cary. Calvin had hated his parents, but he could be a little bit like them at times. He'd probably signed that note using

Melissa's ranch as collateral without even considering the idea he'd be unable to repay it. *Stupid.*

Cary shook his head. "I can't believe he signed that note without telling you." He stood up and walked to the bathroom to grab her some Kleenex. She wasn't crying, but it was close.

Melissa took the tissues he held out. "It probably seemed like so little money to him he didn't even consider it. Besides, Calvin would have been thirty before it came due, and he would have come into his trust fund. We were never going to be short on cash once he had that. I can't even count how many times he said, 'After I turn thirty...'" She heaved a massive sigh. "Life sure has a way of kicking you."

Cary said, "Calvin died just before he turned thirty, so no trust fund."

"The money didn't disappear, it just rolled over to Abby's fund. But I don't have access to it. Neither does she until she's thirty. Those are the terms of the trust his grandparents set up."

"Are they still living? Can they change it? Calvin signed a note that you and your mom are being held responsible for because he's gone. Surely his grandparents never intended—"

"His grandparents are dead. And Greg and Bev have nothing to do with it. It's a law firm in Santa Maria."

"Fuck."

"Yeah." She wiped her eyes. "So I have to come up with seventy-five thousand dollars really fast."

Cary shrugged. "Or you can just go along with things. There's no guarantee the development will happen. The Allen Ranch project may die a natural death because people keep making noise."

"Or it might go through and we'll have two thousand houses at the end of Jordan Valley, chemicals in our water from golf course runoff, and traffic issues from here until forever."

Cary put his hands on his hips, still standing. He was too

pissed off to sit. "It wouldn't be the end of the world," he said. "And you'd still have your ranch."

Melissa cocked her head. "I can't believe you'd even suggest that. I'm not the only one affected by this."

"No, but you know what? You're the only one being asked to put your own neck on the line because of it, Missy. I would *never* judge you for doing what you needed to do to protect your family, and I'd kick the shit out of anyone who questioned your motives."

"But it's not just about me." She reached in her pocket and pulled out her phone. "Oh, and in case you think Greg and Bev are being heartless, read this. She just sent this."

He took the phone and saw an email on the screen.

DEAR MELISSA,

I heard that you and Greg had words yesterday afternoon about the Allen Ranch project. I don't want this to come between our family. It would break my heart.

I want you to know you are always welcome here at the ranch. Always. And though I know you're probably very angry with Greg right now, I have talked to him and convinced him that we don't want to anger you. You're Calvin's widow and Abby's mom. You're family.

If you would speak up in defense of the project at the next council meeting, it would go a long way to smoothing things over with him. If you'd do that, honey, I think we could tear up that note entirely. The money is nothing to us. We just want you and Abby to be safe and happy.

Love always,

Beverly

"That is…" Cary had to read through it twice. "Wow."

"Right?"

"Help us get our development project done and we'll cancel your debt. Speak out against it and we'll take your ranch." He looked up. "Is this woman for real?"

"Did you like how she mentioned the money was 'nothing to them'? I liked that part especially."

"The money *isn't* anything to them." He sat next to her. "This is all about control. About getting their hooks in you whatever way they can."

"And through me, Abby." She looked up at him, her eyes still damp. "I can't do it, Cary. If I give in on this, they'll hold it over me for the rest of my life."

He nodded, knowing she was right. "So what are your options?"

"Right now, nothing. They have to give me notice if they're calling it in, and I already emailed Mom's estate lawyer, hoping he might find a loophole somewhere."

Cary wasn't counting on a loophole. He was already shuffling his assets, trying to figure out where he could grab seventy-five grand. He could put it together, but then he'd have to convince Melissa to take it. That would be the harder part.

She laid her head on his shoulder. "I haven't told Mom yet. She's going to be so pissed. And disappointed."

"At you?"

"No, at Calvin." Melissa heaved a huge sigh. "She adored him."

Cary turned his head and kissed her forehead. "Are you pissed at him?"

She was silent for a long time. "No. Because it's just such a Calvin thing. He was the enthusiastic dreamer. He always figured things would work out. There was no malice there. Just... gross optimism."

"He should have told you when he signed that note."

"I had a hard pregnancy, and I was so damn cranky because I couldn't ride. I was getting three hours of sleep on a good day." She snuggled her head into Cary's shoulder. "He was probably afraid of me."

Cary put his arms around her and marveled at the generosity of her heart. She could have blamed her late husband, could have resented the life of privilege that gave Calvin such an unrealistic attitude toward money.

She didn't. She loved him for who he was.

"What are you going to tell Abby?"

She pulled away and stared at him. "Nothing. Why should I tell Abby anything?"

"Maybe not now, but if they call in the note—"

"She doesn't need to know, Cary."

He bit his tongue. It wasn't his place to say, but Abby was a mature kid and she wasn't clueless. She was going to know something was going on.

"Kiss me," she said.

He stroked her hair and tucked a piece behind her ear. "I want to, but you're upset."

She frowned. "I know. That's why I want you to kiss me."

He smiled, glad that she'd come to him, relieved that he'd become her sounding board even if he had to bite his tongue sometimes.

"I suppose..." He kissed the corner of her eye, which was still a little teary. "...I could kiss you. As a friend."

She looped her arms around his neck. "Yes. Just a friendly kiss."

"Missy," he whispered against her lips before he kissed them.

Soft.

Generous.

Sexy as hell.

The taste of her mouth was addicting. Cary kept his kisses slow and controlled. She wanted comfort? He could give her comfort. She wanted distraction? He was fine with that.

He put his arm around her back and lowered her to the bed, his mouth never leaving her lips. They lay on their sides, and he kissed her over and over again, wanting to drive every tear from her eyes and every ounce of tension from her shoulders.

As he kissed her, he kneaded her back and ran his fingers through her hair.

She let out a shuddering sigh. "You're petting me like a cat."

"Is it working?"

"Meow." She kissed him again and threw her leg over his hips. "This is giving me all kinds of ideas."

"Keep your ideas to yourself tonight," he muttered. "I'm being good, but I'm not that good."

"No." She pulled back and looked into his eyes. "You're not good. You're great. I'm sorry it took me so long to see that."

I am yours.

I am yours.

I am so yours.

Cary cupped her cheek in his hand and stared at her. He rubbed his thumb over her lips. *I love you like crazy, Melissa Rhodes.*

"Can you tell me something?" she asked.

"Anything."

She took his hand off her cheek and looked at it. "How are your hands so soft? Seriously, they're all callused but they're still soft. I don't understand."

Cary chuckled a little. "They make special lotion climbers use because we don't want to lose our calluses. So I order that, and then I also use a very fine sandpaper to smooth them out." He played his thumb along her lower lip. "Don't want to rough you up."

She squeezed his thigh with her leg. "I don't mind a little rough."

"Woman, I am really trying to be good here."

She laughed, a low, wicked laugh that told him she knew exactly how much she affected him.

"Come here." He hooked a finger through her belt loop and pulled her closer. "You kiss me this time."

"I am kissing you."

"You know what I mean."

She put a hand on his cheek and stroked it. Then she ran her fingers up and into his hair, teasing it between her fingers as she leaned forward and took his mouth. Her tongue came out, ran along his lips, and he opened his mouth to welcome her.

Her hand rested on his chest, and she had to feel his heart pounding, had to feel the solid erection he was sporting, pressed against her thigh. She didn't hurry. Didn't rush a single thing.

It was slow, glorious torture, and he loved every minute of it.

She had to leave before it got too late, but Cary was relieved to see that by the time she walked to the truck, the strain was gone from her eyes. He walked her out and opened the door for her.

"You coming to Abby's program next week? We can't do the camping thing because of soccer, but she wanted you and your mom to come."

Abby had invited Cary and Rumi to the fall talent show at her school. She was singing and dancing with a group of her friends and was asking for an audience.

Cary nodded. "We wouldn't miss it. Text me the time of her game this weekend and I'll try to make it if we haven't taken off yet."

"I will. And I'll make dinner after the program if you and your mom want to come over."

"Sounds good." He hesitated, not sure if he should bring up the loan again. "You going to tell your mom about it?"

"Dinner?" Melissa frowned.

"No, the other thing."

"Ah." Melissa took a deep breath and let it out slowly. "Yeah. I have to."

"I still think you should tell Abby. Not to badmouth her grandparents, but just so she knows what's up. 'Cause she's going to know something is up."

She didn't argue with him this time. She stared at the steering wheel and nodded. "I'll think about it."

"Fair enough." He curled his finger toward her. "Come here."

"Again?" Her smile reappeared from hiding. "You're insatiable."

"Just wait. You'll find out how much."

Her lips were flushed and swollen by the time he finished kissing her.

"Soon," he whispered against her mouth. "Very soon."

CHAPTER SIXTEEN

MELISSA SAT NEXT to Cary in the darkened auditorium, trying to ignore the feeling of his finger sliding along her leg. His face gave nothing away; he was watching raptly as Abby and three of her friends lip-synced and danced to "Walking on Sunshine" while dressed in 1980s costumes, sunglasses, and carrying cardboard surfboards.

A slight smile was on his face, but Melissa couldn't tell if he was smiling at the girls' antics or enjoying her torment.

She cleared her throat and shifted. "Stop," she mouthed at him.

He didn't say a word, he just moved his arm from beside her leg to the back of her seat, effectively putting his arm around her.

Her eyes went wide. "Cary."

"What? These seat are tiny," he whispered. "My shoulders don't fit."

She wished she could just relax, lean into his side, and maybe lean her head on his shoulder. He was solid. It would feel so nice.

But her daughter was on the stage. A hundred nosy gossips filled the auditorium. She wasn't embarrassed about Cary, she just didn't want a million different opinions on something that was nobody's business but theirs. So she sat stiffly next to him, pretending the muscled arm around her shoulders was nothing more than the gesture of a friend.

He leaned over to her and whispered, "Our childhood is now a historical musical era."

"Showing your age, old man." She smiled a little. "I was a baby when this came out."

"Oh, that's right. I forgot you're barely legal."

Melissa had to muffle a laugh.

"What was your boy band of choice? Were you an 'N Sync girl? Backstreet Boys?"

"Please." She cut her eyes toward him. "I was obviously the sixth Spice Girl."

His lip twitched. "I apologize. I don't know how I could have made that mistake."

"You think I was a fan of ramen-noodle hair?"

"I don't know what you're talking about, but now I'm hungry for ramen. Thank you."

She smiled. "You never told me how the climb went."

"Good." He nodded. "Very good."

"Was it... relaxing?"

Cary bit back a smile. "Not as relaxing as some things can be."

"*Shhhh.*"

Joan was glaring at them, so Melissa shut up. You could be thirty-four, but that didn't mean you got to ignore your mom when you were whispering during the assembly.

"Be good," she whispered to him.

"Trust me, I'll be *very* good." His thumb slid along her bare shoulder, and Melissa barely contained the shiver.

It wasn't fair for Cary to turn her on in the middle of the Oakville Elementary assembly hall, but when had life ever been fair?

They sat through Abby's dance—which was pretty cute even though the girls had done more laughing than lip-syncing—and two more dance groups. Four trembling singers, three piano solos, and the world's shortest and cutest garage band rounded out the night's entertainment. When the lights came up and everyone turned to go, Melissa looked at Cary.

"I made chili and corn bread, so we can eat when you and your mom get to the house."

Cary was staring at her.

"What?" She looked down. "Did I get something on my dress?"

He murmured, "I want to kiss you right now."

"Because I made chili?"

"No, I just want to kiss you." He leaned close as people shuffled around them. "It's been over a week. I need you and me. Alone."

Her eyes went wide. "I'm going to go pick up Abby from her classroom, then we're going to the house to eat dinner."

"After that?"

Her cheeks felt hot. "After that... I wanted you to check out the new plumbing in the bunkhouse if you have time."

"Sure." His eyes burned her skin. "I'd be happy to do that."

———

"DID YOU SEE WHEN I SLIPPED?" Abby burst into laughter. "I thought Marta was going to fall all over me, and then we were all going to fall over like dominos."

"But you didn't," Rumi said. "You caught yourself and then you all finished very nicely. It was a beautiful dance."

"Thanks, Nana." Abby reached for another piece of corn bread, but Melissa stopped her.

"Nuh-uh." Melissa pointed at her bowl. "Actual food before you take more corn bread."

"Mom—"

"Don't argue. Protein, Abby. Muscles don't grow from corn."

Melissa pretended not to notice when Cary slipped half his

corn bread over to Abby's plate, but she caught his eye when Abby giggled.

"What?" His face was all innocence. He took a bite of his chili. "Great chili, Missy."

Abby swung her head toward Cary. "Hey, adult."

"Hey, kid."

Abby smiled. "Why do you call Mom Missy? You're the only one who does that. Uncle Ox and Grandma call her Lissa sometimes, but you call her Missy."

Cary smiled. "Do you really want to know?"

Melissa said, "Oh Cary, don't."

"What?" He grinned. "It's cute."

"It's embarrassing." She covered her face.

Abby was bouncing in her seat. "What is it? You have to tell me now. You have to."

"It was funny and adorable." Cary turned to Abby. "So when your mom was a little older than you, she was riding over by our house."

Abby turned to Melissa. "Were you riding Sky?"

"I was," Melissa said. "I'd just gotten her a few months before."

Cary smiled. "And I was... a lot older than your mom. I was in my twenties and almost done with college."

Abby's eyes went wide. "I didn't know you were older than Mom."

"Only by numbers. She's much older than me mentally."

"Hey!" Melissa tossed her napkin across the table.

"Can we not start a food fight to prove our youthful energy?" Joan asked. "I'm not cleaning that up."

"If you start a food fight"—Rumi raised a spoon and narrowed her eyes—"I'm taking you all out."

Abby giggled, but she wasn't distracted. "What happened? Why do you call Mom Missy? You still haven't told me."

Cary put his arm around Abby's chair and turned his eyes toward Melissa. "So I'd just come home from college in San Luis to work for the summer, and your mom comes riding up the road from the ranch on her horse."

"On Sky."

Cary nodded. "On Sky. I hadn't seen her in a couple of years and I didn't recognize her. And I knew I'd remember that horse. So I asked her, 'Hey, can I help you? Are you lost?' And you know what she said?"

Melissa covered her face. "I can't believe you still remember this."

"It was unforgettable." Cary turned back to Abby. "She said, 'I'm *Miss* Melissa Oxford, and I always know where I am, thank you very much.'"

"I did not say thank you very much!"

Cary took a drink of his beer. "I'm pretty sure you did."

Abby giggled. "So you called her Missy after that?"

"Yep. Every time I saw her."

"To tease me," Melissa said. "He was making fun of me for being so formal."

Cary's smile was slow and sweet. "I wasn't making fun of you."

She shook her head and reached for Rumi's plate. "You done, Rumi?"

"I am." She rose. "Why don't you and Cary relax and let your mom and me clean up? You've been running around all day."

Melissa glanced at the clock, then at Abby. "It's that time, kid."

"Noooooo." Abby ran behind Cary's chair. "Cary, hide me."

He laughed and stood up. "Sorry, kid. You're on your own. Only a foolish man goes up against *Miss* Melissa Oxford."

Melissa rolled her eyes in his general direction. "Abby, bed. You had a very fun day—please don't end it badly by being stubborn about bedtime."

"Fine." She slumped her shoulders and trudged down the hall. "I can't believe it's already eight thirty."

"It's almost nine. Don't push it. And don't forget teeth."

"Fine." Abby stomped off down the hall.

Melissa's eyes went to Cary and she mouthed, *Fine.*

He smothered a smile.

She asked, "Did you get enough to eat?"

"I did." He ran a hand over his muscled stomach, and Melissa's eyes went straight there. Cary clearly noticed. "I heard Brian was doing some work on the bunkhouse this week."

Melissa glanced at Joan and Rumi. "Uh, yeah. Do you want to see what he's done?"

"I'd love to."

"Cool." Melissa walked toward the front door. "Mom, we'll just be down in the bunkhouse for a few minutes."

"Take your time!"

Melissa felt Cary at her back when she grabbed a flashlight and the keys. "Eventually we'll put lights along the path, but for now it's pretty dark."

"Mm-hmm."

Cary walked behind her as she led him down the porch and around the back of the ranch house.

The bunkhouse sat in a copse of sycamore and oak trees at the east boundary of the ranch. It was the oldest building on the ranch, dating back around a hundred years, and was probably the original house. It was made of adobe bricks and covered in flaking stucco.

Old trees shaded the small house, which sat nestled in the curve of the creek. It was dry this time of year but would fill with water as soon as rain came in the fall. Dry or not, it was one of the prettiest places on the Oxford ranch.

"You gonna put gravel on this road to keep the dust down?"

"I already have a load ordered," she said. "It'll come in a couple weeks."

"You'll want it in before the rain comes or this will be nothing but mud."

"That's what I was thinking too."

He walked closer to her and ran a hand over her bottom. "I've been wanting to do that all night. You've got such a great ass."

Her cheeks felt hot again. "You do too."

His smile flashed in the darkness. "Thank you."

"You like my legs. My ass. My hair." Melissa took the lock and the keys in hand. "Is there any part of me you don't like?"

Cary put his hands on her hips. "I could do without the hair-trigger temper you have sometimes."

She opened the door and flipped on the single light. "I don't have a temper."

"Yes, you do."

She felt her temper rising and took a deep breath. "Do not."

He smiled and pressed her against the dresser. "You're being so good. Look at you, Miss Melissa Oxford."

"I wish you'd forget that story."

"Did you have a crush on me?" He kissed along her collarbone. "That just occurred to me tonight. You must have been what? Thirteen? And you were so formal. Did you think I was cute?"

Melissa couldn't say anything. Her heart was in her throat.

"Did you?" He grinned. "Don't be shy. You were adorable."

"Cary, I was *thirteen*. I had a crush on all cute boys at that age."

He gasped. "You mean it wasn't just me?"

She couldn't stop her smile as she hopped up on the dresser. "Stop."

"My heart is broken. I thought Miss Melissa Oxford, sixth Spice Girl, who always knows where she is, only had eyes for me."

"You were a cute boy with a cool car." She put her arms around his neck. "I'm sure lots of teenage girls had a crush on you."

"I wouldn't want to brag." He ran his hands along her hips and squeezed. "Fuck, I love your legs."

She hooked a leg around the back of his thighs and pulled him in. "You're very talkative tonight."

He leaned in and kissed her. "I'm happy."

Melissa's heart felt like it would burst. "I'm glad."

"I know there's a lot going on, but I'm really happy, Melissa." He kissed the arch of her cheek. "It's all going to work out somehow."

She turned her face to his and took his mouth. She didn't want to talk anymore. She wanted to forget about the skinny girl on the paint horse. She wanted to forget about her responsibilities and her burdens.

"Cary." She let her head fall back as Cary explored every inch of her neck with his mouth. As she braced herself on the dresser, his hands roamed over her body. He squeezed her hip and ran a hand up the curve of her waist. He stroked her breast over her sundress, then dipped his thumb under the low neckline, testing the firm flesh of her right breast and making her temperature skyrocket.

"When do you have another free weekend?" he whispered. "Come to my place. Stay the night."

"I can't." She could barely think. His mouth and his hands were driving her to distraction. He said something, but she didn't hear. "What?"

"Why can't you come over?"

"I can. I can't stay the night."

He pulled back. "Why not?"

"I-I just can't."

"Missy, your mom and mine know what's going on between us."

"I know they suspect, but—"

"But what?" He caged her with both arms. "What's the problem? We're both adults."

She ran a hand along his jaw. "It's not that simple."

"It's not as complicated as you're making it." He reached behind her and with one tug pressed their bodies together.

Melissa could feel the length of his erection. She could imagine it. Imagine how it would feel to be with him. The weight of his body over hers. The solid muscle pressing her into the bed as he kissed her senseless. As he moved in her. She wanted him as badly as he wanted her.

Cary continued to make love to her mouth. His hands stroked her body like his tongue stroked hers. Thoroughly. Teasing her to greater heights as they moved together in the dim shadows of the bunkhouse.

"Mom!"

The sound of Abby's voice threw cold water on Melissa's libido. She shoved Cary away.

"What—?"

"Abby's coming!"

Footsteps were coming closer.

"Tell me something really unsexy. Fast." Cary's shirt and hair were mussed. He looked like he was about to ravish someone, which wasn't far off.

Melissa shoved the flashlight toward him. "Bathroom," she hissed. "In the corner. Go… look at the plumbing!"

Cary stood in the doorway of the new bathroom, untucking his shirt and shining a flashlight into the new construction as Melissa hopped off the dresser and the door opened.

"Hey," she said. "What's up? I thought you were in bed."

Abby's face was pale in the darkness. "I thought you were going to tuck me in."

"It's really late, baby." She ran a hand over Abby's hair.

"What are you doing down here?"

"Just showing Cary the new bathroom Mr. Montoya is putting in. I wanted him to check and make sure it was good enough."

"Oh." Abby narrowed her eyes. "Didn't you and Stu look at it yesterday?"

"Uh…" She shrugged. "You know, it's never a bad idea to get another opinion."

Cary turned and flashed the light in Abby's and Melissa's eyes. "Sorry. Yeah, I think it looks good. It's small though."

"We're going to put a washbasin and counter on the wall

alongside. That way people can still use the sink, brush their teeth and stuff when someone is in the bathroom. Since there's just one bath—"

"That makes sense." He subtly adjusted his shirt to cover the front of his pants. "Well, if you don't need anything else, I should probably get my mom home."

"They're in the living room having cake." Abby's smile was crooked. "I kinda sneaked past them."

So that's how she snuck out. "Head back to the house, Abby. I'll be there in a few to tuck you in."

"Okay. Night, Cary."

"Good night, Abby. Sweet dreams."

He didn't have a smile on his face when Abby ran out the door.

Melissa waited to hear her footsteps fading away before she closed the door, leaned against it, and slid down the wall. "Oh my God."

"Chill." He shut off the flashlight and put it on the dresser. "She was none the wiser. Gonna have to get used to that."

"Cary..." She covered her face. "I can't... I can't deal with this too."

"Missy, it's fine. She's going to see us kissing eventually. It's just a new thing for me and I'll try to—"

"No, we can't do this!" Melissa felt like her world was crashing around her. She wanted to curl up and hide. "What if she'd seen us? She can't see us. She's ten! She'll get all these ideas."

His eyes narrowed. "So let her get ideas. I don't care."

"Do you know how big her hero complex is with you?" Melissa spoke in a low, urgent voice. "You have no idea. She thinks you walk on water. She thinks you are the absolute best."

"And?" His smile was confused. "Melissa, I don't understand what the problem is. I *love* Abby."

She stood. "And what happens when she gets all these ideas and then something doesn't work out? What happens then?"

He started shaking his head. "Oh no. Not this bullshit."

"Are you and your mom still going to come over for family dinners like you did tonight if you're mad at me? Or I'm mad at you? Are you still going to come help her build corrals for her goats? Or go to her school programs? What we had before..." She felt panic rising in her chest. "It was good, Cary. We're friends, and she *depends* on you being there."

"I will always be there for Abby," he hissed. "Always."

"Really? Are you sure? Even if you're sick of me? Sick of us? If we fight or break up or—"

"What are you doing?" He glared at her. "Don't do this! You are not allowed to break this because you're scared of what *might* happen, Missy."

"Except I have to."

Because Abby came first. She had to. Calvin was gone. There was only Melissa now. And she'd been distracted. Flustered. Not focused on her daughter or her ranch.

Because of Cary.

He gripped his hair with both hands and she could see how angry he was, but in a flash of panicked clarity when she heard Abby's footsteps on the porch, Melissa had seen the worst-case scenario.

It ended with Melissa emotionally broken *again* and Abby heartbroken because she'd lost one of the only men in her life she could depend on.

"Why do you insist on looking for the worst thing that could happen every time?" He was fuming. "*Every time*, Melissa!"

"Because it's my job. Because if I don't do it, then no one will, and I have to be prepared."

He walked over and looked her straight in the face. "So you're willing to sacrifice something that could be great—that could be everything for us—because you're content with making some-thing that's just okay for Abby? Is that what I'm hearing?"

Her heart was screaming. She couldn't speak. She could feel the tears threatening in her eyes, so she tried not to blink. She couldn't nod. She couldn't shake her head. She was frozen between what she desperately wanted for herself and what was best for her daughter.

Cary stepped back. "I'm taking my mom home, but do not think this is over. I will talk to you tomorrow."

He walked out, and Melissa's knees buckled. She leaned against the wall, covered her face, and cried silent, hot tears.

CHAPTER SEVENTEEN

HER MOM WAS SITTING at the dining table, sipping herbal tea and reading a book when Melissa made it back to the house.

"Where's Abby?"

Joan looked up. "I am so sorry about that. We were trying to give you two privacy, and she literally snuck out of the house behind our backs." Joan waved down the hall. "I sent her straight to bed."

"She said she wanted me to tuck her in."

Joan gave her the "are you that dumb?" look. "Melissa, she's ten years old. She's been going to bed without you for a few years now. She just didn't want to go to bed, and she was curious what's going on with you and Cary."

Melissa's heart sank. "Nothing is going on with me and Cary."

Joan looked back at her book. "I don't need to know details. You're a grown woman, and it's none of my business what—"

"Mom, nothing is going on with me and Cary." Melissa felt her throat start to tighten up. "Don't get any ideas, okay?"

Joan looked up, put a bookmark in her place, and set her book down. "Melissa, what did you do?"

She sat across from her mom and folded her hands on the

table. "We never should have… There was a reason there's been so much tension. That's my fault. I didn't recognize what was going on. I should have been more self-aware. But we never should have entertained the idea of—"

"Melissa Oxford Rhodes, that man is in love with you."

She felt like her mother just punched her. "He never said that."

"It's as obvious as the nose on my face. What did you do?"

She rested her face in her hands. "I can't deal with this right now."

"Because of the loan?"

"Because of the loan. Because of Abby. Because of the Allen Ranch project knocking at our door. Because I should be getting everything lined up for the mandarin harvest, and I haven't. Because this bunkhouse project needed to be *done* last week and it wasn't because Brian is waiting for another check. Because the ranch—"

"Oh bullshit." Joan lowered her voice and glanced down the hall. "That is bullshit. Now, some of those things are valid reasons to feel overwhelmed, but Stu and Leigh have the herd well in hand. You only have to ride out there anymore if he needs another hand and Leigh's not around—a few times a week at most."

"And Abby?"

"What about her? Abby is *fine*. She's doing well in school. She has a new horse she adores, even if her other grandparents are being difficult. She has her friends. She has her goats."

"Allen Ranch."

"Is not your responsibility." Joan shrugged. "We'll deal with whatever happens. We always do."

"The loan."

"We haven't even gotten notice, but if worse comes to worst, I will cash in my retirement to pay them back. I have enough in my account. I am your *mother*, Melissa Catherine Oxford. Don't even try to argue with me. We are not losing my daddy's ranch because"—she glanced down the dark hall again and spoke in a whisper—"because the Rhodes family are assholes."

Over Melissa's dead body would her mother be cashing out her retirement. "Fine. What am I going to do about the harvest? No one wants to pick half a crop because there's not enough money in it. There aren't enough crews, so instead of ending up with half a harvest, at this rate I'm going to end up with none of one and—"

"You're going to call Phil like Cary told you to weeks ago and see about subcontracting out his pickers when they have spare time. I don't know why you haven't done it already."

"'Cause it's gonna cost him money and time and I'm not looking for a handout!"

"Oh Lissa." Joan took a deep breath and reached for Melissa's hand. "If one of your friends needed a hand—not a handout, a *hand*—you would bend over backward to offer them your help. Why can't you let him do the same?"

"Because…" She couldn't stop the tears. "I don't even know if Cary's my friend anymore, okay?"

"Sweetie." Joan sat next to Melissa and wrapped her arms around her. "That man loves you. He's not going to leave just because you had an argument."

"I can't lose him. You know… he's the only friend I have left. I've lost everyone else. They probably don't even remember I'm alive. I have you, I have Abby, and I have Rumi and Cary. And if I lost him as a friend—"

"You're not gonna lose him." Joan shook her shoulders. "You can't do this. You can't make decisions based in fear. If something bad happened between you and Cary, you'd pick yourself up and you'd move on."

"And Abby?"

"Abby would be fine. Cary's relationship with Abby doesn't run through you. He's mad at you right now?"

Melissa nodded, blowing her nose on a napkin. "Yeah. Pretty mad."

"Do you think he's mad at Abby?"

"Of course not."

"So?"

Melissa had to sit with that one for a minute because dammit if her mom didn't have a point. Even if Cary never spoke to her again, he'd find a way to go to Abby's soccer games and school programs and riding competitions. God knows there had been plenty of times over the years when Cary and Melissa hadn't been on speaking terms for one idiotic thing or another and Cary still showed up.

"I'm more worried about the fact that you feel like you have no friends except me and Cary," Joan said. "Sweetie, that's not healthy."

"I'm friends with Emmie. Kind of." She sniffed. "And Daisy."

"When was the last time you had lunch with Daisy?"

"I don't know. We're both always working."

Joan let out a hard breath. "You know, you moved back here after college with Calvin in tow. Your whole life revolved around him and Abby. After Dad died, both of you worked so damn much. Then Calvin was gone, and it was just you holding everything together."

Melissa shrugged. "Mom, what else was I supposed to do? Leave a pump broken because I wanted to meet Daisy for lunch? Ranching doesn't work that way."

"I know." Joan pursed her lips. "I think the hardest thing about working for yourself is you don't have work friends. It was the same with your grandfather. When I was teaching, I made so many friends. I'm still close with most of the women I worked with, but you don't have that, and I'm sorry."

Melissa shrugged. "I have you. I have Abby." *And Cary.*

"I think you're more afraid of losing your friendship with Cary than you are of Abby losing him. Because she's not going to lose

176

him. That man is Gordon Nakamura's son. Loyalty is as natural for him as breathing."

"I know Cary is loyal."

"Then you know that you need to leave Abby out of this. This is about you and Cary and your fear of things changing."

Melissa sat with that advice for a long time. She took a deep breath. "Most of the big changes in my life haven't been good, Mom."

"Dad leaving."

Melissa nodded.

"Grandpa dying." Joan stroked her hair. "Then the baby. Then Calvin."

"I know why Dad left," Melissa said. "But why didn't you ever get married again? Was it because of me and Ox?"

Joan pulled away. "Is that what you think?" She shook her head. "That I had to devote my entire life to you kids? That's ridiculous logic. And you kids had nothing to do with me staying single."

"Then what was it?"

"I never..." Joan's smile was sad. "I never loved any man as much as I love your father. I still love him. And he loves me too. He's never married anyone else."

"So why did he leave?"

"He's just not cut out for the settled life. He's one of those men who has to drift, and frankly he does better with horses than with people. He tried his best to stay here. Heck, we even tried him living away part of the year."

"I remember that. It didn't work."

Joan shook her head. "We fought all the time. It was better for him to go. I had your grandpa. I had Gordon and Rumi next door. Lots of friends and my job. If I met someone I loved more, I would have gotten married. I just didn't."

"And Dad picked being alone."

Joan nodded. "Yeah. He did. There's a little bit of that in your character too, Lissa. That desire to be independent. That fear of depending on others. I worry about you. Now more than ever."

"I depended on Calvin," she whispered. "And he left me."

Joan sighed. "It wasn't his choice, but yeah. He did."

"I thought I'd gotten the happy ending, Mom. I thought if I did everything right, I'd be safe. But that's not the way it works."

"And now Cary is asking you to open up that door again and you're afraid."

She rubbed her temples, trying to combat the headache she could feel forming. "If you give your heart to someone, they can do whatever they want with it. They could crush it in their hands, not even realizing."

"Or they can take care of it. Guard it. Help it grow."

"I guess."

Joan smiled. "Life is never gonna be safe. You know that. But there's no reason you can't find joy. Even after you've lost the life you wanted. Let yourself find a new dream. There's no reason it can't be just as sweet. But you've got to open up a little bit. Trust a little bit. *Bend* a little bit."

———

THE NEXT DAY, Melissa left Brian Montoya's crew working on the bunkhouse and drove to Cary's office. She didn't see his truck anywhere, but she drove up and flagged Phil, his foreman, down.

"Hey, Melissa!"

"Hey, Phil." She looked around. "He in?"

"He's out at Dapple Ranch looking at the mandarins. We're set to start picking there next week."

"That's early."

"Yeah, but that little spot hits a real high sugar content early because of the exposure. Lets us space things out a little better and gives us an early start. You contract any crews yet?"

"No interest."

Phil spread his hands. "You know we could work something out. We've got groves all around you."

If one of your friends needed a hand, you would bend over backward...

Bend. Just a little.

Melissa took a deep breath. "Yeah. I'd appreciate it, Phil. Let's plan on that. I'm looking at a pretty standard window. Probably late October."

Phil looked surprised, but he smiled. "Cool! I'll talk to Cary and Teresa and get the timing worked out. I know we can handle it. Your trees will be fast."

Part of the knot in her stomach loosened. "Thanks."

She turned her head when she heard Cary's truck. He must have spotted her, but he drove right past, dust flying, and parked near the office door in the shade of an avocado tree.

Phil glanced between Melissa and Cary. "So... you the reason he was in a sour mood all morning?"

Melissa grimaced. "Probably."

"Awesome." Phil backed away. "I'm gonna get out of your hair. I'll have Teresa call you. And I'll make sure no one goes to the office until you leave."

"Probably a good idea if they want to avoid flying objects."

She hopped out of the truck and walked over to the large grey Quonset hut where Cary had built his office.

He was already out of his truck and strode inside, not even looking at her.

Melissa followed.

So this should be fun.

When she opened the door, a blast of cool air met her face.

"Close the door! We're not air-conditioning the whole damn county."

Oh yeah. He's in a great mood. This should be super easy.

Melissa closed the door and stepped into the office. There was a reception room of sorts with a long, L-shaped desk. To the left was a meeting room with a conference table, and two offices were built off the right.

"Phil, was Melissa here to—?"

"It's me."

Cary fell silent.

Melissa walked to his office and leaned in the doorway. "Hey."

"Hey." He didn't get up. He didn't approach her. He crossed his arms over his chest and eyed her warily.

"I came to apologize."

"For?"

Melissa took a deep breath. "First, for assuming that you'd ever abandon Abby or ignore her if something didn't work out between us."

He waited a long moment before he nodded. "Okay."

"I know you wouldn't do that. I know it, and so does she. That's why she can be kind of a brat with you sometimes, because she knows that you're not going to stop caring about her."

Cary kept staring, but he didn't move and his expression didn't soften. "Okay."

Bend. Just a little.

"And second, I want to apologize for…"

Why was this so *hard*? Stripping off her clothes and dancing naked down Main Street in Metlin would be easier than this.

"For?"

"For being afraid," she said in a small voice. "You're probably my best friend, Cary—when we're not at each other's throats because we're fighting about something stupid—and the thought of changing that is terrifying. Because if…" She cleared her throat. "If I didn't have you, I don't know what I'd do."

He unfolded his arms and leaned his elbows on his desk. The black outline of a dragon on his forearm was all she could look at. His muscles were flexing, and she wanted to touch them. Somehow, if she just touched him, she knew everything would feel better.

180

Cary asked, "So what are you saying?"

"I'm apologizing."

"What do you want?"

You. She couldn't say it. Not when she was so exposed.

He continued, "You want us to be friends again? *Just* friends? Because I can't lie, Melissa, that's not what I want anymore, and I'm not saying I can't get back there, but I kind of need some time."

"I want..." She let out a breath. "I don't know exactly what I want. I know I want you to not be angry with me. Can we pretend my freak-out and our argument last night didn't happen and start from there?"

"I don't know," he said. "I have to think about that."

See? When you handed someone your heart, they could do whatever they wanted with it. Including crush it in the palm of their hand.

"Right." Melissa nodded and turned to go. "Okay."

Cary didn't say anything. He let her walk to the door. But just as she was opening it, he came storming out of the office. He slammed one hand on the heavy metal door, smashed it shut, and flipped the dead bolt.

"I thought about it."

CHAPTER EIGHTEEN

HE KNEW how much it had taken for her to come to him like that and bare her soul. Because that was exactly what she'd done. She'd bared her soul. Or at least as much as Melissa was ever going to bare.

You're my best friend...

Changing that is terrifying...

If I didn't have you, I don't know what I'd do.

"I know you're not clear on what you want." He leaned down and spoke in her ear. Her back was to him, and her hand was on the doorknob. His hand held the door shut as his body came to life in her proximity. "So I'm going to tell you what I want."

She didn't say anything, but she nodded.

"I want you to be my girlfriend, as ridiculous as that word sounds to a forty-six-year-old man. I want to see you exclusively, I want you to exclusively see me. No other people involved. That's not negotiable."

She nodded.

"I want to kiss you whenever I want. I know you probably have your own timeline about telling your daughter, and I respect that, but I'm not going to hide you or us from anyone else. I'm not going to pretend the only thing I feel for you is friendship, whether it's to our friends, our employees, or our families."

She took longer to nod on that one, but she did.

He put his hands on her hips and pulled her closer. "I want to make love to you. Not in this office. Not in the bunkhouse. Not sneaking around like a couple of kids. I want you to come to my house and stay over the next time Abby is at her grandparents' house."

Goose bumps rose on her neck.

She wanted that. She definitely wanted that.

Cary slowly bent down, brushed her braid to the side, and laved her nape with his tongue. He placed openmouthed kisses over her shoulders and her neck. He wrapped his arms around her waist and turned her until their mouths met.

The fire went from simmering to explosive in the space of a heartbeat. Melissa threw her arms around his neck, and Cary reached down to pick her up. He placed his hands on her ass and lifted. Melissa wrapped her legs around his hips.

"Conference table," she muttered.

"We are not having sex on my conference table." He spoke between kissing her. "I'll never be able to have a co-op meeting in here again."

"Need…" She put her hand over the erection that had sprung to life the minute she walked through the door.

Fuck. Melissa left Cary feeling like a teenager. He batted her hand away. "Thursday night. After the market." He kissed her mouth. Her cheek. Her neck. "Put Abby to bed and come to my place." He placed her on the edge of the sturdy conference table and cupped both cheeks in his hands. "You don't have to stay, but come over, okay?"

"Yes."

She was saying yes, but she was also trying to unbutton his shirt.

"Missy—"

"I just"—she pulled her mouth from his and rested her forehead against his chest, panting—"I need you. I need to know I didn't ruin this."

"You didn't ruin this." He shook his head. "You didn't— Ahhhhh."

She'd unbuttoned his jeans and drew his zipper down, putting both her hands on his erection.

"Fuck, Melissa."

The corner of her mouth turned up. "You said we couldn't do that in here."

"You don't have anything to prove to me." He put his hands on hers. "I don't want…"

Her hand stroked up and down over his boxers. "You don't?"

"Melissa." Cary put his hand on her cheek and kissed her hard and deep. "Of course I do. I'm just saying you don't have to—"

"I know I don't have to. Who says I don't want to?" She hooked one arm around his neck and leaned into him, capturing his mouth as she pushed him back. She slid off the table, tucked her hands in the sides of his jeans, and pushed them down as she sank to her knees.

Cary couldn't take his eyes off her.

She looked up at him, his cock in her hand. "Okay?"

All he could do was nod.

This is a dream.

This is a dream.

"Fuck!" He slammed his hand on the table when Melissa took him in her mouth.

If this was a dream, it was a really fucking good one.

She took her time, stroking in and out, tasting the length and thickness of him. Cary braced one hand on the table so he didn't fall over and the other on the side of her cheek, going slowly insane as he saw, felt, and heard Melissa giving him head.

She scraped her nails lightly along the back of his thighs, and he thought he might just die from pleasure right then.

The tightening anticipation of climax approached too quickly.

"Missy," he groaned. "Missy, I'm going to—"

She took him deeper and he came in her mouth.

Cary's knees nearly buckled. Melissa stood, her hand over her mouth, and grabbed the tissue box in the center of the conference table. She wiped her mouth and lay back on the table, stretching out on her side. She had a small, smug smile on her face.

"Give my apologies to the co-op," she whispered.

Cary started laughing and he couldn't stop. He hitched his pants up, leaned over her, and kissed her smiling mouth. Then he started to tease her shirt up.

She gasped. "What about the sanctity of the conference table?"

"This table has lost all sanctity. Might as well ruin it completely." He kissed up her belly, teasing his fingers along her waistband. He stopped just south of her rib cage and ran his fingers up, pushing her T-shirt out of the way.

He glanced up to see her watching him, her lips swollen and red, her blue eyes trained on him. "You like seeing me with my mouth on you?"

"Yes."

"How long have you wanted me?"

Her breath caught. "Honestly?"

"Yes."

"Four years."

Cary propped his chin on her belly and silently unhooked the clasp of her bra, spreading it so her breasts were exposed.

"You hid it well," he said. "Not hidden now though."

"No." Her breath was coming fast.

He stood, bent down, and took her breast in his mouth, covering the sensitive tip with his mouth and teasing it with his tongue. Melissa's body arched up and her knees bent.

Cary held her as she twisted on the table. He teased the top of her pubis beneath her jeans as he kissed her breasts. Her nipples were hard in his mouth. Her skin was flushed and hot.

"Cary—"

"Do you like my mouth on you?"

"Yes."

"Good." He lifted his head, snapped her bra back into place, and pulled her shirt down.

Melissa blinked. "What?"

"I want you thinking about my mouth on you for the next few days until I see you Thursday night."

"What?" She kicked at his leg, but he dodged her, laughing. "You're mean!"

"Just a little." He bent over her and took her mouth again. "But I love kissing you. I could kiss you for hours."

"I love kissing you too."

His smile was slow and he felt it down to his bones. "We're gonna be fine, Miss Melissa Oxford. After all, you always know where you are."

She put her hand on his cheek. "You think so?"

"I know so." He turned his head and kissed the inside of her wrist. "Do you know what you want yet?"

"Do I have to know right away?"

"No." He smiled a little. "I know what you need."

She raised her eyebrows. "Oh really? What's that?"

"I'll tell you Thursday."

———

CARY OPENED his computer up after Melissa left. Abby was getting out of school soon, and Melissa wanted to check on the workmen for the bunkhouse before she had to pick her up. She also needed to help her mom create a plan for the evening farmers' market on Thursday.

Where they would share a booth.

And then they'd share a bed.

About damn time. Though his dick wasn't complaining. It was feeling very happy just then. So happy, Cary wanted to take a nap on the couch in his office.

He didn't. He looked at his financial portfolio and picked up the phone that he'd put on hold when he heard someone walk in the office. He'd thought it was Phil.

It wasn't.

He dialed his broker again, waited a few rings for her to pick up. "Paulette. Sorry about that. Had an unexpected meeting. What did you find out?"

While he was talking with Paulette, he brought up a picture he'd taken at Abby's birthday of Melissa and Abby laughing and pointing at the camera. He hit Print from his phone and was waiting for the printer to warm up.

"Okay, I understand that, but how long would I have to pay it back?"

He waited for the printer to finish before he grabbed the paper. It wasn't the best quality, but it would do until he could get a proper picture of the three of them on the wall.

"Ten years is more than enough. Would there be an early-payment penalty of any kind?"

He folded the white edges back, took two blue pins from the corner of his corkboard, and stuck the picture of Melissa and Abby to his wall.

"Okay, cool. Fax the application to me. If I don't end up needing it, that's fine. But it'll be there if I do. How long?"

He stood and surveyed the new faces on the corkboard.

"Sounds good. Call me when I need to sign something."

Most of the pictures were of his workers. Luis, Shannon, and David at the company barbecue. Phil and his clan at the family trout derby in Lower Lake. Someone had caught a picture of Cary at the top of a picking ladder a few years ago. There was an old picture of his mom and dad standing in front of a tree laden with oranges, posing in their 1970s finery. His dad was even wearing a hat.

I miss you, old man.

And now Melissa and Abby were up there.

Cary smiled. Melissa might get pissed off, but he didn't care. He was used to Melissa getting pissed off, and he was starting to understand what calmed her down.

The image of Melissa on her knees flashed brightly for a second before he shoved the memory to the back of his mind.

He'd take that out later when he wasn't at work.

Until then, he'd have to distract himself with scheduling because harvest was bearing down on him, the packing house was talking about a worker shortage *again*, and in three weeks picking crews would be filling his groves. Not to mention the town council vote on the Allen Ranch project would happen the middle of next week.

Whatever was happening between Cary and Melissa, his life was about to get more than a little crazy.

CHAPTER NINETEEN

MELISSA KNOCKED LOUDLY and shoved Abby's door open at dawn the next day.

Her daughter sat up and rubbed her eyes. "What is it?"

"Nothing. Let's go for a ride before school."

Abby blinked. "Really?"

"Yep."

"What if I'm late for school?"

Melissa shrugged. "If you're late, you won't be *that* late."

And Abby was hardly ever late. Her daughter breezed through school. Unlike Melissa, Abby was a natural student, and she nearly always got straight As. Melissa credited Calvin, because while she'd been a good student, she'd had to work her butt off.

"Get dressed." Melissa tossed her a helmet. "I'll meet you in front of the barn."

Nothing got Abby more motivated than horses and goats. She loved both with equal passion, though her heart was with the horses and her mind and pocketbook were with the goats.

Abby had spent dinner the night before detailing the steps of making goat-milk soap, which she'd recently learned from YouTube. Her grandmother was eager to try it out, even if it meant she had to sacrifice some of the milk. They had plans for the weekend after next.

Watching Joan and Abby the night before, Melissa had a revelation.

This wasn't just her ranch.

Just like Melissa had started making plans for Oxford Ranch when she was a kid, Abby was making her plans too. Those plans might change, but for now Abby had to assume that Oxford Ranch would be a four-generation affair.

Which meant that anything that happened to the ranch was Abby's business too.

Melissa readied Moxie and PJ and tied PJ to the corral. Then she mounted Moxie and waited for her daughter to come running.

Abby flew down the dirt road in the early-dawn light, her hair streaming behind her helmet and her boots kicking up the fall dust. There was a bite in the air and, like her mother, she'd thrown on a flannel shirt over her jeans and T-shirt.

Look at her, Calvin. Melissa's heart swelled. *Look at that stunning girl. We made that, babe.*

"You ready?"

PJ turned his head to greet Abby, offering a sweet nicker when his second-favorite person grabbed his reins. Abby used the fence to mount the gelding and nudged him toward Melissa and Moxie.

"Ready now," Abby said. "Where we going?"

"I thought we'd just take a quick ride up to Christy Meadow."

"Is the creek running?"

"Just a little bit, but you're with me."

"Cool."

If the creek was running, Abby knew she wasn't allowed to cross it without being with her mom or her grandma.

Mother and daughter started up the road at a nice trot, going easy until the horses were warmed up.

"Is he feeling it?" Melissa asked.

Abby leaned forward and hugged PJ's neck. "Oh yeah. Aren't you, buddy? You feeling it?"

The air whipped against their faces as they picked up speed. By the time they reached the creek, they were riding at a smart lope. They slowed down to cross the creek, both horses knowing exactly where to go. It was a familiar route, and Melissa could feel Moxie's anticipation when they reached the other side of the wash.

As they made their way through the scrub, PJ tossed his head and let out a loud whinny.

Abby giggled. "He wants to run."

"Oh yeah he does."

"You ready, Mama?"

Melissa leaned forward and felt Moxie beneath her. "Just keep to the path."

"I know!" As soon as the scrub cleared and the pasture widened, Abby urged PJ into a canter, then a gallop, letting out an excited whoop as she and the horse ran the length of the pasture. Melissa and Moxie weren't far behind.

She felt the wind on her cheeks, the cool air teasing her neck. She chased Abby around the field, keeping to the wide, well-trodden path along the outer edge where the ground was even. They ran two laps around the meadow before they slowed to a stop.

Abby and Melissa were both grinning. Abby leaned forward, hugging PJ and turning her face to Melissa as they walked slowly back toward the creek.

"I wish Sunny lived on the ranch." Abby's eyes were sad. "He would love this place. He only goes on the trails around Grandma's house. And I don't think I've ever galloped with him."

"Don't rush it. You're still getting to know each other." Melissa reached over and patted Abby's leg. "And I'm sorry he doesn't live here either. I know he's a fancy horse, but I think Moxie and PJ would love to be his friends."

"He's only ever in his stall or out with the groom getting exercise. He doesn't have any horse friends. They never hang out in the pasture or anything."

"Baby, I'm sorry." They crossed the creek and continued walking back to the house. "I wanted to talk to you about your grandparents."

"About Sunny?"

Melissa frowned. "Not really, but kinda?"

Abby looked confused.

"Here's the thing about your dad's parents, and I'm not telling you anything that your dad didn't tell me, okay? So please don't think I'm being disrespectful or I'm trying to make you think badly of them or anything like that, okay?"

Abby frowned, but she nodded.

"Your dad and I chose to live out here for a couple of reasons. Great-grandpa Oxford needed help with the ranch when I got out of college because he was getting older. So your dad and I could help with that. And then you were born and your dad and I decided that this would be a great place to raise kids since there's so much open space and lots of freedom to run around." She glanced at Abby. "Were we right?"

Abby laughed. "Yes, Mom."

"I know we were right, because I grew up here too. And I had sheep instead of goats for 4-H, but I learned how to take care of animals and work hard and respect the ranch."

Abby nodded. "I know."

"And your grandparents... they didn't really like that too much. I mean, it's normal to want your kids around, so I totally get that. But they were very unhappy with your dad and me."

"And now they're unhappy with you because Dad is dead and you won't move to Paso Robles."

Melissa nodded. "Pretty much. But there are good reasons I'm not going to move, and it's not just because I love this place." She paused, picking her words so carefully. "All people have things they think are really important. In our family, it's really important to take care of each other and our neighbors. It's important to take care of our animals and treat them well, even though they can't talk to us."

Abby leaned forward and patted PJ. "PJ talks to me."

In answer, PJ let out a friendly nicker and flicked his ears.

Melissa smiled. "We also want to make sure the ranch is healthy. That we're not using chemicals that are going to hurt the pastures or putting anything in the water that could poison it. And we want to help our neighbors keep their land healthy too."

"I know, Mom." Abby was frowning. "What does this have to do with Sunny?"

"What I'm trying to say is that not every family thinks the same things are important. Sometimes it's just different. Your dad and I thought that your grandparents valued different things than we did. Things we didn't think were as important as the ones I was talking about."

Abby had a thoughtful expression on her face. "Grandma and Grandpa Rhodes like being rich."

Bingo.

Melissa nodded. "Yes, they do. And money isn't a bad thing. I am absolutely not saying that. When you're older, because your great-grandparents were very generous and worked very hard, you're going to have a lot of money. And I bet you're going to do great things with that."

Abby smiled. Then her smile fell. "Grandma and Grandpa like having money a *lot*."

Melissa's heart sank at the conflicted look on her daughter's face. "Yeah. They do."

"They're not very nice to Aunt Audrey either. They said she doesn't make any money. Even though she has two little kids. And I don't get that, because Trevor and Austin are a lot of work. I mean, they have a nanny, but they get into everything all the time."

"I am very sorry to hear they're giving Aunt Audrey a hard time." Melissa wanted to rage, but what could she do? She and Audrey weren't close. They didn't even like each other much. Melissa still felt for her. Audrey's parents had raised her to be a pretty girl who would marry someone rich, give them attractive grandchildren, and that was about it. When your whole identity revolved around your looks and your marriage potential, what kind of life did you have?

"I want you to remember something," Melissa said. "Having money or not having money isn't what makes you important, okay? Some of the best people I know have had a hard time making money. Sometimes because they're really generous with people who have even less. Money is not what life is about."

"That's not what Grandma and Grandpa think though." Abby bit her lip. "Are they the ones who want to build houses on the Allen ranch?"

Melissa blinked. "What makes you say that?"

"I heard Uncle Devin talking about it with Grandpa the last weekend I was there. They didn't realize I was listening."

"Yeah. I hate to tell you, but they're part of the business that wants to build a bunch of houses here."

Abby wrinkled her nose. "I like having neighbors, but that seems like a lot of neighbors. Maybe too many."

"I know. Personally, I don't like the idea of looking out that way and seeing nothing but houses instead of hills."

"Yeah." Abby sighed. "I don't think Grandma and Grandpa think the right things are important."

"But that doesn't mean they don't love you," Melissa was quick to add. "And that doesn't mean you can't love them. It just means…"

Abby waited with a small frown on her face.

"That means," Melissa continued, "that you have to know who you are. And what you think is important. You have to know

194

those things for *sure*. And never forget what is the most important."

Abby nodded. "I can do that."

"Good." She glanced at her daughter. "I figured you could."

———

THE THURSDAY-NIGHT FARMERS' market only happened once a month, and it was more of a social event than a market, but Melissa and Cary set up their booths nonetheless. They wanted to pass out flyers about Jordan Valley preservation in Metlin while they were there. A lot of Metliners picnicked, hiked, and enjoyed Jordan Valley. If they could get some new supporters, maybe Melissa could back off.

Melissa had brought crates of Joan's jam and marmalades along with a fresh batch of lemon curd. Cary was making gallons of lemonade in every flavor imaginable. Strawberry lemonade. Blueberry. Peach. Tangerine.

Joan and Abby had stayed home, so the only backup they had was each other.

Melissa walked back from the bathroom at INK, waving to Cary as she returned. "Thanks. You need a break?"

He smiled and looked her up and down. "I'm good."

She flushed just from the look. "Stop," she murmured when she sat on the stool next to him.

"Stop what?"

"The looks."

He leaned closer, his delicious arms crossed over his chest. "Do you feel like I'm undressing you with my eyes?"

"Yes."

"Good. That's exactly what I'm doing."

Her face was so hot she probably looked like one of her mom's tomatoes. "Cary—"

"Hey, guys!" Tayla's bright voice interrupted Melissa's embarrassment.

Cary gave her a small smile. "How you doing, Lizard?"

"Lizard?" Melissa looked at Cary.

"Your..." Tayla's smile was wicked. "Sorry, not sure what's going on with you two lately. Is it friend? Boyfriend? Kissing buddy? I heard something about making out on Main Street."

Melissa ignored her completely. "Why is Cary calling you Lizard?"

Cary said, "Because when she's at the climbing gym, she just sticks to the wall." He spread his arms out with his hands wide. "Like this. Stuck there. Sometimes she stays for hours."

"Ha ha," Tayla said. "Nice attempt to avoid the question. So, kissing on Main Street?"

"I have no idea what you're talking about," Cary said. "Would you like to buy some lemonade?" He nodded behind her. "Because those people do."

Tayla stepped to the side, allowing Cary to help the customers behind her. That only put her closer to Melissa.

"Tell me," Tayla muttered.

"None of your business."

"Tell me anyway." She smiled at a lady who handed over seven dollars for jam. "I have been waiting for you to tap that for years now. Is he as strong as he looks, because hot damn, that man looks—"

"Tayla, you're scaring the children." Melissa gritted her teeth in the semblance of a smile.

"There're no children around." Tayla looked. "Don't try to evade! Emmie and I saw you kissing in front of Jeremy's, and we have been very, very patient because we know you're busy, but *come on!*"

Melissa plastered her mouth shut and managed to keep it closed until Daisy made her way through the crowd.

"Hey," Daisy said. "Did you ask her?"

"Not you too!" Melissa glanced at Cary, who was still swamped with lemonade customers. "Daisy, we're not in high school."

"I know." Daisy planted her hand on Melissa's table. "She's in a relationship. I've been married forever. We need excitement. Spill. What's going on with you and Hottie Nakamura?"

"We're…" How had her face not exploded by now? Was that possible? Had she been sad that she didn't have female friends? Why was that again? "We're… dating?"

"I know that much. One of my waitresses works at Café Georgette on the weekends. Tell us more than that."

"How is this town three times as big as Oakville and yet somehow even more nosy?" Melissa walked over to Cary. "Hey, the ice in the bucket for the lemon curd is melting. Can I grab some of yours?"

"No problem." He put a hand on the small of her back and dropped a fast kiss on her mouth. "Just grab some from the ice chest in the back of the truck."

Melissa stood, frozen. "Okay."

Cary caught her expression. "Told you I was going to kiss you whenever I wanted if we weren't in front of Abby."

She nodded woodenly, then walked to the truck and came back with a small bucket of ice to refill the bowl with the lemon curd.

Tayla and Daisy were waiting with triumphant expressions.

"I knew it!" Daisy said.

"You two are insanely hot together. How old is Cary again?"

"Forty-six," Melissa muttered.

"Damn, that man has aged like fine wine." Tayla leaned over the table and craned her neck. "And he has an amazing ass. I can't lie, I love my boyfriend, but I can't *not* check that out when we're climbing." She held her knuckles out to Melissa. "Nicely done, my friend."

Melissa leaned back to block Tayla's gaze. "Why are you staring at my…" She almost said boyfriend but stopped herself because honestly, it felt weird to be calling a grown man a boyfriend. "Why are you staring at my significant other's ass?"

Tayla's eyes went wide. "You can stare at Jeremy's if you want. It's very cute."

"He's my little brother's friend! Ew!"

Daisy cackled. "This is awesome. But you've got to think up a better name for Cary than significant other. That sounds like a legal term."

"What sounds like a legal term?"

Melissa turned her head and saw Adrian Saroyan perusing the flyer that read SAVE JORDAN VALLEY! at the top.

"Adrian! How are you doing? I have been meaning to call you for literally weeks now about this thing, and I keep forgetting because my life is insane. Has anyone from the committee called you?"

He looked confused. "What committee?"

Adrian Saroyan was a commercial real estate agent in Metlin, but he did a lot of work out in Oakville too. He was trusted by most of the community because his grandparents had pistachio acreage on the west side of town and were founding members of the Armenian church. He was a good guy who dealt fairly with farmers and ranchers, which made him well-respected in Melissa's neck of the woods.

He frowned. "You know, I got a voice mail from someone, but I wasn't sure what they were talking about and I thought they maybe had a wrong number."

"I'm sorry. Seriously, I meant to call and explain things, but I forgot. How are you doing? How's business?"

"I'm doing good." Adrian was frowning as he scanned the flyer. "When did this start?"

"The Allen Ranch thing?" Melissa said. "A few weeks ago. Maybe the initial proposal was at the end of the summer. I'm not sure. They've been cagey about it. I wanted to call you because the town council is refusing to do an environmental impact study, and I'm not sure if that's legal or not."

Adrian's mind seemed to be elsewhere. He turned to Tayla. "Do you know if Gus knows about this?"

"Jeremy's grandpa?" Tayla shook her head. "I don't think so. I haven't heard him mention it." She took a flyer too. "Wait, is this Gus's old ranch?" Her eyes went wide.

Adrian muttered, "Sure is."

Cary walked over. "Am I missing something?"

Melissa nodded at Adrian. "Adrian hadn't heard about the Allen Ranch project."

"Yeah, I mentioned it to Jeremy, but he didn't think Gus could do much, so he was debating whether to tell him or not."

"I'll call Gus," Adrian said. "Give me a couple of days."

Cary crossed his arms. "You heard of JPR Holdings?"

Adrian glanced at Melissa. "Yeah. I know who that is."

"Don't worry," Melissa said. "I know it's them."

Daisy looked around. "I am so lost right now."

"The holding company trying to develop the land next to my ranch—the land that used to belong to Jeremy's grandpa—is partly owned by my late husband's parents. They're trying to put two thousand condos and a golf course on it for rich retirees."

Tayla gasped. "Jeremy and I had our first date there. They can't turn it into a golf course!"

"They're trying," Cary said. "The council is supposed to vote on it next week."

Daisy asked, "Oakville people are usually pretty private. Why would they want this?"

"Because of the budget shortfall," Melissa said. "No one wants to lose the middle school and high school."

"Oh, that's rough." Daisy shook her head. "But surely there has to be another way."

Adrian lifted a flyer. "Melissa, you mind if I take a couple of these?"

"Take as many as you like," she said. "Call me or my mom if you have any questions."

Cary asked, "You know Les Arthur?"

Adrian nodded. "I know Les."

"He's on the council. Might be worth talking to him."

Tayla turned her eyes back to Melissa and Cary. "Just because you've distracted us with a big bad real estate developer, don't think you've escaped giving us more details about your love life."

Cary put his arm around Melissa. "Okay, Lizard. Sure thing. We'll get back to you on that."

"Lissa!" Ox's booming voice cut through the crowd, and Melissa turned to see her baby brother—all six foot and two inches of him—walking through the crowd.

"Ox!" She walked out from behind the table, grateful that most of the crowd had drifted down Main Street to where the band had started playing. "You weren't in the shop earlier."

"Nope." His grin was half a mile wide. "Come here."

He motioned her to a quiet bench across the street from her booth. "Check it out." He pulled something from his pocket.

Melissa stared. "Ox, that's a ring box."

"Yep." He opened it. "It's Emmie's grandmother's ring."

Melissa's eyes went wide. "Are you—?"

"Yep."

She threw her arms around him. "I'm so happy for you! I know she's going to say yes! I know it. But how did you get the ring? Did Emmie already have it? Have you already talked about getting married?"

"Well, yeah." His face was a little red. "In general. Not in detail. We both want to, we just haven't made it official yet. But she doesn't know about the ring. See, when I went to talk to Spider—"

"Oh Ox. You didn't ask for his *permission*, did you? Emmie is a grown woman. She doesn't need permission to get married from—"

"Chill." He held up a hand. "I went to get his *blessing*. He's the closest thing to family that she has."

"Okay, that's cool."

"And a few days later he calls me, says he and Daisy have Betsy's old wedding set. She'd given it to Spider because Spider didn't have any money when he asked Daisy to marry him. Well, Daisy only wears her wedding ring because she works at a bakery all day. So she and Spider both agreed that they wanted Emmie to have it back."

Melissa put a hand over her heart. "Oh Ox." She had tears in her eyes. "It's perfect. The ring is perfect. Spider and Daisy are the best. And Emmie is perfect for you." She threw her arms around him. "I'm so happy for you."

"And I'm happy for you." He smiled. "I heard about you and Cary."

"How? How does everyone in this town know about my business?"

"You two were making out on the street, Lissa."

"We were not making out!"

He shrugged. "Whatever. I really don't want details. Really." He shook his head. "Please, no details."

"You think I want to share them with you?"

"Please don't."

"Good." She nodded. "So that's settled. Cary and I are... whatever we are. Abby doesn't know anything yet, so don't mention it. And you and Emmie are getting engaged." Melissa grinned. "This is so great."

"I know."

"Tell me when it's official." She felt her phone buzz in her pocket. She got it out and read the message on the screen. "Oh, you've got to be kidding me."

Ox frowned. "What is it?"

She sighed. "Probably nothing, but Abby is throwing up. No

fever, but Mom needs me to come home and pick up some Popsicles on the way."

"Oh rotten. Poor kid."

Melissa glanced at her table. Everyone was drifting away, and Cary was starting to pack up. "I better get going."

"Cool. I'll help."

"No need." She was going to have to explain to Cary that she couldn't come over. Dammit. "Cary and I rode together, so he'll help me."

"Okay. Tell the goat queen I hope she feels better soon."

"Thanks, bud."

Ox gave Melissa one more hug before he headed back to his shop, and Melissa made her way through the falling darkness to Cary, who was loading crates and jugs in the back of his truck.

"Hey," he said. "Good news from Ox?"

She smiled. "Not official good news yet, but soon. Unfortunately, it's bad news from Mom." She held up her phone. "Abby's puking."

His face fell. "Seriously?"

"'Fraid so. I have to head home, and can we pick up some Popsicles?" She spread her hands. "I'm sorry, Cary."

He shook his head. "Don't worry about it. Kids get sick. That's life."

"Tomorrow?" she asked. "I'm dropping Abby off in Kettleman after school. Well, as long as she's over whatever this is. I could come over after that."

He smiled. "Yeah. That sounds perfect."

"Okay."

Cary took the last crate off his table. "Ox and Emmie are good together."

"They really are."

"Almost as good as we are."

Melissa's heart nearly stopped, but Cary didn't say anything more. He just kept loading the truck. "Help me with the table?"

"Sure." She flipped the table to the side, and they folded it and loaded it in the truck. Then they gathered the bits and pieces of their booths, tossed the trash in the dumpster, and walked back to the truck.

Cary paused before he opened the door.

"What is it?"

He gave her a small smile and held out his hand. "Can you spare five more minutes?"

She cocked her head but walked around the truck. "She'll live five minutes without me."

Cary linked their hands together, and they walked around the corner, cutting through an alley to get to the plaza near the old Fox Theater where a band was playing a slow song. A crowd had gathered, but Cary and Melissa stood on the edge, both in their work clothes, and he spun her around.

Melissa looked around. "Are we dancing?"

He nodded and pulled her closer. Cary pressed her against his chest and wrapped one arm around her waist while he took the other in his and kissed her knuckles as they turned with the music.

His quiet sweetness made her weak.

Cary smiled down at her. "Hey."

"Hi."

"One song?"

She nodded. "One song."

"Good."

Melissa tilted her head up. "Kiss me."

He raised an eyebrow. "Right here on the sidewalk in Metlin? I'm shy."

"We have to; it's tradition."

He smiled slowly. "That's right, it is."

Cary took her lips with quiet, devastating thoroughness, leaving no doubt in her mind that whatever he had planned for the following night would destroy any and all defenses she had remaining.

Melissa had been slipping for a while, but in that moment, on a busy street in downtown Metlin, she fell. Her heart landed at Cary Nakamura's feet, and she prayed to everything merciful in the universe that he wouldn't break it.

She broke off their kiss and slid her fingers into his hair, resting her head over his heart as they swayed back and forth.

CHAPTER TWENTY

FRIDAY WAS MADNESS. The crew was finishing up the final renovations to the bunkhouse, Teresa was coming to the orange grove to finalize the schedule for her mandarin harvest, and Stu called her because the water pump for the lower pastures was acting up. If she couldn't fix it, they'd have to move the entire herd up to the north pasture that afternoon, which would completely screw up her day.

Melissa was running around so much she couldn't remember if she'd eaten anything. Maybe? Something around breakfast? Possibly?

She pulled off her gloves and shouted, "Okay, try now!"

Thankfully, this time when Stu flipped the switch, she heard the welcome gurgle of water coming up the pipes. So did the herd. They mooed and started moving toward the water troughs fed by the pipes that came from the storage tank on the hill. It would take some time for the water to make it down to them, but they were thirsty.

"I cannot wait for the rain to come." She sighed and tossed her gloves to Stu. Then she mounted Moxie and put her hat back on. "You good here?"

"Yep." He turned to the side and lit a cigarette. "Cooper's is due for a break, so they'll be good wandering round here till next week. We culling soon?"

"How many?"

He squinted. "I think around a dozen."

Melissa nodded. "Sounds about right. Check with me next week on timing. I'll try to take a look over the weekend and see if my numbers are the same as yours."

"Sounds good." He drew on his cigarette. "Got a friend in Utah that's due to have a litter of dogs in the next month. Been thinking about getting a female, training her up to work, and maybe breeding her to Dex. Maybe even doing a litter a year if it works out. Nothing big. Just raising good, strong working dogs. I can train 'em to work with the horses and the cattle. Sell 'em when they're old enough. Would you be okay with that?"

"With you breeding dogs on the ranch? Little tiny, cute border collie puppies? You're already on track to be Abby's favorite person, Stu. You don't have to work so hard."

His face creased into a grin. "So you're saying you wouldn't mind a few balls of yappy fluff running around the place?"

Melissa threw up her hands. "We got cows, horses, barn cats, chickens, goats. Hell, my mom was talking about getting ducks last week. Dogs are hardly the craziest thing going on around here. I'm only surprised no one has brought a llama home yet."

"Give it time. They're great with sheep, you know." Stu nodded and tipped his hat before he nudged his horse Magnum down the hill.

"No sheep, Stu!"

"Sure thing, Miz Rhodes."

"I'm serious. No sheep!"

Melissa followed him down the trail, wondering if she had time to eat anything before she headed over to pick Abby up from school.

She glanced at her watch. Two forty-five.

Nope.

Here's hoping Cary hadn't eaten all the granola bars in her purse.

———

SHE DROPPED Abby off with not a single word to her father-in-law, made it back to Oakville, and dropped by the bunkhouse just as Brian and his crew were finishing up.

Brian waved a set of keys as she brought her truck to a stop. Melissa opened the truck door.

"Perfect timing." He tossed her the keys. "We just finished cleaning up."

When she'd left, the outside of the bunkhouse was patchy, newly primed stucco over the old adobe bricks. Now it was a tidy cream-colored building with green trim around the red-tiled roof and windows. The porch had been shored up and painted the same green.

"Brian, it looks fantastic."

"I'm really pleased with it." He grinned. "It's not often you get to work on old buildings like this, so it was pretty cool. I'm glad you called me for it. I was thinking I wouldn't have time, but Cary…"

"Cary what?"

Brian smiled. "Anyway, my guys have had fun."

Hmmmm. Interesting. "And the structure is all looking solid?"

He nodded. "These old adobes last forever as long as they don't get water damage, and the roof on this one only had like… one leak, maybe? We replaced the tile—that was really old—and the subroofing. You've already seen the bathroom. The trim is all cleaned up and the floors are refinished. Stay off them for a couple of days and you're golden."

She shook his hand. "I'm excited about this."

"It's a sweet spot. You gonna rent it out?"

She nodded. "Gonna set it up as a vacation rental. Grab some park traffic."

"Cool." He crossed his arms and looked around. "You know, I was just fixing up an old barn the other day to be a wedding venue. The setup out here is pretty close, only you've got the whole citrus grove too. If you built some kind of bigger deck under the trees there with a pavilion or something along those lines, I bet you could do something similar out here. You get a lot of wildflowers spring and early summer?"

She cocked her head. "Tons. All along the creek. I hadn't thought about it."

"I'd start thinking about it if I were you. I wouldn't have time to start right away—we're busy through the rest of the fall. But I could give you an estimate on what I'm seeing for a deck and pavilion."

"That works out because I don't have the money to pay you for more right now."

Brian laughed. "I know how that is."

"But send me the estimate," Melissa said. "I'll take a look and talk to my mom."

"Will do."

She shook his hand again, walked over to the bunkhouse, and peeked in the windows, careful not to step on the newly refinished floors. She could already imagine the rustic bed she'd put in the corner. They had some old furniture stored in the barn that would be perfect. A rag rug on the floor. Maybe she could get some of Cary's pictures for the walls.

She heard her mom honk the horn to grab her attention. Joan was coming up the road in her ancient Subaru. Melissa walked back to the house and waited for Joan to park.

"Groceries?" she asked.

"In the back."

Melissa popped the trunk. "You remember I'm meeting Cary for dinner tonight, right?"

"Lissa." Her mom got out of the driver's seat, a pile of mail in her arms. "I went by the post office." She held out a large envelope marked NEXT DAY EXPRESS.

Melissa looked at the return address.

Bristol, Brooks, and McDonald

Santa Maria, CA.

She opened the envelope with a sense of inevitability and pulled out the cover letter. She read it, nodded, and put it back in the envelope. "They're doing it."

Joan shook her head. "You have got to be kidding me."

"Somebody must have told them I was handing out flyers at the market. They're calling in the note." Melissa tucked the envelope under her arm and reached for the first grocery bag. "I have ninety days to come up with seventy-five thousand dollars."

———

"OW!" She pulled her foot back. "You stepped on my foot."

Cary lifted an eyebrow. "I called your name four times and you didn't even turn your head. I was beginning to worry."

They were sitting on the patio at Flora's by the River, enjoying fresh Mexican food and a pretty view. So far, their date had gathered a few looks but no comments. Melissa had been staring at the water when Cary stepped on her foot.

"I'm sorry I'm distracted."

"Are you getting weird about the two of us again?" Cary crossed his arms over his chest. "Just give me a heads-up if you're going to freak out, and I'll plan my response accordingly."

"I'm not thinking about that."

"Then what is it?"

She sighed and turned her attention back to him. "I got an envelope from the Rhodes family law firm in Santa Maria today. Next-day express."

He shook his head. "Unbelievable."

She put a hand over her face and felt the anger and guilt wash over her. "I thought I was juggling all the balls in the air, but I dropped this one. I've got ninety days."

"It's not your fault Calvin's parents are jerks." He picked up her hand and kissed the knuckles. "You finished with your food?"

"Yeah."

"Then let's get out of here."

———

"NINETY DAYS." Melissa rubbed her temple, wishing she could get her mind off the looming deadline. She was at Cary's house. His mother was visiting her sister-in-law on the coast. They were actually alone, and Melissa had a bag in the car if she wanted to stay the night. She could do sexy, illicit things to the man she'd been dreaming about for four years!

Ninety days was three months. Right around the end of the year. After Christmas but not after New Year's.

"I could sell cows," she said.

"Didn't you tell me prices were crap right now? That's why you're waiting to cull?"

"Yeah." She was sitting at the small table in Cary's room, and he was opening a bottle of wine for them. "But I could sell some, even if I took a hit."

"Which would screw up both your herd and possibly your income for the rest of the year, right?"

She shrugged. "Ninety days, Cary."

He handed her a glass. "No problem."

She smiled. "Do you have a magic money tree I don't know about? I thought we were friends who kiss. You holding out on me?"

He sat across from her. "I already talked to my banker, okay? Give me the word and I'll have one hundred grand in your account in four weeks."

Melissa froze. "Cary, you can't just give me one hundred grand."

"I'm not giving it to you. It's a loan. Not a gift. You're gonna pay me back, just like you were gonna pay Greg and Beverly back. I'm just not gonna be an asshole about it."

She shook her head. "I can't take money from you."

"The terms of this loan would be ten years. And you'd pay me back in two, right?"

She kept her face blank. "The harvest next year should be enough. But *should* is not definitely, Cary. I can't guarantee—"

"No one can guarantee anything in farming, okay? I get that. That's why I got approved for a ten-year note. You'd have to pay the interest, but you'd have ten years."

"I can't take your money."

"Why?" He leaned forward. "Why not? I have a hell of a lot more confidence in you than I do in anyone else I work with because I know you take care of your shit."

"But I haven't taken care of this, have I?" She shook her head. "This is my fault. I should have read that note before—"

"No, fuck that!" He lowered his voice and reached for her hand. "I'm sorry, but fuck that, Missy. Calvin should have told you what the terms were. He should have told you, and he shouldn't have waited three years to do it. If you were my wife, I wouldn't borrow a hundred grand from Mother Teresa without telling you."

She squeezed his hand. "She was a nun. I'm pretty sure she didn't have that kind of cash to loan out."

"Missy—"

"My mom is threatening to cash in her retirement account."

"And she will take a huge financial hit if she does that. Let me help you."

She put a hand on her forehead and squeezed her eyes shut. "Why are you doing this, Cary?"

He stood, took her wineglass, set it down, and drew her to her feet. Then he put his arms around her and held her close. "I'm doing this for all the reasons I said. I'm doing it because I'm your friend. Because you're a good businesswoman and I trust you. And I want to help."

She slid her arms around his waist and pressed herself into his body.

He kissed the top of her head. "And I'm also doing this because I love you, Miss Melissa Oxford. I want to make your life a little bit easier."

She froze, but Cary kept swaying back and forth.

"You're probably going to freak out that I said that, but let's be honest, you already knew. I've loved you for years. I've wanted you for years."

She looked up at him with wide eyes. "Cary—"

"I don't want you to say it back to me right now, because I'm a suspicious bastard and I'd probably think you were saying it to be nice, but I think you love me too." He bent down and kissed her long and hard. "I think you love me, and I know I love you."

She put her arm around his neck and drew his mouth to hers. Melissa kissed him long and slowly.

I love you, Miss Melissa Oxford.

I think you love me too.

Of course she did. That's why everything was so scary. She drank from his mouth in long, slow sips as he spun her around and backed her to the bed.

"Were you finished with your wine?"

"Yes." She unbuttoned his shirt at the neck. "You still need to tell me."

"I love you."

She couldn't stop a smile from flashing across her face. "Not that."

He frowned. "What?"

"You told me." She kissed his chin. "Last week you said you knew what I needed."

"Oh." He pushed her back until her knees buckled and she sat on the bed. "Yes. I know what you need."

"Which is?"

He hitched her up the bed, sliding her from the base all the way up to the pillows.

She gasped a little. "Damn, you're strong."

"I lift."

She ran a hand over his shoulder, all the way down his arm. "Did you always?"

"No." He lay next to her and cradled her face, taking her mouth before he reached for her thigh and drew it over his hip. "I started lifting when I started climbing. I needed to be stronger."

"It worked."

"Glad you like it." He bit her bottom lip. "Now take off your shirt."

CHAPTER TWENTY-ONE

MELISSA'S CHEEKS flushed and her fingers returned to the buttons on his shirt. "I thought I was taking yours off."

"Leave it." Cary shrugged her hands away and bent to her ear to whisper, "Didn't I tell you that I know what you need?"

He could feel her confusion, along with more than a hint of anxiety, but he was hoping to wipe it all away. Wipe away the tension, the worry, the constant, constant pressure.

"Cary, I don't understand what—"

"Do you trust me?"

She frowned. "Always."

"Good." He took her mouth in a hard kiss and unbuttoned her jeans. His hand spread wide and slid up her belly. He could feel the goose bumps on her skin. Her energy felt like a rubber band about to snap.

He released her mouth. "You are in charge of everything on your ranch, all the time, all year round. Am I right?"

"Yes." Her voice was small.

"Then what I want you to do is take off your shirt. Do what I say. Don't argue. Don't think. Just take it off."

Without another word, she rolled away from him and pulled it up and over her head.

Thank fuck.

"Toss it on the ground. Leave your bra on."

She tossed it.

"Now your pants."

She unzipped her pants and shimmied them down her legs with Cary's help. He took his time after he'd thrown her clothes on the ground, stroking slow hands over her bare legs, teasing the sensitive skin around her thighs and the curve of her ass.

"I'm going to take your panties off."

Goose bumps rose all over her body, and she released a deep breath. He could see her shoulders relax. Her abdomen went soft. The lines on her forehead smoothed out as she stopped thinking about what she was supposed to do and simply did what he asked.

Cary slid her panties down her legs and smoothed his hand up the inside of her thigh, spreading her legs as he lifted one so he could roll between them.

He kissed up her legs, going higher and higher. He slid his arms under her knees and pushed them up, opening her body to his gaze.

"You are so beautiful," he said.

"You too." She breathed out. "Sorry. Little bit nervous. It's been a while."

"Yeah, me too." He kissed her once. Twice. "Let's see if we can figure out what goes where, huh?"

Her nervous laugh turned into a moan. Then she was panting, gripping his hair as he went down on her. He hummed in satisfaction, which just made her grip harder.

"Cary, Cary, Cary..."

She didn't say anything intelligible, just his name, and when she came, she didn't say anything at all.

He stood while she was still breathing hard. A light sheen of sweat covered her skin, making her glow in the low light from the bedside table. She watched him silently as he took off his shirt. His pants. He stripped down to his skin before he joined her back in bed, lying next to her, skin to skin.

"Hey." He traced a finger around her lips.

"Hey." She slid her fingers into his hair. "Have I mentioned I love your hair?"

"Yes." He spread hers across the pillow, a golden-brown waterfall on his ice-white sheets. "I love yours too. You never wear it down."

"It's long. Usually a braid is easier when I'm working."

"Keep it down when we're in bed."

"Okay." Her cheeks turned pink again. So did her breasts. Cary put his head down and tasted each one.

"Cary." She was squirming underneath him.

"Stay still."

Melissa fell motionless, and he felt the tension drain out of her again. He lifted her upper body to his mouth and tasted every inch of it. Her neck. Her breasts. Her belly. He was hard as a rock, but he didn't want to miss an inch.

"Do you have condoms?" she whispered.

He came up to kiss her mouth and laid her back on the pillows. "Yes."

She smiled. "Good."

Cary reached for the drawer in his bedside table, opened it, and grabbed one. Then he ripped it open with his teeth and rolled the condom on, all while teasing her breasts with his other hand.

"I love the size of them," he muttered.

"They're small."

"They're perfect." He tasted them again. "And they're so sensitive."

She was twisting beneath him, but it wasn't nerves. It was need. Cary knelt between her legs and lowered his body, pressing his chest to her breasts. Her fingers ran over his shoulders and down his arms.

"So strong."

"Mm-hmm." He nudged her legs open. "Melissa."

She looked into his eyes. "Yes."

"Keep looking at me."

She nodded and Cary slowly slid inside, keeping their eyes locked together.

He let out a guttural breath.

Yes.

Finally.

Tears came to her eyes, and a soft smile spread over her face. "I really love you, Cary."

He felt like his heart would burst out of his chest. "Love you, Missy."

He saw it in her eyes. He saw everything. He lay completely still within her, letting her get used to the feel of him. He stroked her cheek, kissed her mouth.

When he felt her start to move, he reached down and gripped her leg. "Put your legs around me."

She wrapped her legs around his hips, changing the angle and letting him go deeper. They groaned in unison as he began to move.

"Wrap those legs tight." He bit his lip and thrust. "You are so *fucking* sexy."

"Oh... Cary." Her voice was high and needy.

"Are you going to come?"

"I already did but..."

The wave of climax was going to hit him faster than he wanted, but there was no stopping it. A few more minutes. A few more rough commands, and he was there.

Cary came in a heady rush of pleasure, clasped between Melissa's legs, her name on his lips. Before she could catch her breath, he slid down. "Lift your hips."

She arched up, he hooked her legs over his shoulders, and he put his mouth on her again, flipping her into a second climax within minutes.

He held her quaking body, enjoying the way her muscles tensed and relaxed. The look of euphoria on her face.

"Come here." Her eyes were closed, but she was reaching for him.

"Let me..." He set her down, turned, got rid of the condom before he lifted the sheets on the bed and slid next to her. "Missy."

"Hmm?"

He smiled at how exhausted she was. "Slide under the covers before you fall asleep."

"Oh. Right." She scooted over, and Cary lifted the covers up. She moved back and he pulled the sheet over them as she nestled herself in his arms.

Cary kissed her temple, enjoying the heat of her skin against his. His whole body felt lit up. The only other time he'd ever felt this good was climbing a new mountain. His heart was racing; he felt light-headed with pleasure.

Melissa murmured. "Are you going to try ordering me around when we're not in bed?"

His eyes were drooping. "Pretty sure doing that when you're not naked will just result in more arguments than I want to deal with."

"Yeah, probably." She sighed. "I feel so relaxed. I can't remember the last time I felt this relaxed."

The low laugh rumbled in his chest. "I told you I knew what you needed."

She looked up, her eyes narrowed. "Oh hey. This *is* the most relaxed I've seen you."

Cary reached down and pinched her bottom. "Go to sleep. I want to do this again in the morning."

———

THEY DID DO it again in the morning. By the time Cary was done with her, Melissa had come so many times he'd stopped counting.

Not really. It was seven. She came seven times. Mission accomplished. She was looser than he'd ever seen her.

He made her breakfast after they got up. He didn't have a ton of food, but he could do eggs and toast. She managed to put away four eggs; clearly she was starving.

"I forgot to eat yesterday," she said between bites.

"Did you eat lunch at all?" He dipped his toast in the egg yolk. "I know you didn't eat much dinner."

"I didn't have time for lunch."

He shook his head. "You need to not do that shit, Missy. You know it's not good for you."

"I had a granola bar."

He reached for her purse and peeked inside. "Are there any left? You might eat all my food. I better take a couple."

"Hey!" She grabbed her purse, laughing as she tugged it away. "You can't just look through my purse."

"I'm your boyfriend now. I can't look through your purse?"

Her cheeks turned pink. "You're my boyfriend?"

"You told me you love me. I better be your boyfriend."

She wrinkled her nose, but she looked pleased. "Can we be boyfriend and girlfriend at our age? Aren't we too old?"

"I don't give a shit." He gulped some coffee. He was out of milk, but luckily Melissa didn't mind it black. "I'm not gonna call you my significant other. What does that even mean?"

"That you're significant. And... other?"

"Exactly." He took another bite of eggs. "I'm fine with being a boyfriend as long as I'm yours."

She set her fork down. "Okay, seriously?"

He frowned. "What?"

"How are you so unintentionally romantic?"

"Am I?"

"Yeah, kinda."

The corner of his mouth turned up. "Cool."

"Ox and Emmie are coming for dinner tonight. You should come."

"Can I kiss you in front of your mom?"

She shook her head, but she was smiling. "Yes, you can kiss me in front of my mom. I'm sure she'll be thrilled."

"Good."

"I can't wait for you to see the bunkhouse."

He smiled. "Yeah, Brian said it turned out really well."

"Did you call him and tell him to make time for me?"

"Yep." He took a bite of toast and locked gazes with her. "You gonna argue with me about it?"

She narrowed her eyes. "Since he was booked through the fall, no."

Cary grinned. "So, dinner tonight. What time and what can I bring?"

"Six o'clock and bring your muscles." She grinned. "We're scavenging in the barn."

Oh joy.

———

CARY STOOD NEXT TO OX, staring at the solid block of tangled furniture pushed into the storage closet of the barn.

"Good Lord," Ox said.

"She said she wanted a dining set out of here and a bed for the bunkhouse. And there's a coffee table too, but she wasn't sure if it was here or in the attic."

"I can't see anything other than cobwebs."

"You scared of spiders, Ox?"

"No, but I hate dust."

Emmie and Melissa walked into the barn and Emmie's eyes lit up. "Oooh! It's like a treasure trove back here!"

"Right? Anytime we get new furniture for the house, we just put the old stuff out here. We never throw anything away."

Ox said, "Why are you saying that like it's a good thing?"

"Because there's so much good stuff in there."

Cary took a deep breath and elbowed Ox. "Okay. We're doing this."

Ox pulled a bandana from his back pocket and tied it over his mouth as Emmie and Melissa picked through the other storage areas in the barn.

"Man," Ox said, "you are so whipped."

"Yes, and?" Cary glanced at Emmie. "Aren't you leading a middle school book club now?"

Ox's face lit up. "Those kids crack me up."

"Just... move your ass." Cary started lifting pieces from the closet and setting them on the empty floor of the barn. All the while, Emmie and Melissa were talking a mile a minute about Ox and Emmie's engagement—no surprise there—and plans to expand the second-floor apartment above the shop.

"I own the whole building, and right now Ethan and his dad are just using their second floor for storage. So I think if we lowered their rent a little, they'd let us use the space. We could just knock down the second-floor wall to expand the apartment." Emmie's smile was shy. "I mean, we love living over the shop, but..."

Ox said, "Eventually we'll want more bedrooms."

"Exactly."

Melissa's eyes went wide. "What? Really?"

Emmie held up her hands. "Not right now. Or even right away. You know... eventually."

Melissa's face was glowing. "I'm so excited for you guys. *So* excited."

Cary's heart lurched in his chest. They were talking about Ox and Emmie having kids. Did Melissa want more kids? She was young enough to have more. He'd always wanted children, but after his first marriage broke up, he figured it wasn't in the cards. Could it be? His eyes must have given more away than he realized, because Melissa caught his gaze and looked away quickly.

Shit.

It wasn't a deal breaker for him. Not even close. She might be happy with one kid and didn't want more. Since Cary loved Abby like she was his own, that would be fine. It'd be great, in fact. But the idea of having more...

It would be like climbing El Capitan successfully and then coming down and finding out you'd won the lottery while you were on the side of the mountain.

But how did he bring it up? It was probably too soon. Wasn't it?

He watched Ox and Emmie giddily making plans for the future and realized something surprising.

He was jealous as hell.

CHAPTER TWENTY-TWO

THE OCTOBER MEETING of the Oakville town council was held at the Veterans Hall, just like it typically was, but the hall ran out of chairs fifteen minutes before the meeting was due to start.

That was not typical.

Instead of a scattering of residents, the hall was packed to the gills. There were people wearing bright yellow T-shirts in the back with banners saying SAVE JORDAN VALLEY. There was a contingent from the Yokuts tribal government sitting in the second row. There were residents and store owners, young parents and senior citizens.

And lots and lots of farmers.

The farmers, conventional and organic, ranchers and herders and tree growers, had all clustered on the right side of the hall. Melissa walked into the meeting with Cary and had to bite back a laugh.

He frowned. "What?"

She waved her right hand toward the farmers. "A sea. A veritable sea of plaid."

Cary glanced down at the blue chambray shirt covering his national park T-shirt. Both were ripped up from citrus thorns, and the blue chambray had an old coffee stain on the sleeve. "I always did try to be different."

"And that is only one of the reasons I love you."

He smiled. "Come on. We may not be wearing plaid, but they are our people."

Melissa and Cary moved to the right side of the hall, exchanging nods with all the farmers, growers, and ranchers they knew.

They were a solitary crowd by nature, but from the mutters and mumbles Melissa could hear, not a single one of them was a fan of the Allen Ranch project. Too many people. Too much water—water was a big issue. The farmers were worried about new people complaining about the dust and the smell of animals. About large equipment moving down the roads.

City people meant problems, even if they appreciated the scenery. That was the general consensus.

Cary found a clear spot of wall to lean against, and Melissa leaned against him. They got a few looks, but not many.

Had she really been that oblivious? Not a single person looked surprised to see them together.

She felt the atmosphere of the room change as soon as the representatives from JPR Holdings walked in. There was Kevin Fontaine, whom they'd met before; Devin Peres, Melissa's brother-in-law; and a face she didn't recognize, a middle-aged woman with a smartly cut blond bob.

"She looks like a lawyer on television," Cary said. "Not like a cheesy injury lawyer, like one of those actresses *playing* a really smart lawyer."

"Is it the hair?"

"Maybe it's the hair."

Bud Rogers had actually brought a gavel to the meeting. At five minutes before the hour, he started banging it.

"We're a little early, but let's get started. Uh... now I know that this is an unusual meeting because we're having a vote tonight, but we still have to follow protocol. So right now I'm going to read the minutes from last month."

As Bud read the meetings from the month before, Melissa mentally reviewed everything that had happened since that first meeting.

She and Cary had become friends who kissed. And then more.

The note on her ranch had been called in.

Her first harvest of mandarins was almost ready to pick.

She'd hired a new employee who had taken over a lot of duties on the ranch.

The bunkhouse had been renovated.

She discovered her in-laws were even bigger assholes than she'd realized.

And Abby had a new goat.

"I really need a vacation," she whispered.

"And that is nearly impossible until Christmas."

A tiny whimper left her throat.

Cary leaned forward and kissed her temple. "Maybe we can find a weekend to take the goat queen camping."

"That would be nice."

Bud finished reading the minutes of the meeting and banged the gavel again. "Now," he said, voice booming, "because of the unusual nature of this meeting, we'll be opening the floor for questions."

Everyone started talking, and Bud banged the gavel again.

"You know, I thought it was maybe overkill," Cary said. "But that gavel was a good call."

"It's very loud."

"This will not work unless we have order!" Bud shouted.

Nobody was listening.

Tammy Barber stood and shouted, "Everybody, be quiet and listen!"

Tammy had been a teacher in the high school, and half the people in the room had probably taken biology or chemistry from her. She didn't mess around, and within seconds the room was quiet.

She pointed at the front of the room. "Okay. On either side, we've set up microphones. Form two lines so everyone can ask their questions."

Everyone started shuffling around and lining up while Tammy kept shouting directions.

"You get *one* minute for your question, so you better not ramble. The people from the developers will have three minutes to answer." She glared at the JPR Holdings people. "Three minutes, and we want real answers for real questions. I'm sorry we have to put such a tight schedule on you all, but there are a lot of people who want answers and we only have two hours."

More muttering, but the lines formed.

One of the first people up was the Yokuts representative. "There are several members of our community who have important family sites on the Allen ranch. It is our understanding that when the land was sold, one of the provisions Mr. Augustus Allen made was that those families would continue having reasonable access to those sites that are sacred to them. Will JPR Holdings be honoring that part of the sales contract? We're in the process of obtaining those records right now."

The woman who looked like a lawyer leaned forward. "Since the property has not changed hands since the Allen sale, all original contract provisions stand. If reasonable access is part of the sales contract, that will be honored."

The Yokuts representative tried to speak again, but Bud Rogers cut him off. "I'm sorry, Claude, if you want another question, you're gonna have to line up again."

"I'm just trying to figure out what 'reasonable access' means to them, Bud."

Muttering around the room.

"He's right," Melissa whispered. "That phrase is way open for interpretation."

"Yeah."

The next question came from a parent who wanted to know if the property taxes would cover all the renovations needed for the high school.

Tammy answered that one. "Yeah, they would. It'd be more than enough to cover the bill for all the plumbing. And from what I've seen about the development proposal, because this is a retirement community, the impact on our schools is gonna be very minimal. The people moving in aren't going to have kids. So the schools wouldn't get crowded."

A general murmur of appreciation from the room.

The next person stepped up. It was Melvin Raphney, who was on the Committee to Save Jordan Valley and wearing a truly eye-searing yellow shirt.

"Has anyone answered what we're going to do about the roads?" he asked. "I read that proposal, and what they're talking about doesn't seem like it would work. Who says that the farmers in Jordan Valley are going to want to sell their land to these people so they can widen the highway to four lanes? Two lanes have been fine for as long as I've lived here. Why do we need four lanes? Is it gonna be divided? Are people gonna be able to park along the road during wildflower season? What about traffic? Are we gonna need more traffic lights in town, because if there's one thing I hate, it's a—"

Bud slammed the gavel down. "Melvin, that's your minute." He looked at the JPR group. "Traffic?"

"All our civil impact studies have shown that the effect on traffic will be minimal," the blond woman said to widespread muttering. "We do not anticipate a problem obtaining the land to widen the road."

"And if they do have a problem"—a rancher spoke up from the right side—"they'll just use the government to pressure us to sell."

Bud banged the gavel as everyone started talking. "Kurt, that is not a question and you do not have the floor."

"This is bullshit, Bud."

"I don't appreciate that kind of language!"

Tammy Barber had to stand up to quiet the room again. "Let's settle down! Next question."

The questions came fast and furious. People wanted to know how much the houses would cost. Could people from Oakville buy them? If there was a golf course, could they play it? What kind of restaurants would be coming in? Did the Allen ranch have enough groundwater to support two thousand houses? What about solar panels, would the houses have solar panels? Would this development raise property values in town? How much?

Melissa caught Devin's eye about halfway through the meeting. He nodded at her and gave her a shit-eating grin. Devin thought this was going well, which worried her. Because in Melissa's opinion, the mood of the room was not on JPR's side. So if Devin was confident the vote would go their way... why?

"Les is being real quiet," Cary said. "You notice that?"

"Les is always quiet."

"But look at him." Cary nodded toward the old man. "He knows something."

If Devin looked smug, then Les Arthur looked *sure*. The old man sat at the end of the council table, and his expression swung between mild annoyance anytime the JPR people were speaking to bemusement.

People were moving in and out of the room. Residents got in and out of line as questions were asked, presumably sitting down if someone else asked the question they wanted an answer for. And people wanted to know about everything.

What are the houses going to look like?

How much are they going to cost?

What about beekeepers?

Can we revisit the dispensary idea before we build houses?

What about the fire department? Would we need a new station?

Melissa heard the rumble of the crowd before she heard the

next speaker through the microphone. She couldn't see him, but she'd recognize that voice anywhere.

"I've been listening to all this for about an hour now," Gus Allen said from the far side of the room. "And what I want to know is why on earth you people think you can get away with this development?" The crowd began to murmur, but Gus Allen kept speaking. "It's specifically spelled out in the contract that I signed with you, Miss Delaney, that any residential subdivision of the Allen ranch can only occur under very specific circumstances and must be limited to no less than four-acre divisions."

"Oh... shit." Cary chuckled. "Hey there, Gus. Nice to see you. Glad you brought your hammer."

Melissa's eyes went wide. "It's in the sales contract? Can you do that?"

Cary shrugged. "Maybe?"

The blond woman's smile was brittle. "It's so nice to see you, Mr. Allen. Thank you for coming tonight. If you examine the plans submitted to the planning committee of the Oakville town council, you will see that, in fact, all the particular addendums to the sale of your land have been met."

There was shuffling and a new voice spoke into the mic. Melissa craned her neck and saw Adrian Saroyan reaching for the microphone.

There was a squeak, and then he spoke. "Miss Delaney, with all due respect, I would disagree with your assessment of the submitted plans. Jeremy, you want to hold up that board?"

Jeremy Allen, Gus's grandson, walked to the front of the room and held up a board half the size of a Ping-Pong table. On it, Melissa could see the outline of two thousand houses nearly surrounded by a massive golf course.

"Hey, folks. I'm Adrian Saroyan. A lot of you knew my grand-parents, Jan and Ana. They went to Saint Gregory's, so I spent a lot of holidays out here as a kid." Adrian paused while the crowd made friendly noises. "What JPR is trying to do here is a pretty classic underhanded tactic. As you can see from the diagram Gus's grandson is holding up, they've divided the Allen ranch into these weird property parcels so that it looks like they're all four acres, but all the condos would be in the middle of the development" — Adrian pointed to a cluster of houses in the middle of the board— "and then the golf course would surround it."

"Huh," Cary said. "Clever. Devious, but clever."

"And then the homeowners' association is going to lease the land from the purchasers for the golf course, I guess. Now, we can challenge this in the court as a breach of contract—"

"I hope your friend has deep pockets, Saroyan." Devin Peres leaned forward and spoke loudly. "Very deep pockets."

Les Arthur cleared his throat and spoke for the first time. "Oh, I wouldn't worry about Gus, Mr. Peres. He's a smart man with his money." The old man shot a pointed glance at Devin. "And he's got more than a few friends in Oakville willing to back him up if he needs it."

Melissa said, "You were right. Looks like Les does know something."

Cary said, "I wish I had popcorn right now."

Melissa reached in her purse and handed him a bag of air-puffed cheesy corn. "Knock yourself out. It's Abby's favorite, but she'll live."

Cary's jaw dropped open. "You are the best girlfriend ever." He threw his arm around Melissa and opened the bag of popcorn.

Adrian started to speak again, but Bud banged his gavel. "Time is more than up, Mr. Saroyan."

The farmer standing on the other microphone said, "I'm gonna go ahead and yield my time to Mr. Saroyan, if that's all right. Adrian, you have more to tell us?"

"Sure do, Carmen." Adrian held up a sheaf of papers and turned around, speaking to the room. "Now, what I think is really important for the council and all of you to know is, they're going to try to screw Oakville on taxes with this plan."

Cary munched on a handful of popcorn. "I'm shocked."

"So shocked." Melissa grabbed a piece.

The muttering in the room turned angry.

Adrian kept talking. "They've reserved a very small space around the edges of the property." He walked over and pointed to the boundaries of the golf course with one finger. "See that shaded area right along the edges? That appears to be reserved for some kind of agriculture. It's not much—not really productive—but it'll probably be enough to keep the land taxed as agricultural use instead of residential, which will save them a whole truckload of money and significantly reduce the taxes Oakville will be able to collect."

The murmurs from the crowd gained in volume.

"What's this?" Bud Rogers was glaring. "I didn't see this part of the plan. What's this?"

"Did you read the actual proposal, Bud?" Adrian held a folder out to him. "Here. Have a copy. I don't know what they're going to do with that amount of land, breed llamas or something? God knows. Maybe a chinchilla herd?"

Laughter scattered around the room.

Melissa said, "I knew llamas were going to make an entrance in this somehow."

Cary said, "I've heard they're really good with sheep."

"The point is," Adrian continued, "they're going to do everything in their power to screw you out of as much tax money as possible." He turned to address the council. "I know this seems like it might be a solution to the budget shortfall. But it's not." He pointed at the JPR representatives. "These people have no interest in this town. They're out to make money. They don't care about the health of the community. Not even a little."

Devin Peres, Kevin Fontaine, and Blond Lawyer Delaney were all glaring at Adrian.

He didn't seem to care. "I very much doubt the residents they attract are going to shop on your Main Street," he said. "They *might* go to Metlin. Maybe. But they don't care about Oakville. I know you need development, but this is not the way."

Bud looked defeated. "I don't want to close the high school, Adrian."

"No one wants that," Adrian said. "And if you want, I will volunteer my time with you guys to figure out some better solutions. But don't do this." Adrian looked at each council member, one by one. "Let's figure out a way that keeps Oakville the town you love."

Someone in the back started clapping, then the whole room joined in.

Melissa bumped Cary's shoulder. "It's a good thing I love you."

He frowned. "I don't disagree, but why?"

"Because if I didn't, Adrian Saroyan is looking surprisingly attractive right now."

"You know, I had the exact same thought, only about Gus Allen."

Melissa burst out laughing and slid her arm around his waist. "Well, it appears that the Allen Ranch Retirement Community is on life support and things are not looking good. My father-in-law is going to be pissed, but I don't really care. Let's go home."

CHAPTER TWENTY-THREE

"Yeah?" He looked up from pounding nails in a small shed for Abby's goats. "What's up?"

Abby popped her head up from behind the box she was cleaning. "Want to hear a goat joke I just thought up?"

He smiled. "Yeah."

"So there was a mama goat and she went home, and the dad goat was giving their three baby goats a bath."

Cary smiled. "Uh-huh."

"And the mama goat says to the dad goat, 'Hey, you'll never guess what happened. I went to the vet and I found out that I'm gonna have three more babies. Surprise!' And the dad goat is really shocked and says, 'Wait, how can that be possible? You just had these goat babies.' And the mama goat says, 'Don't worry. I was just kidding.'" Abby burst into laughter. "Get it? Because a mama goat having a baby is called kidding!"

Cary hung his head and laughed along with her, as much from her laughter as the joke. "That was pretty funny."

"Princess." Abby danced in front of her goat. "Do you get it? You were just kidding!" Abby continued to crack herself up.

It was Saturday morning and Cary had the morning off. Melissa, Emmie, and Joan were cleaning and painting furniture for the bunkhouse, so Cary was hanging with Abby and helping her fix her pens.

"Hey, kid."

"Yes, adult?"

"How often have you fixed these pens?"

Abby stood and cocked her head. "Uh… maybe three times this year I think."

"Have you ever thought about investing in stronger fencing? Something with more metal?"

She chewed on her lower lip. "How much would that cost?"

"I don't know. Want me to find out?"

"Yeah, that would be cool. Thanks."

Looks like the goat queen is getting fencing for Christmas. Cary could think of worse presents.

A floppy-eared brown goat with yellow eyes was staring at him, a piece of grass hanging out of his mouth. "Hey, dude."

"That's Mr. Tumnus!"

"Ah." Cary nodded. "The devourer of roses."

Mr. Tumnus let out a bleat that sounded an awful lot like a laugh.

Cary picked up another screw and stared Mr. Tumnus right in his weird yellow eyes as he took the electric drill and screwed it into the new corner post. "See this? You're not gonna be able to knock this one down. We're on to you."

Mr. Tumnus bleated again.

"That's concrete at the base of that post. Two feet of it."

The goat snorted and moved to the tire tower Abby had built in the middle of the pen. With Cary's help last summer, she'd filled old tractor tires with dirt and stacked them together to make a kind of obstacle course for the goats. It seemed to be working. With all the toys and all the places to climb, the escape artists were getting out less.

"Hey, Cary?"

"What's up, buttercup?"

"You knew my dad, right?"

"Yes, I did." He smiled. "Did you have a question? Want to hear a funny story?"

She was staring intently into Princess's stall. "What do you think my dad would want me to do about Grandma and Grandpa Rhodes?"

Cary let out a long breath and sat back on his heels. He stood and walked into the shed where Abby was cleaning out Princess's stall. Mama and baby were in the small corral and the baby was nursing.

Abby leaned on the top of the stall and stared at him.

Cary brought an old stool over and sat across from her. "What's going on?"

"Okay, so you can't tell Mom."

He shook his head. "I can't guarantee that, Abby."

She huffed out a breath. "I heard Grandma and Mom talking about a letter from a lawyer and I could tell it was important and it had something to do with the ranch, so I went looking in Mom's desk—"

"Abby!"

"I know! I shouldn't have. But I did and I found the letter from my grandpa's lawyer." She blinked back tears. "Why would he do something like that, Cary? I don't understand." She took a deep breath, trying to control her tears. "It's my ranch too."

"Come here." Cary held out his arms, and Abby came to him. He wrapped the little girl up and she hugged him tight. "First of all, I don't want you to worry about having to leave the ranch. Your mom has it figured out. You're not going to lose the ranch, okay?"

She nodded. "Okay."

"Do you believe me?"

"Yeah." She sniffed. "I know Grandpa doesn't like Mom some-times and he thinks she's too proud—"

"Ignore him. Your mother is exactly the right amount of proud." He kissed her head. "And you are too. You're both proud of your accomplishments. You know what accomplishments are?"

"Things you... accomplish?"

"Yeah, things you do. Like planting mandarin groves or raising goats. Or getting good grades in school or helping your friends."

Abby nodded. "I have a lot of accomplishments."

Cary smiled. "You do. Especially for only being ten. Being proud of your accomplishments is good. You should be proud of them. Being proud of other things is stupid."

"Other things like what?"

Cary frowned. "I'd say anything you're born with that's just chance? Don't be proud of that. I mean, you should always like who you are, right? But don't think you're better than anyone else because of it, because that's just luck. You get me?"

"Like having straight teeth or curly hair?" Abby sighed. "I wish I had curly hair like Marta."

"And I bet Marta's curly hair is really pretty, but is that some-thing you should be proud of? You're born with whatever hair you have, right? I mean, is it the most important thing about her?"

"No. She is a *really* good singer. And dancer." Abby sighed. "She really carried our group at the talent show."

Cary muffled a smile. "See? Way more important. Those are accomplishments she should be proud of."

"Are Grandma and Grandpa proud of the wrong things?"

Cary shrugged. "What do you think?"

"I think... they think they're better than Mom and Grandma Joan."

"Do you think they're right?"

She frowned. "No!"

"Why do you think they want the ranch?"

"If I can't live here with Mom and Grandma, I'd have to live at our house there." She rested her chin on Cary's shoulder. "They want me to live at their ranch. And go to school with my little cousins. And ride English instead of Western."

"And what do you want to do?"

"I like riding English *and* Western. I think it's good to learn both."

"Agreed. That way if you go to England, you'll be able to talk to the horses."

Abby giggled, then she put on her serious face. "People and horses in England speak English, Cary. Everyone knows that."

"Yeah? I've heard the accent is way different though."

Abby grinned and threw her arms around him. "I love you, adult."

"Love you too, kid." He rubbed her back. "And you know how you were asking about what your dad would do about your grandma and grandpa Rhodes?"

"Yeah. What do you think?"

Cary thought hard. He didn't want to overstep, but he'd also been Calvin's friend, and he knew exactly what the man had thought of his parents. He tried to imagine what Calvin would say. What he'd do. How he'd counsel his ten-year-old daughter coming face-to-face with the fact that part of her family really weren't very good people.

"You know"—he patted her shoulder—"I think I have an idea."

———

AFTER SCHEMING WITH ABBY, Cary gathered his tools and walked over to the bunkhouse, curious if Melissa needed help with anything. He walked up the new gravel path, which was wide enough for a car, that ran along the north side of the main house. The truck had come to spread the gravel a few days before. It was still dusty, but it would look great when the rains came.

"Missy?"

"Inside!"

He took his shoes off on the porch and set his toolbox down, walking in to the newly refinished bunkhouse that still smelled like wood oil, varnish, and paint.

"Wow." He looked around, turning in place. When he got to the corner, he saw Melissa, lounging on the repainted four-poster queen bed that had been placed in the corner. "That looks great there."

"Doesn't it? The blue is perfect, right?"

He nodded and looked around the room. "Blues, greens, and grays inside."

She nodded. "Color of the mountains. With the red accents…"

He perched on a wooden chair in the small dining area. "It's like visiting the sequoias. Green, red, and blue skies."

"Do you have some pictures I could buy for the walls?"

Cary frowned. "I have some pictures you can *have*."

"You sell your work because it's good. I'm not going to—"

"Melissa, don't try to give me money for pictures. That's ridiculous." He pointed to the long wall next to the old iron stove. "You know what would go great there?"

"What?"

He wiggled his eyebrows. "That portrait of you from branding day."

She covered her face. "No."

"It would though."

She shook her head. "Not a chance. Do you still have that?"

He scoffed. "Of course I still have it."

"Did you get any offers for it?"

He smiled slowly. "Yes."

She was dying to ask. He could tell.

"I wasn't going to sell that one. Ever. It didn't even have a price listed."

"Why not?" Her cheeks were red.

He walked over, braced himself on the bed frame, careful that his dirty hands didn't touch the clean white sheets, and leaned down to kiss her.

"It's not for sale because you're mine," he whispered.

The smile spread slowly and surely across her face. "And you're mine."

He kissed her, over and over again, only drawing back when he heard voices coming up the path. "We have company."

"Did you and Abby get the goat pens fixed?"

He nodded. "We did. Mr. Tumnus has been foiled again."

"That damn goat." She shook her head.

"Hey, Melissa."

"Hey, Cary."

"Did you know that goats can see up to three hundred and forty degrees in the periphery with their weird demon eyes?"

"Noooo." She put a hand over her face and laughed. "Don't tell me there are two of you now."

"Goats are fascinating creatures."

She reached for his hand, and he lifted her off the bed just as Emmie, Ox, Abby, Leigh, and Joan came in the bunkhouse.

"...think it's a great idea," Joan said.

"It'll be so beautiful in the spring with the wildflowers," Leigh said. "I could do the cooking for you."

Joan was beaming. "Melissa, you'll never guess what."

Melissa said, "Ox and Emmie want to get married at the ranch."

"Yes! How did you know?"

"Crazy, wild guess when you're walking around with a glowing engaged woman and talking about wildflowers and catering."

Emmie laughed. "We love it here, and it's the family place." She took Ox's hand. "It feels right."

Ox said, "I am one hundred percent on board with this as long as there are no cows in the pictures."

Melissa scowled. "Why the hate?"

"But you want goats, right?" Abby was bouncing up and down. "Goats make the perfect wedding guests! We can tie the ring on Princess's back and have Lala carry a basket of flowers and—"

"Wouldn't Mr. Hummus eat the flower bouquets?" Ox said.

"His name is not Mr. Hummus!"

Cary leaned against the wall. "Now I'm hungry."

"This place is gorgeous now," Emmie said. "You could easily host weddings here. There's lots of parking in the pasture. There're beautiful trees and the creek." She motioned around the bunkhouse. "You even have a honeymoon cabin."

Melissa said, "We'd need to build some kind of deck or pavilion if we want to host any events that aren't family, and I'm tapped out since we finished this. I'm all on board for a simple wedding here at the ranch for you guys, but if you want something bigger, then you're going to have to wait for a while."

As everyone chatted happily about Ox and Emmie's wedding, Cary was overwhelmed by that familiar burning in his chest.

Jealousy.

He was happy with Melissa. So fucking happy. They were getting closer every day, but he had to wonder if it took him four years to convince her to be his girlfriend, how long would it take her to say yes to being his wife?

Because he definitely wanted to marry her. Maybe even add another kid if it was in the cards. Ten years ago, the thought of getting married again would have caused him to flee. Now it was all he could think of. He wanted to get married. He wanted to be Abby's stepdad. He wanted Melissa to have another baby.

Did men have biological clocks, because seriously, what the fuck?

He couldn't rush her. If he rushed her, she'd just dig in her heels.

And Melissa was giving him another odd look.

Snap out of it. Cary said, "Ox, if you want to work on a deck with me, we can probably build something ourselves. I've built decks before. It can't be that different."

Ox nodded. "That's an idea. Would definitely save some money if we did it ourselves."

Melissa said, "Free labor for me? Cool. I'll take it."

Cary said, "Oh, don't worry. I'll figure out some kind of payment structure for you."

Ox laughed, and Emmie stepped on his toe.

Abby said, "What's a payment structure?"

CHAPTER TWENTY-FOUR

HOURS AFTER OX and Emmie had gone home, Melissa sat with her feet kicked up on the front porch of the bunkhouse, watching the sun set over the valley as hawks cried overhead, searching the meadow for one last meal before the light disappeared.

Cary had left in the early afternoon to meet Jeremy at Halsey Rock. Stu, Leigh, Rumi, and Joan had driven into Metlin to see a movie they were excited about.

And Abby was stuck in a new book, engrossed in dragon-riding adventures with her goats.

She heard Cary's quad before she saw it. He drove down the trail along Halsey Creek, crossing the stream with a quiet splash before he came up the bank and into her view.

His silver and black hair flew back as the wind whipped it. He was wearing climbing pants and a thin tank top, a bandana around his neck and sunglasses shielding his eyes. His arms were braced wide on the handlebars, and his skin glowed golden in the waning sunlight.

God bless mountain climbing muscles; I get to have sex with that man.

There were lots of other amazing things about Cary Nakamura, but seriously, that couldn't be understated. She got to see that man naked basically whenever she wanted, and he ordered her around in a bone-melting voice when they were having sex.

It was… very nice. Very, very nice.

He smiled when he approached the bunkhouse. "Hey."

"Hey." She swung a beer by the neck. "You want one?"

"I'll have a taste." He crooked his finger at her and shut the bike off. "Come here."

Melissa glanced around, but Abby was in her room reading. She walked to the quad, putting a little extra sway in her hips because she had just remembered that she got to have sex with that man.

Which was very nice.

She walked beside him and threw her leg over his lap, straddling him face-to-face. She slid over and hugged his thighs with her legs. "Hey."

He grabbed her beer. "Hey." He took a drink with one hand and slid his other hand down her back and onto her ass. "How's my girlfriend today?"

"Feeling a little…" She leaned toward his lips. "Lonely."

"Are you?" He reached over and set the beer down. "We can't have that."

He took her lips in a long kiss. His mouth tasted like green tea and honey. His skin smelled like sweat with a hint of sweetness. She reached back and ran her fingers through his hair, careful to work out the tangles from the wind.

"I knew it!" Abby's voice rang through the air.

Melissa froze.

Cary froze. Then he immediately removed his hands from Melissa's ass. They both turned to see a triumphant ten-year-old marching toward them, pointing an accusing finger.

"I knew you guys were in love!" Her face was beaming. "I bet you thought I didn't notice!"

"Uh… hey." Melissa's heart was racing. "Hi. Um, what…"

Nothing. She had nothing.

Cary narrowed his eyes. "Hey, kid."

She crossed her arms and watched them with a smug smile. "Hey, adult."

"How long have you known?"

Abby rolled her eyes. "Only like… a year now."

Cary snorted. "Oh, look at that! She knew before you did, Missy."

"Will you be quiet?" she muttered. Melissa awkwardly climbed off Cary's lap, which was not as easy as climbing onto it. Not even a little bit. "So… Uh, Abby, what do you mean that you knew we were in love?"

The eye roll was epic. "Oh come on, Mom. It was so obvious."

He wasn't laughing out loud, but Cary's shoulders were shaking.

"What?" She put her hands on her hips. "I don't know what you mean. What was so obvious?"

Abby waved her hand. "Whatever." She bounced over to Cary. "So, Cary."

"Yes?"

"Since you're my mom's boyfriend, will you teach me how to mountain climb?"

"Yes."

"No!" Melissa was furiously shaking her head. "She's already jumping giant horses. Give me a break."

Cary glanced at Melissa. "When your mom says it's okay, I'll start teaching you the basics."

"Cool." Abby glanced between Melissa and Cary. "So you're gonna get married, right?"

Melissa closed her eyes. "Abby, despite what you may think, this is pretty new and we have not talked—"

"Yeah," Cary said. "We'll get married."

"Cary!" Melissa gaped. "What are you doing?"

"Missy." Cary spread his arms wide, a giant smile on his face. "Come on. This is us."

This is us.

He made it sound so easy. Sitting there, looking beautiful and free on his bike, his arms open. His heart wide open.

He loved her. He loved Abby. She loved him.

This is us.

Maybe he made it look easy... because it was. Melissa blinked back tears. Maybe for the first time in a very, very long time, something wasn't a fight. Or a struggle. Or an uphill battle. Maybe this... just was.

Cary crooked his finger at her. "Come here, Miss Melissa Oxford, who always knows where she is."

Melissa walked over to him, and he was every dream she thought she'd lost. A friend. A lover. A partner. A father to her daughter.

Cary got off the bike. "Why are you crying?" He wiped her eyes. He kissed her cheeks. "Don't cry. You've got the smartest kid in the world. I love you. I was getting things all twisted around in my head too, but Abby's right. It's so obvious."

Abby looked between them. "Well, *obviously* you have to talk about this, and probably argue about it a while. But I, for one, am in favor of Cary marrying you and living on the ranch."

Melissa wiped her eyes. "Oh yeah? Why's that?"

"I feel like he's a goat ally."

Melissa burst into laughter through her tears.

———

THEY MADE love in the bunkhouse after they'd eaten dinner and put Abby to bed. It was slow and achingly sweet.

"Right there?" Cary moved in her.

Melissa breathed out and nodded without saying a word. Her

eyes were drifting shut in pleasure when he said, "Look at me. Keep your eyes on me."

Her eyes flew open and locked with his.

Cary's lips were flushed and swollen from her kisses. He was braced over her, his thick hair falling around them. Their bodies were pressed together and he moved with torturous precision, taking her apart piece by piece.

"Bend your knee up." He nudged her right knee and moved deeper, changing his angle.

Her mouth fell open with a wordless gasp.

"There." The corner of his mouth tilted up. "Right there."

"Please," she whispered. "Please."

Her climax didn't come with a rush. It came in an inevitable, crushing wave, spreading over every inch of her body as she cried his name into the darkness. It waned and surged, overtaking her three times before Cary groaned with his own release, gripping her hair as he closed his eyes and pressed his face into her neck.

He rolled to the side, his chest heaving. "Oh fuck, that was good."

"I don't even know what that was." Her whole body was shaking. "I'm not sure I can walk."

Cary reached over and pulled Melissa's head onto his shoulder, stroking her hair, running his fingertips over her skin, and generally making her feel like she'd received a full-body massage while simultaneously galloping a horse and taking a double shot of tequila.

"I don't know how you keep giving me different orgasms," she mumbled against his chest. "I thought there were just a couple of different kinds. But there's a lot more."

His chest shook in silent laughter. "That's the benefit of being with an old guy. We like taking our time."

She ran her hand over his defined abdomen. "Oh yeah. Super old."

Cary fell silent. He took her hand and squeezed it tight.

"What is it?"

"My dad died when he was seventy." Cary's voice was quiet. "He thought he was in perfect health. I think about that a lot. He had no signs of heart disease."

She twisted herself around and propped her chin on his chest. "So you get your heart checked early and often. You do all the tests and stuff exactly when the doctor tells you. And if you don't, I will give you absolute hell until you do."

He smiled a little. "Understood." His hand stroked up and down her arm. "Since we're getting married now and everything."

"Assumptions from my daughter do not count as a proposal, just so you know. And we still have... a lot to talk about."

"I know." He stroked her hair. "Like... would you ever consider having more kids?"

Her eyebrows went up. "Do you want kids?"

"I always wanted kids. I just didn't think it would happen."

"I would... be open to having more kids if I had some help. I can't imagine being a full-time mom now like I was with Abby. My life is too crazy."

He nodded. "That's fair."

"But I always wanted more." She worried her lip. "I lost a baby. About three months before Calvin died. I was four months along."

The hand that was stroking her hair froze. "Missy."

"I wasn't really showing yet, so we hadn't told many people. I was just really bitchy and cranky because the doctor said I couldn't ride. And then..." She shook her head. "The doctors never knew what happened."

He leaned down and gently kissed her forehead. "I'm sorry."

"She would have been six this year. Born between Christmas and New Year's." Melissa wiped her tears away quickly. "It happened a long time ago. I'm just bringing it up because I don't know if I can have more kids, you know? It might not happen."

"We have Abby." He smiled. "You don't get much better than that. Anything else is just a bonus."

247

And she fell for him all over again. "Thank you for literally saying the most perfect thing you could just now." She reached for his cheek and pulled it down for a kiss. "Thank you for being great."

"Miss Melissa Oxford," he whispered, "do you know where you are right now?"

"Yeah." She snuggled closer and laid her head over his heart. "I'm right where I need to be."

———

ADRIAN SAROYAN SAT in Café Maya, Daisy's restaurant downtown, sipping a coffee and eating a piece of blueberry-and-sourcream pie. Melissa and Cary were meeting with him after he'd called and told them he had an update on the Allen ranch.

"As of right now, the Allen Ranch project has been tabled," he said. "The property owner has put it back on the market and is asking around about buyers who might be interested."

"Seriously?"

"Let's hope we get an actual farmer or rancher this time." Cary dug into his own piece of sweet potato pie. "So Gus isn't going to have to sue them?"

Adrian raised an eyebrow. "Honestly? It would have been a tough case. Gus was sentimental and put a lot of addendums in the contract that probably wouldn't have held up in court. But it would have eaten up time and cost JPR Holdings a lot of money. And Les Arthur all but told them he'd bankroll the whole thing if he needed to."

"So Les isn't a development fan?" Melissa waved at Daisy, who made the "call me" motion with her hand. Melissa nodded and turned her attention back to Adrian.

"Oh, I wouldn't say that," Adrian said. "He's bought quite a few properties that have needed investment and he's turned a good profit. Invested quite a bit here downtown on 7th and

Main. But he's also not a fan of your father-in-law, Melissa. No offense."

"None taken. I'm not a big fan of his either."

"It is interesting though." Adrian took a bite of pie. Swallowed it. "I was getting all my stuff together last week, pretty sure we were going to have to find a lawyer, and Gus called me. Said the current owner had called him and said all his partners were pulling out. Said he couldn't fight it on his own. Said both Devin Peres and Greg Rhodes had called him up and said they were out."

"Huh." Melissa frowned. "That's kind of weird. They'd already invested quite a bit. Why would they just pull out like that?"

Something flickered on Cary's face, drawing Melissa's attention. It was a little smile. A flash in his eye.

He knows something.

She was certain of it. She was also certain he'd never share it with Adrian.

She took a deep breath. "I guess that means the Allen ranch is back on the market, huh?"

Adrian nodded. "Yes. And from what I'm hearing, there's quite a bit of buzz."

Melissa asked, "From ranchers?"

Adrian smiled a little. "Initial interest has definitely come from the agricultural sector. Uh-huh."

Melissa frowned. "But...?"

"But not from where you might expect."

"Is that so?" Cary frowned. "Who's looking at it?"

"There are a few companies interested. Nothing for certain yet. Some inquiries. Some pretty *interesting* buyers, as well."

"More interesting than a citrus grower?" Melissa squeezed Cary's hand under the table.

"Impossible," he muttered. "We're the most fascinating men in the world."

Adrian laughed. "I would never argue with that. But let's just say that these new farmers are looking to take advantage of an old cash crop that's currently very popular in California and a few other select states across the country."

Cary frowned. "What?"

Melissa's mouth dropped open. "No way."

"Land all over the valley is at a premium, and people want crops that bring premium prices." Adrian couldn't stop his laugh. "Wasn't Bud the one that was turning apoplectic about allowing a marijuana dispensary in town, even though it would have brought in a ton of tax revenue?"

Cary laughed, a full, roaring sound that came from his gut. "You have got to be kidding me."

Adrian shook his head. "My friend, I am not. Nothing is certain, but at least half the people looking at the Allen ranch are legal marijuana growers."

Melissa closed her eyes and shook her head, trying to imagine the look on Bud Rogers's face when he heard the news. "Well... at least we know they'll probably be organic."

CHAPTER TWENTY-FIVE

CARY TOSSED HIS CARDS DOWN. "You little hustler."

Abby giggled and grabbed all the M&M's in the middle of the table. "What?"

"You know what!"

They were sitting on the front porch of the ranch house while Rumi, Joan, and Leigh cooked dinner inside. Abby had convinced Cary she needed to "learn" how to play poker.

After a few fumbling hands, she had destroyed him.

"Who taught you how to play cards?" he asked.

Ox walked out of the house and set two beers on the table. "Did she get you too?"

"She got *you*? I assumed you were the one who taught her."

He shook his head and sat down. "Nah. I fell for it too."

Cary narrowed his eyes on Abby. "Okay, who was it?"

Abby blinked innocently. "I just looked on YouTube."

"Lying. No one learns that well from YouTube."

"I learned about making goat-milk soap on YouTube. I even made some orange-blossom soap, and your mom says it's the best soap she's ever used." Abby picked up her bottle of Coke and sipped it. "I'm going to try honey-and-lavender-scented soap next."

Cary leaned forward. "That sounds like a great idea, and stop avoiding the question."

"I don't know what you want me to say." Her eyes were wide and innocent. She shrugged her tiny shoulders. "Just beginner's luck, I guess."

"Ooooh." Ox started chuckling. "I know who it was."

Abby gasped. "You better not."

"I know because she used the same 'beginner's luck' line on me."

Abby scrambled up and put a hand over her uncle's mouth. "No! Don't tell him!"

"Tss dfffly Mmmmy." Ox was laughing behind Abby's hand.

Cary drank his beer. "Emmie, huh?"

"No!" Abby threw her head back. "I promised I wouldn't tell!"

Cary drummed his fingers on the table. "So Emmie's the card shark in the family?" He nodded slowly. "Good to know."

Ox's eyes were laughing when he pulled Abby's hand away from his mouth. "At least she's got that part of being a cowgirl down."

Cary squinted into the bright autumn sun. The leaves were changing colors on the hills, the grass was brown and thirsty. And in the corral nearest the house, Melissa was sitting on the fence next to Stu, shouting instructions to Emmie, who had just started trotting PJ around the ring.

"Eyes forward!" Melissa shouted. "Keep your hips loose and trust your mount, Emmie."

Abby leaned on the porch rail and watched. "You know, Emmie's seat isn't bad."

Ox smiled a little. "Her seat's pretty damn fine, if you ask me."

"Dude." Cary sent him a withering look.

"She'll learn fast," Abby said. "Don't worry, Uncle Ox."

Cary was relieved the innuendo flew completely over Abby's

head. For now. He was bracing himself to have a teenage daughter. He wasn't sure quite how he was going to handle it, but he was going to do his best.

The more time he spent at the Oxford ranch, the more he realized…

He had no idea how girls worked.

There was squealing.

There were slamming doors.

There was attitude to spare.

There were multicolored bottles in the bathroom in quantities heretofore unknown by man. Cary had no idea what they were all for. Did you need more than three or four? That seemed like the maximum number of bottles you needed in one bathroom, especially for someone less than five feet tall.

There was also laughter.

And hugs.

Hilarious conversations about horses, fractions, and the probability of dragons actually existing at some point in history.

And lots and lots of food.

"Another hand?" Cary nodded at the cards.

"I'm in!" Abby said.

He started shuffling. "Yeah, I bet you are."

"What are the moms making for dinner?" Ox asked.

Cary started dealing again. "Leigh is making beef stew, and I think Joan is making chile rellenos."

Abby bounced up and down. "Did Nana Rumi bring rice balls?"

"Yes, she did."

"Yesssss."

Ox, Cary, and Abby all picked up their hands. Ox tried to cheat. Badly. It cracked Abby up and produced a near-constant stream of ten-year-old shit-talk that made Cary feel like he really needed to up his game.

The girl could never sit still, so Cary noticed when her feet stopped moving.

"Abby?"

Her head had turned to the west. "Someone is coming up the road."

Were all Oxford girls telepathic when it came to their ranch? Melissa had a near-perfect awareness of the changes in her land. Abby appeared to be following in her footsteps.

A few seconds later, he saw dust in the distance. He heard the sound of a motor just a moment before a truck crested the hill and stopped at the gate.

Abby's eyes went wide. "It's Grandpa Rhodes."

"What?" Cary set his cards down. "Was he supposed to come today?"

"Nope."

"Hey." He waited for her eyes to meet his. "So you did?"

Abby's mouth was set in a firm line. "Yeah."

"Okay then. I'm with you, kid." Cary looked at the corral. Melissa was already walking toward the house, leaving Emmie in Stu's capable hands. Ox and Cary stood up as Abby walked down the steps toward her mother.

Ox muttered, "You know why they're here?"

"I have an idea."

They weren't driving the Range Rover, they were driving their heavy truck, and a fancy silver horse trailer stretched behind it.

"That better be what I'm hoping it is," Ox said.

Cary said nothing. He walked down the steps to Melissa and Abby as Joan came out on the porch.

"Ox? Is that Greg and Bev? Did Melissa invite them for dinner?"

Cary walked down the gravel path and stood behind Melissa, who had her arm around Abby's shoulders.

"Uh, Mom. I should probably tell you something."

"What?" Melissa looked at Abby, clearly confused. "Did you know they were coming today?"

"No, but..." Abby looked at Cary in desperation.

Cary said, "A few weeks ago, Abby found the letter from the attorneys in Santa Maria. She figured out what was going on."

Melissa's eyes went wide. "What?"

"I'm sorry, Mom." Abby's eyes were anguished. "I know I shouldn't have looked in your desk."

"She knew it was wrong and she asked me what she should do," Cary said.

"You mean you knew?" Melissa's face went pale. "The whole time, you knew?"

The note wouldn't be an issue for much longer, and Cary hadn't even needed to help. Melissa and Joan finally sat down with their banker, who explained that as much as their ranch was worth, taking out a small loan to clear the debt to the Rhodeses would be fast and easy. They could pay it back as soon as the mandarin crop came in or take more time and breathe a little easier.

As much as Melissa hated putting any kind of debt on the ranch, she knew it was better than owing money to her in-laws. As soon as the loan processed, she'd send them a check and that would be that.

Abby had tears in her eyes. "I was really angry, and I didn't know what I should do about it. I was mad about Sunny. I was mad that they were trying to build all those houses next door, and then I found the letter..." Her face was tormented. "I had to do something."

Melissa took her daughter by the shoulders. "What did you do?"

"She wrote a letter to them." Cary rubbed Abby's back. "That's all. I helped her write a letter to them, and we talked through what she wanted to say. She told them how they'd been making her feel. We sealed it up and I left it with Abby. Told her it was up to her if she mailed it or not." He raised an eyebrow. "I guess you sent it."

"If you write something and don't send it, what's the point?"

He muttered, "That's definitely the Oxford way of looking at it."

All three of them waited for the truck and trailer to stop. Greg shut off the truck, and he and Beverly got out. A young man jumped out of the seat behind them.

"Hey, Greg," Melissa said. "Hey, Bev. This is a surprise."

Beverly was looking at Abby. "We came to a decision this morning, and we didn't want to wait."

Melissa and Cary stood behind Abby, their hands on her small shoulders.

"Just so you and Greg know," Melissa said, "I am just now hearing about the letter Abby sent you. But just because I didn't know about it doesn't mean I don't approve of Abby expressing her feelings in a respectful way."

Cary put his hand on the small of Melissa's back. "It was very respectful."

Greg looked at Cary and Melissa. "You two seeing each other now?"

"Yep," Cary said.

Greg and Beverly didn't say a word.

Greg came to stand in front of Abby. "Princess, I'm sorry."

"Mr. Rhodes," Cary said, "she told you she doesn't like that nickname."

Greg's face was tight, but he kept his eyes on Abby.

"You used to call Aunt Audrey that," Abby said. "She told me. And now you say mean things to her."

Beverly flinched, and Cary wondered if someone had called her princess in the past, only to discard the affection once its usefulness had run out. But worrying about Beverly wasn't his job.

"I'm sorry," Greg said. "I forgot. I will try not to call you that anymore, Abby."

The back of the horse trailer levered down, and Cary heard hooves on metal.

"We brought Sunny," Greg said. "He'll be living here at the ranch with you from now on, and you'll be responsible for his upkeep. The points you listed in your letter were all valid and very well thought out." The corner of his mouth turned up. "I think I remember receiving a similar organized list from your father when he was around your age."

Abby beamed. "About what?"

"About his desire to ride on the ranch without a chaperone," Greg said. "It's what made me think he would make an excellent attorney someday."

Cary felt Melissa tense under his hand.

"But instead of doing what I expected," Greg said. "He followed his own dreams. And if he hadn't followed those dreams, we wouldn't have you, Abby." He cleared his throat. "And your grandmother and I would not trade you for anything."

The young man in the Rhodes Cattle Company polo shirt led the tallest horse Cary had ever seen. He blinked.

Seeing Abby next to the Thoroughbred was enough to have him feeling as nervous as his mother. "Is she big enough to ride that horse?"

Melissa looked at him like he was crazy. "Yeah, it's totally fine."

"Sunny!" Abby ran over to her horse, who immediately lowered his head and nickered. She put her arms around his neck. "I missed you every day." She turned to her grandparents. "Thank you. I promise I will take very good care of him. I *promise*."

Beverly said, "We still want you to take jumping lessons. Antonio says you have so much potential and you're a natural horsewoman."

Greg cleared his throat. "Obviously it runs in the family."

Melissa softened. "Thanks, Greg." She walked over to Sunny

and held out her hand for the big horse to sniff. "Hey buddy. How much do you like horse trailers?"

"He's very comfortable in them," Greg said. "And we're paying Antonio to come from Los Angeles twice a month anyway. I suppose it's just as easy to have him come here." Greg looked around at the serviceable corrals.

"You know," Melissa said. "I have an old friend in town who breeds warmbloods. She's got a wonderful stable and training arena for her school. I'm sure we can work something out."

Greg nodded. "That would be... good."

"Maybe Audrey could come over and check it out," Melissa said. "Make sure it'll work for Abby and Sunny."

Stu, Ox, and Emmie had wandered over, drawn by the spectacle of the giant horse in the front yard.

"Grandpa and Grandma, this is Stu—Mr. Hagman," Abby said. "He works on the ranch with Mom and he has the coolest dog. Dex is almost as smart as a goat."

Stu tipped his hat at the Rhodeses. "How you doing?"

Bev smiled tightly. "It's very nice to meet you."

"Well, Miss Abby"—Stu held his hand out to the horse, and Sunny immediately responded to him—"I suppose it's a good thing we have three more stalls in that barn, huh?"

"Sunny, you're going to meet so many new friends!" Abby hugged his neck again. "You're gonna meet Moxie and PJ. And Magnum and Lucy. Uncle Ox, isn't he the most handsome horse ever?"

Greg left Abby introducing Sunny to Ox and Emmie. He drew Melissa to the side, and she grabbed Cary's hand to come with her. Greg cut his eyes toward Cary but didn't say a word.

"I'm glad the ranch is doing well enough to hire some help," Greg said.

"Tell your lawyers they can expect a check next week. It'll be coming from my bank."

"Melissa—"

"No." She raised a hand. "I should have paid off the note long before this. If I'd known I could, I would have. It's left this… thing between us. And it's better that it's gone."

Greg crossed his arms over his chest and stared at the ground. "Fair enough."

"I want you to take that house out of mine and Calvin's name," Melissa said. "If you want to put it in Abby's name to do what she wants with it when she'd older, that's up to you. But it's not my house. It's not my home. This place is my home, and it always will be."

Greg nodded slightly. "Yes, Abby made that point in the letter she sent us."

"Gifts aren't gifts when they come wrapped up in strings, Greg."

Greg looked at Abby and Sunny. "That's why we brought the girl her horse."

Cary rubbed Melissa's shoulder. "Can I offer a suggestion as someone who loves Abby and sat with her while she wrote that letter?"

Melissa nodded. "Yeah."

He looked at Greg. Then Melissa. Two very stubborn and opinionated people who would probably never see eye to eye in their entire lives. But Cary could also see the love on Greg's and Beverly's faces. They might have had their issues, but they adored their granddaughter.

He looked at Melissa. "I think you should let Abby get a phone. She's a smart, responsible girl. It doesn't have to be a fancy one, just one so she can call her grandparents directly without asking you. And they can call her."

"But—"

"You're busy, and she knows the three of you don't always get along. She needs to be able to call them without asking you for permission."

Melissa took a deep breath and let it out slowly. "I think we can work something out."

Greg smiled. "Thank you."

"Just know that I will be checking that phone, Greg," Melissa said. "No subtle suggestions about moving. No hints about school at Saint Anne's."

He held up a hand. "I get the idea." He glanced over his shoulder. "She's an extraordinary girl, Melissa. You've done so well with her." Greg grimaced. "It kills me that Calvin can't..." He took a rough breath.

Melissa dropped Cary's hand and put her arms around Greg. The older man hesitated for a moment before he hugged her back hard.

"I miss him every day," Melissa said. "But he's here. He'll always be here."

God, she was tough. Cary watched her hugging the man who'd threatened her ranch and her community with his arrogance and selfish intentions. He was also the man who had raised Melissa's husband, lost his own son, and loved his granddaughter fiercely. He wanted the absolute best for her, as misguided as his methods could be.

Cary asked, "Why don't you and Bev and your guy stay for dinner? I promise there's plenty of food."

The groom was saddling Sunny as Abby held the reins. She was patiently explaining the differences between English and Western saddles to Leigh, who had come over to see what was going on. In short order, Abby was on Sunny's back and Stu had ridden PJ over, mounting up so he could ride with the little girl.

"She's surrounded by people who love her," Greg said. "That's the best you can ever hope to have for your children." He nodded at Cary. "We can stay."

"If it gets too late, the guesthouse is done," Melissa said. "You and Bev are welcome to stay. It really turned out nice."

"We'll see," Greg said. "The trailer has living quarters too."

He walked over to the horse corral and stood next to Bev, the two of them watching Abby show Sunny around his new home. PJ was as excited as Abby. He was the most social of the Oxford horses and the only one Cary felt comfortable riding.

Melissa leaned against the fence. Cary put his arm around her.

"You changed the sheets in the bunkhouse, right?"

She smiled. "Yes. Definitely."

"Good."

Melissa leaned her chin on the fence post. "What did she write in that letter, Cary?"

"I can't remember the exact words, but it was along the lines of what she just told you. She said she was angry at them for trying to hurt the ranch because it was her home. She was angry that they bought her a horse, but she couldn't keep it even though she could take care of him."

"She made a list for that one?"

"Five points with additional subpoints, including approximate yearly cost of feed and her projected income from goat-milk soap."

"Yeah, that sounds like my daughter."

"I can't decide whether I should hire her or just hand her to the keys to my office now."

Melissa smiled. "What else?"

"Just that." He kissed the top of her head. "There was one bit that I remember exactly."

"What was it?"

"She wrote, 'If you take my home away, I will know you don't love me. Your mouth can't say one thing when your actions say something else.'"

Melissa let out an audible groan. "Oh, that's harsh."

"But true." He watched Abby ride around the ring, strength, determination, and joy written across her face. "That's *your* daughter, Missy. Be so damn proud."

"I am." She looked up at him. "I know why Abby thinks we've been in love for so long."

"Oh yeah? Why?"

"Because of that. Because of what she wrote. Our actions were talking even when our mouths were arguing."

Cary wrapped both his arms around her waist and leaned his chin on her shoulder, watching their golden girl gallop in the afternoon sun. "I love you, Miss Melissa Oxford. Thanks for always knowing where you are."

EPILOGUE

Five months later...

"I HOPE you don't mind the noise too much!" Melissa cringed at the sound of an electric saw as she helped a couple from Switzerland carry their bags from their rental car into the bunkhouse. "My fiancé and my brother are working on the deck, but I promise it's only during the day and they don't start too early. They both have day jobs."

"I think we will be at the park most of the time they will be working?" the young man said. "So I think it will not be a problem."

"Wow," the young woman said. "Is this house very old?"

"It's around one hundred years old," Melissa said. "Fixed up recently, of course. It was here when my family first bought the ranch. When I was a kid, it was the bunkhouse for the cowboys. It's been a guesthouse for a few months now."

A hammer was pounding on wood, and Melissa could hear Cary shouting at Ox to bring him more screws.

The young man's face lit up. "Real cowboys lived here?"

"You bet. This is a working cattle ranch. If either of you two ride, we can put you up on a horse and give you a tour of the place if you like."

Both of them laughed.

"Oh no!" the woman said. "We are hikers only, but we will walk around if that is okay."

"Just keep to the roads and you'll be fine," Melissa said. "And my daughter will try to show you her goats. All the soap in the bathroom and kitchen she makes from goat milk, and you're welcome to take that with you."

The woman looked around the tidy guest cottage. "This is very nice."

Melissa, Joan, and Emmie had spent two months making everything in the old bunkhouse feel fresh and clean, with just a hint of California ranch. They'd painted the walls and trim, hung some of Cary's best pictures of the Sierra Nevadas and the foothills on the walls, along with some original touches to make the bunkhouse feel like an updated, down-home hideaway. A line of old horseshoes hung over the door. They'd turned a vintage water pump into a lamp. And warm Pendleton blankets hung on a rack near the freshly blacked wood-burning stove.

It was March at the ranch, and the winter had been a wet one. From the bunkhouse, guests could hear the rushing creek flowing down from the mountains as the snow melted in the warming temperatures. Wildflowers were beginning to peek out in the meadows, and the orange trees spread the heavenly scent of their blossoms on the wind.

Traffic to the park had been steady, even through the winter, and once Melissa earned her first three reviews, the bunkhouse had stayed busy through much of January and February. If occupancy kept up, it was set to bring in as much as Melissa paid Stu, which meant Melissa could give him a raise or hire Leigh on the ranch permanently. Since Leigh was doing a lot of the guest welcome and cleaning, she was leaning toward the latter.

"Your nightly rate comes with dinner included," Melissa said.

"We serve that up on the porch about six thirty this time of year. And no food allergies for either of you?"

"No," the man said. "We eat everything. We travel a lot."

"Make yourself at home. My number is on the wall there, and make sure you put a pin in the map." Melissa pointed to the hanging map on the wall where dozens of pins had already been added. "We love keeping track of where our guests are visiting from."

Gold pins had already been stuck in the East Coast, the Pacific Northwest, Southern California, Australia, a few scattered across Europe, and even two in India! It was fun and Abby always asked a million questions if guests were up for a visit.

She handed over the keys and walked back into the trees where Ox and Cary were muttering back and forth about screws versus nails.

Once they were finished, a raised wooden deck would run along the creek, weaving through the trees, with a wide dance floor stretching into the small meadow near the bunkhouse and a pavilion near the creek. Ox and Cary were facing the creek, arms braced on a table where materials and plans were laid out along with Coke cans, a couple of beer bottles, and a stack of old paper plates.

"You guys good?" She glanced at the table. "You need a trash bag?"

"I'll grab one in a bit." Cary glanced at the bunkhouse. "They gonna complain about the noise?"

She shook her head. "Don't think so. Dinner tonight, Ox?"

"Can't. I'm heading back to Metlin in another hour. Emmie's hosting book club tonight."

"Tell her to bring more cards the next time she's up. And those coupons. I'm out of them for the welcome baskets."

"Sure thing." He wiped his forehead. "Back to work. I want to get the rest of these brackets screwed in so we can put the last boards down tomorrow."

She squinted up at Cary, who was wearing a loose tank top that showed off his arms. "Things are looking good."

The corner of his mouth turned up. "You talking about the deck?"

"That too."

Ox said, "Walking away now." He disappeared around the corner, leaving Melissa and Cary alone at the creek bank.

Cary sat on the edge of the raised deck and spread his legs. Melissa stepped between them, and he immediately put his arms around her, sliding his big hands into the back pockets of her jeans.

"Hey, Missy."

"Hey, Cary."

He leaned forward and took her mouth in a long, lingering kiss. "You taste good."

"I just ate an orange." She breathed deeply, enjoying the sound of the water and the feel of Cary's arms around her and the taste of his lips on hers. "Did you get lunch?"

"I did. Your mom brought sandwiches out." He nudged her chin up and began kissing her neck. "I'm still hungry though."

"Yeah?"

"It's been a while"—he gripped her bottom with both hands —"since I had a really full meal."

Oh, thaaaat kind of hungry. "Well, in two more months you'll be able to have..." She started to go cross-eyed from the feel of his mouth on her collarbones. "You'll get an all-you-can-eat... buffet."

Cary snorted and stopped kissing her neck. His shoulders started shaking with laughter. "Did you just call yourself an all-you-can-eat buffet?"

"I admit that metaphor got away from me." She had to smother a laugh. "But you get my point."

"Two months." His smile was slow and wide.

"Yep. Just two months."

Since Emmie and Ox wanted to invite most all the same

people to their wedding that Cary and Melissa wanted to invite to theirs, they decided to do a double wedding at the beginning of May. It wasn't a fancy occasion, but Abby was getting a *very* fancy dress, lots of friendly people were coming, and there would be an old-fashioned Santa Maria barbecue with lots of beer.

Goat participation was still being negotiated, but the most important thing was that Melissa would be marrying the best man she knew.

It was exactly what she had dreamed of.

"You know, I was thinking about your mom when she brought out lunch," Cary said. "Is she sure she wants to move? I don't want her to feel like she has to move out just because I'm moving in."

Melissa shrugged. "She says we'll be newlyweds and she wants to give us as much privacy as possible."

"Okay." Cary lowered his voice. "Do you think we could get her to take Abby with her?"

"Ha!" She laid her head on Cary's shoulder. "I have no doubt sleepovers will be common."

"Careful, I'm sweaty."

"And I smell like horses."

He kissed the top of her head. "My favorite."

Plans were already in the works to build Joan her own cottage on the ranch, but in the meantime, she'd be moving in with Rumi, taking over Cary's old apartment.

"Personally," Melissa said, "I think your mom and my mom have wanted to start a wild retired-lady commune for a while now."

Cary started to laugh. "Really?"

"Just think about it," Melissa said. "They can sleep in. Only cook for themselves. No laundry to wash but their own. They'll read all the sexy books Emmie can get her hands on and drink wine all night."

"You're right. We may never see them again."

"I may leave you and Abby to fend for yourself and join them."

"Really?" Cary kissed her long and hard, pulling her body into his. By the time he let her up for breath, she really was cross-eyed. "*Really?*"

"No, not really."

"Good. You know the kid would only use me for brute labor and I'd end up serving the goat queen."

"I just got a very clear mental picture, and it's not that far from believable." Melissa glanced at her watch. "Okay, sexy. We have five more minutes to kiss before I have to go get the goat queen from school."

"Five minutes?"

"That's it."

"Hmm." He slid his hands up her back, teasing her spine. "That's not much time."

"You don't think so?" Melissa pulled him closer. "I bet you and I could do a lot in five minutes."

"I told you before, Missy. I never bet against you."

THE END

SIGN UP FOR A FREE SHORT STORY.

Dear Reader,

Thank you for reading *Grit*. I truly hope you enjoyed Cary and Melissa's story as much as I loved writing it.

I also hope you'll take a few moments to leave a review where you bought your copy of the book. Honest reviews are a great way to help other readers find books and authors they'll love. Just a few words can make a big difference.

Also, if you're looking for more about my work, I hope you'll sign up for my monthly newsletter, where I send out writing updates, insider info, free fiction, and news about giveaways and promotions of my work. As a thank you, I'll send a link to a free short story, Too Many Cooks.

Thanks for reading,

Elizabeth

ABOUT THE AUTHOR

ELIZABETH HUNTER is a *USA Today* and international best-selling author of romance, contemporary fantasy, and paranormal mystery. Based in Central California, she travels extensively to write fantasy fiction exploring world mythologies, history, and the universal bonds of love, friendship, and family. She has published over thirty works of fiction and sold over a million books worldwide. She is the author of Love Stories on 7th and Main, the Elemental Legacy series, the Irin Chronicles, the Cambio Springs Mysteries, and other works of fiction.

ElizabethHunterWrites.com

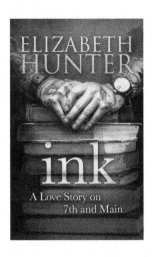

It's everything but business as usual.

To reopen her grandmother's failing book shop, Emmie Elliot knows she'll need a hook. She'll need a strategy. She'll need an... Ox?

Miles Oxford is a tattoo artist without a space to work, and the last thing he wants is to get involved with anyone after his last disaster of a relationship.

She sells ink. He tattoos it. Unusual? Yes. But working together might be the ticket for both Emmie and Ox to find success on their own terms. As long as they keep their attention focused on business.

Just on business.

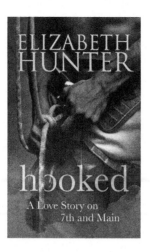

She's in high heels; he wears hiking boots.
Can these two opposites make romance in Metlin work?

Tayla McKinnon is not a small town girl. The fashion blogger moved to Metlin with two goals in mind: help her friend start a book store and have a little fun.

Jeremy Allen has been playing the long game with Tayla, even though the avid outdoorsman was certain she was the one from the minute he set eyes on her.

When a job opportunity from a new fashion start-up lands in her inbox, Tayla takes it as a sign that it's time to leave town, leaving Jeremy no choice but to turn up the heat.

ALSO BY ELIZABETH HUNTER

Contemporary Romance
The Genius and the Muse

7th and Main
INK

HOOKED

GRIT

The Elemental Mysteries
A Hidden Fire

This Same Earth

The Force of Wind

A Fall of Water

The Stars Afire

The Elemental World
Building From Ashes

Waterlocked

Blood and Sand

The Bronze Blade

The Scarlet Deep

A Very Proper Monster

A Stone-Kissed Sea

The Elemental Legacy
Shadows and Gold

Imitation and Alchemy

Omens and Artifacts

Midnight Labyrinth

Blood Apprentice

The Devil and the Dancer

Night's Reckoning (Winter 2019)